PROPERTY OF A LADY

PROPERTY OF A LADY

Sarah Rayne

This first world edition published 2011
in Great Britain and the USA by
SEVERN HOUSE PUBLISHERS LTD of
9–15 High Street, Sutton, Surrey, England, SM1 1DF.
Trade paperback edition first published
in Great Britain and the USA 2011 by
SEVERN HOUSE PUBLISHERS LTD.

British Library Cataloguing in Publication Data

Rayne, Sarah.
  Property of a lady.
  1. Abandoned houses–Fiction. 2. Supernatural–Fiction.
  3. Shropshire (England)–Fiction. 4. Psychological
  fiction.
  I. Title
  823.9'2-dc22

ISBN-13: 978-0-7278-8028-4 (cased)
ISBN-13: 978-1-84751-347-2 (trade paper)

All Severn House titles are printed on acid-free paper.

Severn House Publishers support The Forest Stewardship Council [FSC],
the leading international forest certification organisation. All our titles that
are printed on Greenpeace-approved FSC-certified paper carry the FSC logo.

MIX
Paper from
responsible sources
FSC® C018575
www.fsc.org

Typeset by Palimpsest Book Production Ltd.,
Falkirk, Stirlingshire, Scotland.
Printed and bound in Great Britain by
MPG Books Ltd., Bodmin, Cornwall.

ONE

Maryland. October 20—

M ichael,
Is there any possible chance you could sneak a day or two away from Oxford and take a look at a house for me? We just had this amazing letter straight out of the blue, from some English lawyers I never heard of, saying Liz has inherited a house from a great-aunt or tenth cousin or something who she never knew existed!

It's like the start of a Victorian English novel, isn't it – the long-lost heiress from overseas coming back to the ancestral home. *Bleak House* or one of those huge tomes you teach to your adoring female students who hang on to your every word, only you never notice it. Except I don't think we'll be coming to the ancestral home until at least the end of the year, and I shouldn't think there's likely to be much of the 'ancestral home' about it. It'll most likely be an ordinary house in a village, and from the sound of it pretty derelict as well, because the lawyer says it's been empty for years. Apparently they didn't know they held the deeds to the place until some ninety-year-old partner in the firm died four years ago and they went through his files! They've been trying to find a descendant of the original owners ever since.

Anyway, the house is in a place called Marston Lacy (???!!!) in Shropshire. I looked it up on one of the Internet maps, and it's the tiniest speck of a place you ever saw, just about where England crosses over into Wales. Why do they say Salop on some maps, by the way?

I want to sell the place without even seeing it – the lawyer over there could do it – but Liz is wild to keep it if we can. She has this crazy idea of discovering her English ancestors, (since she never knew she had any English ancestors until this week, that strikes me as pretty off the wall, but there you go, that's Liz). She says why don't we restore it and use it for vacations or even rent it. Either way it will be an investment for when Ellie's grown up and at college or getting married or taking a trip round the world, or whatever kids will be doing in about fifteen years' time. I guess Liz has a point; real estate values bounce up and down according to the season, but when you come down to it, land is still the best investment. Land doesn't get up and walk away.

So we've agreed on a compromise. And since I value your common sense and intelligence highly (ha!), you get to be the compromise. Could you possibly go over to this Marston Lacy any time soon, and look at this house for us? The address is Charect House, which sounds pretty grand, although I've no more idea of what a charect is than fly to the moon.

Typing this email, I'm imagining you in that dim English study with all the books and the untidiness, and Wilberforce snoozing in a patch of sunlight from the quad.

Anyhow, what we'd really like is a few photos so we know what the place looks like, and some idea of how many rooms there are. Also whether it really is Bleak House or somewhere for ordinary people.

Till soon,
    Jack.

It was typical of Jack to send an email of this kind, and it was typical of him to think it would be easy for Michael to travel to the unknown Shropshire house. Americans always had the impression that England was tiny enough to make darting from one end of the country to the other a matter of a couple of hours.

Michael folded the letter into his wallet so it would not get lost, because important letters had an extraordinary habit of going astray if he left them on his desk. Shropshire might be manageable at the weekend. He could probably stay overnight, although he would have to be back on Sunday night. This term was quite a lively one; a gratifying number of students were taking his course on the metaphysical poets – it was true that more than half of them were females, but that was pure chance.

He got up to look up the exact meaning of charect, switching on the desk lamp to see better, because his study was in a small rather obscure corner of Oriel College, as befitted a junior don. The windows overlooked a tiny quadrangle which most people forgot was there, but which in summer was harlequined with green and gold from the reflections of trees in upper-storey windows. Just now it had the faint cotton-wool mistiness of autumn, with scatterings of bronze leaves on the stones. Michael liked his study, and he liked the view, although at the moment it was slightly obscured by Wilberforce, who had gone to sleep on the window sill.

Here it was: *charect*. An obsolete word for a charm: a spell set down in writing – literally in characters – to ward off evil.

He thought he would tell Jack and Liz this, and then he thought perhaps he would not. It begged the question as to why the house had been given such a name. What evil had to be warded off?

Maryland, October 20—

Michael,

That's great news that you think you can get to Marston Lacy this weekend. I've emailed the lawyers, authorizing them to hand the keys to you. They suggest you book into the Black Boar for Saturday night, and they'll get the keys to you.

We haven't mentioned this to any of the family here – Liz's cousins would go wild with curiosity and excitement, and some of them would demand why it's Liz who's inheriting the place and not them. We'd never have any peace. And her godmother would want to pay for all the work, which we wouldn't allow, and even then she'd end up taking over the entire project. You met Liz's godmother at our wedding, didn't you? If you remember her (and everyone who meets her always does), you'll know what I mean.

But one thing Liz has done is get in touch with an antique dealer in the area, to see if any of the house's original furniture can be tracked down. The dealer is called Nell West, and she runs Nell West Antiques in Marston Lacy itself. She's already found a long-case clock that apparently belonged to the house, that's being auctioned locally on 10th of next month. I'm mailing you the catalog.

We'll try to get to England for the Christmas vacation. It's far too long since we saw you, and Ellie was seven last birthday, so she's due some attention from her godfather. She's already making up stories about the people she thinks lived in Charect

House – including someone called, of all things, Elvira. I
swear the child will end up being a writer, which means
permanently broke. I certainly won't be able to help her – this
English house will have bankrupted us long before then.
   Jack

As Michael worked on his students' essays about Byron and
Shelley, Jack's letter, which had arrived that morning, was
propped up on the edge of the desk.

He finished marking the essays, added a few notes, then
reached for the catalogues Jack had sent. Lot No. 521 was
circled in ink, and Jack had stuck a yellow Post-it note next
to it, on which he had scribbled the words 'Note the reserve
price! See what I mean about impending bankruptcy!'

> Messrs Cranston & Maltravers, Auctioneers of Fine Arts
> and Furniture (est.1922)
> *Lot No. 521.* The property of a lady. Nineteenth-century
> long-case clock by Crutchley's of Shropshire. Mahogany
> inlaid with rosewood, made c.1888. Brooke Crutchley
> was the last of the famous clockmaking family, and this
> piece was made for William Lee. In view of the manner
> of William Lee's death, this item is expected to realize a
> high figure.

Michael glanced at the reserve price and was not surprised
Jack was prophesying bankruptcy. But as he stared down at
the smudgy reproduction of the photograph showing the long-
case clock, he was aware of a vague unease. In view of the
manner of William Lee's death . . . What did that mean?
Something slithered within his mind, and for a moment it was
as if a soft voice whispered a warning. You'd be much better
not to meddle, said this voice. You'd be much better to throw
the whole lot on the fire and tell Jack you're too busy to trek
into the wilds of Shropshire.

But of course he would go into Shropshire, and of course
he would take a look at Charect House. He went downstairs
to ask the porter about feeding Wilberforce over the weekend,
promising to leave some tins of cat food and an extra pint of
milk in his rooms. He would be back on Sunday night, he
said. Yes, he would have his mobile phone with him in case

anyone needed him. No, he would not forget to charge it this time.

He drove out of Oxford early on Saturday morning. He would have preferred to travel by train, because even though he had mapped out the route with diligence, he knew perfectly well he would get lost. Several of his students had said he should buy satellite navigation, which was really cool and you absolutely couldn't get lost with it. Michael had promised to consider the idea.

In the event, he did not go out of his way too many times, and he reached Marston Lacy shortly before lunch. The Black Boar appeared to be the traditional oak-beamed inglenook-fireplaced inn. Charles II had hidden here, Elizabeth I had slept here, and Walter Scott had written something here.

'At separate times, of course,' said the manager with the automatic geniality of one who produces this epigrammatic gem for all newcomers.

'Of course.' Michael signed the book, collected the keys which the solicitors had left for him as promised, and deposited his overnight case in a chintz-curtained room on the first floor. Then he went in search of Jack and Liz's house.

'It's along the main street towards the A458,' said the Black Boar's manager. 'Turn left at the end by the old corn market, then left again into Blackberry Lane. It's about a quarter of a mile along. You won't miss it, Dr Flint.'

Blackberry Lane was a winding bouncing lane with bushes and thrusting thorn hedges that pushed against the sides of the car, and whippy branches that painted sappy green smears on the windscreen. A thin rain was starting to fall, making everything look mysterious and remote. Michael began to wonder if he had fallen backwards into somebody's gloomy metaphysical elegy without realizing, and whether he might encounter flitting shades among tombstones, or disconsolate wraiths, wringing their hands. The lane wound round to the left, and quite suddenly the house was there, set a little way back from the track, standing behind a tangle of briar and blackberry. There were no shades or wraiths, but seen through the rain the house was misty and eerie. Michael regarded it for a moment, then got out of the car, turning up his collar against the rain. There was a low brick wall enclosing the house, and a rusting gate half off its hinges that shrieked like a banshee when he pushed it open. I'm stepping into a house whose name was once a spell against evil, he thought.

Charect House was larger than he had expected. It was a red-brick, four-square building with the tall flat windows of the Regency and crumbling stone pillars on each side of the front door. The brick had long since mellowed into a dark, soft red, and some kind of creeper covered the lower portions. Even with the rain it was possible to see the dereliction. The upper windows had shutters, half falling away, and all the window frames looked rotten. The roofline dipped ominously.

But the locks still worked, and the door swung open easily enough. The scent of age met Michael at once, and it was so strong that for a moment he felt his senses blur. But this was not the musty dankness of damp or rot; this was age at its best and most evocative: a potpourri of old seasoned timbers and long-ago fires, and a lingering scent of dried lavender. A gentler age, when ladies embroidered and wrote letters on hot-pressed notepaper and painted dainty watercolours, to the gentle ticking of a clock . . .

The ticking of a clock. He could hear it quite clearly, which was unexpected because he had thought the house entirely empty of furniture – in fact the auction that included the long-case clock was not until next week. Perhaps there was an old wall clock or a kitchen clock somewhere.

He walked through the rooms, listing them carefully and making notes about them. Three reception rooms on the ground floor – one of which was a beautiful long room with windows overlooking the tanglewood gardens and a deep window seat. There was a dingy fireplace with bookshelves on each side.

At the back was a big stone-floored kitchen. When Michael tried the water in the outer scullery something clanked and shuddered in the depths of the house, then a thin reddish stream came from the tap. He turned the tap off and went back to the front of the house. The clock was still ticking away to itself somewhere. It was rather a friendly sound; people did not have ticking clocks very often these days.

The main hall had the wide, elegant stairway of its era. The stairs went straight up to a big landing, then swung back on themselves in a hairpin bend, a smaller, narrower flight obviously winding up to the second floor. Attic stairs.

It was barely half-past four, but the light was already fading, and Michael thought he would come back tomorrow and see the rest of the place in daylight. He had reached the front door when unmistakably and disconcertingly three loud knocks sounded somewhere inside the house – peremptory, fist-on-wood rapping, startlingly loud. Michael's heart jumped, and he turned back to the hall, but nothing moved anywhere and the only sound was the ticking clock still faintly tapping out the minutes somewhere. Probably, it had been his imagination, or a bird in the eaves or even old timbers creaking somewhere. Or someone outside? He opened the front door and looked out, but there was only the dismal drip of rain from the leaves, so he came back in and rather apprehensively looked into all the downstairs rooms. Nothing. But as he went into the long drawing-room there was movement in the shadowy garden beyond the windows, then something pallid pressed itself against the glass. Someone's out there, thought Michael, trying not to panic, but feeling his pulse racing. Someone's standing in the garden, knocking at the window to come in.

And then he saw that after all it was only the remains of an untidy shrub that had dipped its boughs against the window pane. As he watched, it moved again, claw-like branches brushing the glass with a faint, goblin-claw scratch. That was certainly not the sound he had heard.

He was in the hall when the rapping came again, and this time it was unmistakably overhead. It was coming from the bedrooms.

It was probably perfectly innocent – a window open and banging against the wall, or a trapped animal. No, an animal would bark or yowl. Wilberforce had once been accidentally shut in a cupboard on one of Oriel's landings, and the entire college had heard his indignant demands to be rescued. And this sound was sharp and echoing and somehow filled with desperation. Michael remembered, and wished he had not, the Rachmaninov suite that began with three sonorous piano chords intended to represent a man buried alive knocking on the underside of his coffin lid to get out. He was so annoyed with himself for remembering this that he started up the stairs before he could change his mind. The stairs creaked ominously, and he expected the knocking to ring out again at any moment. It did not, but Michael had the strong impression that someone was listening.

As he reached the main landing, the knocking suddenly came again, louder and more frenzied. Did it spell out a plea? Was it saying: *let-me-out* . . . Or was it: *let-me-in* . . . ? On the crest of this thought something moved on the edge of his vision, and Michael looked across to the attic stair.

Fear rose up, clutching at his throat, because there was someone there. Within the clotted shadows was a thickset figure crouched against the banisters.

For several seconds Michael stood motionless, staring at the figure, a dozen possible actions chasing across his mind. There was a confused impression of a pallid face, with the eyes so deep in the shadows that they appeared to be black pits, and of thick fingers curled round the banister rails.

Michael heard himself say, challengingly, 'Who are you? What are you doing here?' and at once the man moved, flinching back into the shadows. There was a scrabbling movement, and the man turned and ran up the narrow stairs to the top floor.

Michael thought he was as brave as most people, but he was damned if he was going to confront an intruder in a deserted attic with nobody in calling distance. He ran back down the stairs, slammed the door and locked it, then dived into his car and reached for his phone to call the police.

By the time a portly constable arrived, the intruder appeared to have got away.

'Very sorry indeed, sir, but it seems he's escaped us.'

'It's impossible,' said Michael as they stood outside the house, staring up at the windows. 'He was on the stairs, and he went up to the top of the house – I saw him go up there. There can't be any way for him to have got out. In any case, I locked the front door when I came out – to keep him in there. And I waited in my car until you got here.'

'You saw for yourself, Dr Flint,' said the policeman. 'We went in every room and every last cupboard.'

'Yes, we did,' said Michael, puzzled.

'And the two other outer doors were locked. The scullery door, and the garden door at the side, as well.'

'There were no keys in any of the locks,' said Michael,

frowning. 'Which means that if he got out that way, he could only have done it by unlocking a door and locking it again behind him.' He looked at the policeman. 'And that's absurd. Unless—'

'Unless what?'

'Unless he's got keys to the house,' said Michael slowly and unwillingly.

'Surely not. Likely, he managed to climb out through a window at the back while you were phoning. It'll have been some tramp looking for a night's dosshouse.'

'He didn't look like a tramp,' said Michael, remembering the round, pallid face and the black-pit eyes. 'I think I'd better have the locks changed while I'm here. Is there a locksmith who'd do an emergency job at the weekend?'

'No one in Marston Lacy, sir, but I can give you a couple of numbers a bit further afield.'

Michael wrote down the numbers and drove back to the Black Boar, puzzled and vaguely disturbed.

It was not until he was showering before dinner that he realized there had been something else that was even more disturbing. All the time he was in the house he had heard the ticking of a clock – at times quite loudly, at other times fainter, as if the ticking was coming from behind a closed door.

But he and the policeman had searched Charect House from cellar to attic, and every room had been empty. There had been no clock anywhere.

TWO

Charect House, seen in Sunday morning sunshine with the faint sound of church bells somewhere across the fields, had emerged from its semi-haunted state, and it presented a bland, innocuous face to the world. It was elegantly derelict and appealingly battered, and Michael suddenly liked it very much.

He had borrowed a colleague's camera, which the colleague had said was the easiest thing in the world to operate, but which Michael found confusing. It was fortunate that the locksmith, summoned from a nearby town, turned up and helped out. Michael was grateful, and while the man was cheerfully fitting new locks, he managed to get what he thought were several reasonable shots of the house's outside, which should give Jack and Liz a fair idea of the place. Encouraged, he ventured inside, pressed a series of buttons for the flash, one of which seemed to work, and captured the long drawing-room and also the wide hall and staircase. He stood in the hall for a moment, looking up at the stairs, remembering the face that had seemed to stare out through the banisters of the attic stair. Could it have been a freak of the light? Could the loud knocking sounds have been the old timbers after all, or an animal? Such as squirrels with hobnail boots, demanded his mind cynically, at which point he went back outside, closing the door firmly on Charect's ghosts. He paid the locksmith's modest bill there and then, added a substantial tip for the twofold service of Sunday call-out and photographic advice, and drove back to the Black Boar, leaving the locksmith promising to deliver the keys to the solicitor's office on Monday.

Sunday lunch at the Black Boar consisted of something called Chicken á la King, which, as far as Michael could tell, was a chicken portion immersed in chicken soup from a tin. He ate it without tasting it, declined something called Death by Chocolate by way of pudding, and had a cup of coffee in the bar. After this he drove back to Oxford, relieved to be heading for familiar ground. That evening he managed to find the camera-owning colleague, who was reading a batch of second-year essays, and persuaded him to download the Charect House photos on to the computer so they could be emailed to Jack and Liz. Yes, he said, he knew it was the easiest thing in the world – of course he did – but since he was not familiar with the camera . . .

Maryland, October 29th

Michael,

That's a great batch of photos you sent. Liz is thrilled with every last one. It looks a beautiful old place, despite the neglect – and a whole lot grander than we expected! We'll hide the photos from all the cousins!

Liz is already working out color schemes for that long room with the windows looking over the gardens. She says Wedgwood blue and ivory, whatever Wedgwood blue might be. Beveled bookshelves in the window recesses, and cream silk drapes. (And probably Ellie's grubby fingerprints all over them to add a touch of *avant-garde*.)

We're having a survey done next week, and we'll try to send in local builders and electricians once we've got the surveyor's report. It'll be difficult from such a distance, but we want to get the really disruptive work done by Christmas. Wiring and plumbing and roof work – oh God, *is* there going to be roof work? Wouldn't it be great to spend Christmas in the house? Assuming there's still money in the bank for food by then. But you'd be part of the festivities, even if it had to be bread and gruel round a single candle, like a scene from Dickens.

The efficient Ms West just emailed to say a rosewood table's being offered in the same sale as the long-case clock, and the provenance indicates it also belonged to Charect House. (One day you've got to tell me what that word *charect* means, because I can't find it in any reference books here and for all I know it could be anything from one of those old Edwardian after-dinner games to an obscure English law nobody's used for a thousand years. I'm kidding about the after-dinner game, but I'm not kidding about a thousand-year-old law). Ms West said would we like her to bid for the rosewood table at the same time as the clock, and Liz said yes before I could so much as look at a bank statement.

Liz is upstairs with Ellie – Ellie's got herself really upset over her beloved 'Elvira' this last couple of days. She had fierce nightmares last night and, after breakfast, we found her huddled into a corner of her room crying to herself. Liz is keeping her off school today. It's fine for kids to have imaginary friends, but we might have to find a way of ditching Elvira. Maybe she could go off to do missionary work in Indonesia or to rescue the rainforests? I don't think Ellie would accept anything less altruistic. She wants to save the world, can you believe that? Seven years old and already she's a philanthropist.

It looks as though you sneaked a romantic weekend into the schedule somewhere. Except that if you were trying to keep your girlfriend a secret, you should have told her not to stand at the window while you photographed it. I couldn't see much detail, but I hope she's a cracker. Maybe we can meet her when we come over. When I *think* of all the knockout girls who've lain siege to you over the years, and how you've never even realized it . . . Well, I could just spit, that's all.

Till soon,
Jack.

Michael hardly registered Jack's last sentence, because by this time he was scouring the computer to retrieve the photos of Charect House. It was astonishing how difficult it was to find things on a computer: he opened several files which appeared to contain nothing but incomprehensible hieroglyphics; lost himself amidst technical folders, alarmingly labelled 'System File Do Not Delete'; but finally ran the photos to earth.

Blown up on to the computer monitor, Charect House looked benign and bland. The first three or four shots showed the frontage and views of the back. Michael remembered taking those to the sound of the locksmith's cheerful whistling.

It was the fifth photo that caused an icy hand to twist into his ribs. He had moved a little way back into the garden for that one, hoping to get a good shot of the roofline and the chimneys. People worried about roofs and chimneys in old houses, and Jack would appreciate shots of them.

Almost all of the windows were splintered with sunlight, but the top row – the small attic windows directly under the eaves – were in shadow. At the very smallest one was the clear outline of a female figure pressed against the glass, obviously looking down into the gardens. One hand was raised as if she might be waving.

Or as if she might be banging on the glass.

Michael sent a non-committal email to Jack, saying he was glad the photos had been helpful, that he would of course go back to check the progress of the various work, and that he hoped Ellie would get over her spell of nightmares. It upset him to think of the small Ellie with her heart-shaped face and bright hazel eyes suffering nightmares and crying. He would send her a light-hearted email as if Wilberforce had written it, making up a Tom-and-Jerry-type story about the family of mice who lived under the stairs at Oriel College and who always got the better of Wilberforce, jeering and blowing raspberries at him from holes in the skirting boards. He sometimes did this, and Ellie always loved the stories and wanted more of them.

He made several attempts to respond to Jack's veiled questions about the face at the window, but the first draft sounded as if he was discussing a silent horror movie, the second had an air of worried apology, and the third appeared to have been written by a too-eager estate agent trying to sell Borley Rectory or the Bloody Tower . . . ('You get a lovely view of the river by night and the only ghost who's in any way troublesome is Ann Boleyn and that's only once a year on the anniversary of her beheading . . .')

In the end he did not comment about the photo at all. He would prefer to let Jack and Liz suspect he was having a secret (and therefore presumably illicit) fling, rather than plant the idea that their house had a ghost. It did not, of course, because there were no such things and, even if there were, Michael was not going to believe in them. As for the meaning of charect, he would wait until Jack saw the house before he disclosed that it was a kind of rune – an ancient spell for warding off evil.

The photo apparently showing a female at the top window would have a rational explanation, and if Michael understood more about cameras and computers he would no doubt be able to provide that explanation. The obvious explanation was a freak reflection from a cloud. He looked at the photograph again, and this time he managed to increase the size to 150 per cent. He instantly wished he had not done this, because if it was a cloud, it was a very unusual one. It appeared to have a mass of dark hair, a slender neck and a garment with striped sleeves, and it could not be anything other than a human female form. Or could it? How about it being the remnant of an old curtain inside the room – or a piece of striped fabric that had blown against the window? He seized on this idea gratefully and was able to end the email to Jack by saying he hoped the house did not consign Jack to a debtors' gaol and the rest of them to gruel by candlelight at Christmas.

Nell West hoped she would manage to buy the long-case clock for Jack and Liz Harper without it breaking their budget. They gave the impression of being fairly prosperous, but Charect House was said to be in such a tumbledown condition that it would probably bankrupt a Texan oil millionaire.

It seemed vaguely unfair that the Harpers had to pay for things that had once belonged to Liz Harper's family, but business was business and their loss could be Nell's gain. She had quoted a buying commission of twenty per cent of the eventual purchase price, which was pushing it a bit, but Liz Harper had said that was fine and they would love to have the clock and the table and pretty much anything else that could be found.

Nell had not been in Marston Lacy very long, but most people knew her quite well already because her shop was in the main street and she tried to have really striking displays in the bow window.

In the main, life was still bleak without Brad, but occasionally something pleasant or amusing happened and at those times Nell felt as if she had stepped out of the darkness into an unexpected splash of sunlight. And there were a number of things to be grateful for – it was important to remember that. Beth seemed to be getting over the loss of her father; she liked her school and had made friends there. This was a huge relief, because after his death Beth had woken sobbing each morning, because her daddy had been in her dream, alive again and smiling. Nell did not say Brad was in her own dreams as well.

On a purely practical level, she was surviving. There was

enough money to live on – not a massive amount, but enough – and she was even starting to have a modest social life in Marston Lacy. Last month the Chamber of Commerce had issued a rather stately invitation for her to join their ranks. That was the kind of thing that would have made Brad smile in the way he always smiled if she achieved something new. She wondered if she would ever get over the knowledge that she would never see him smile again, and whether she would ever be able to stop thinking about his car skidding out of control on the icy road that night. But I'm coping, thought Nell, determinedly. It's over a year now – it's one year and nine months to be exact. And I'm all right.

The Harpers had emailed to say a friend of theirs, Michael Flint, was driving into Shropshire to take photos of the house – they were really keen to see what it looked like. Their daughter had drawn a bunch of pictures of how she thought it would be, but she had a crazy idea that all English houses had either thatched roofs, Elizabethan beams, or ghosts. They were not mad about thatched roofs, which might harbour rats, said Liz, or about old beams that might harbour infestation, and they certainly did not take kindly to the possibility of a resident ghost.

Nell was looking forward to meeting the Harpers. Liz Harper's last email said they would love to know a bit about the house's past and its occupants; if Ms West had time to do a little local research, they would happily cover her expenses. This was an intriguing idea – Nell had not seen the house yet, but she would love to find out more about it. She had already asked Cranston & Maltravers about the clock's history, but they had only been able to tell her that Brooke Crutchley had been the last of a locally famous clockmaking family whose work had been considerably sought after in the county. You came across Crutchley clocks in any number of local National Trust or English Heritage houses in this part of the world, and this particular one was believed to have been made for William Lee in or around 1888. They did not know anything about William Lee, they said firmly, and Nell gave up on them and looked at land registers and transfers of title in the archives department of the local council. She wasted a lot of time trying to find Charect House until she found it had been known as Mallow House until 1890.

There was not very much to discover about William Lee or any of its owners, but early in 1940 it had been requisitioned by a rather obscure Ministry of Defence department. Nell glanced rather perfunctorily through a sheaf of letters clipped inside the file, thinking they would relate to the requisitioning of the house.

But they did not. The letters had apparently insinuated themselves under a paper clip on one of the MOD memos and been misfiled. They bore dates from the early nineteen sixties. Nell skimmed them, then began to read with more concentration.

THREE

Letter from: Joseph Lloyd, Planning Department, Council Offices.
To: Dr Alice Wilson, Special Investigator for Psychic Research.

D ear Dr Wilson,
    I am in receipt of your letter dated 10th ult. and will try to answer your questions to the best of my ability.

Charect House was built around 1780–1800, but its ownership is complicated and the Council is in a difficult situation. The last known owner vanished in 1939. However, in February 1940 the Ministry of Defence requisitioned the place, and it was not decommissioned until 1950. Those ten years ensured the fabric was kept in good condition, but since then the house has fallen into considerable disrepair. There are no funds to maintain it – National Trust and English Heritage were approached, but both declined, primarily because of the absence of a legal owner.

The title deeds cannot be traced – it's believed they may have been destroyed in WWII bombings – but since the place cannot be allowed to deteriorate further, the County Council have appointed my committee to act in a caretaker capacity. We have passed a resolution that Charect House be leased to small business concerns on short-term tenancies until the legal owner can be found. The income can be utilized for repairs, and any monies remaining can be placed on deposit.

However, because of its reputation as the local 'haunted house', currently no suitable tenants can be found. We feel it is therefore necessary to quench the persistent and damaging rumours that surround the house, and for that reason I have (most reluctantly) agreed to an investigation by your organization.

I must tell you that I believe a normal explanation will be

found for the reports of so-called 'supernatural' activity. The evidence all indicates that the problems are caused by one of the following:

1. Settlement in the foundations.
2. A fault in the plumbing, which admittedly dates to around the time of WWII.
3. A fault in the electrical wiring, which dates to the Abdication of Edward VIII.

No doubt you will bear these points in mind when conducting your investigations.
Yours sincerely,
    J. Lloyd

From: Dr Alice Wilson to J. Lloyd

Dear Mr Lloyd,
    In 20 years of scientific research into the paranormal I have never heard of settlement, plumbing, or electrical wiring that caused psychic disturbances of the kind being reported to your council.
    Please let me have copies of the reports of all sightings, and advise whether the culprit house is actually empty. Of living people, that is.
    Yours,
        Alice Wilson.

From: J. Lloyd to Dr A. Wilson

Dear Dr Wilson,
    Charect House is unoccupied.
    I am enclosing copies of reports of what you term 'sightings', but do not feel any credence can be placed on these. I would point out that most come from:
    – Teenagers, who might be thought to have taken illegal substances.
    – Three typists who are known to be devotees of late-night television horror films.
    – Revellers, whose testimony cannot be trusted, since they are known to frequent the Black Boar's real-ale bar.

– A character known locally as Arthur the Quaffer, whose predilection for methylated spirits causes him to regularly see all manner of strange things.

If you can let me know when you could come to Marston Lacy, I can arrange accommodation for you at the Black Boar.

With good wishes,

J. Lloyd

Alice Wilson to J. Lloyd

Dear Mr Lloyd,

Please don't tell me how to do my job; your council is paying my organization very handsomely to investigate this house, and I would prefer to earn that payment.

I will arrive on the 18th.

Good wishes to you as well.

Alice Wilson.

Nell read these letters twice. So Charect House really was Marston Lacy's haunted house – to the extent that in the 1960s a ghostbuster had been called in. She considered Alice Wilson's letters for a moment, rather liking the sound of her and wondering if it would be possible to find out the results of her investigation. She would like to find out more, purely for her own curiosity.

The auction took place the following afternoon in the barn-like auction rooms of Cranston & Maltravers' offices. Nell found a seat near the front and settled down to wait, enjoying the buzz of speculation all round her. There were several dealers whom she recognized and a sprinkling of locals.

The clock was Lot No. 521. Nell did not like it very much. She had seen it on one of the viewing days, when she had checked it for signs of woodworm and repairs – if it had showed either she would have told the Harpers it was not worth the reserve price. But whatever William Lee's reputation might be, his clock was unblemished.

It was described as a moon-phase clock – the face of the moon was set in its own secondary arch-dial above the main, conventional one. The workings would move around to mark the passing of the moon's cycle, and the sphere representing this had been fashioned in blue enamel and lightly marked to indicate human features. Nell supposed it was intended to look a little like illustrations in children's books of the Man in the Moon smiling benignly down from the night sky, but seen from this angle it did not look at all benign. The face was half visible, which presumably meant it was midway between moons when it stopped, and although it was probably a trick of the light or dust on the surface, it looked exactly like a full-faced man peering slyly over a wall. A Peeping Tom, thought Nell, studying it. However much you're worth, and however famous a workshop you've come out of, I wouldn't want you in my house.

When the bidding opened, the room fell silent. Nell had no idea which way this would go: bidding might go through the roof and beyond her budget, or no one would bid at all and the Harpers would get it for a song.

The reserve price was declared, and Nell made a nod of assent to the auctioneer.

'Three thousand pounds on the table,' said the auctioneer. 'Three thousand five-hundred, anyone?' He looked round the room invitingly. 'Come on, this is a nineteenth-century clock from a well-known workshop. Solid mahogany, with brass. Once the property of a lady. Three thousand five-hundred, anyone?'

The silence stretched out. Nell discovered she was gripping her catalogue so tightly that she had dented the corners. This was absurd. She would like to get the clock for the Harpers, even though she did not like it herself, but it would not be the end of the world if she was outbid. She would be annoyed not to have the £600 commission, but she could find other pieces for them. There was still the rosewood table to come.

'Once, twice, third time,' said the auctioneer with the air of one washing his hands of such a lacklustre audience. The gavel smacked down on the desk, and at once a faint thrumming came from the clock, as if the force of the blow had disturbed something deep inside its mechanism. For a moment the sly moon-face seemed to pulsate, then the moment passed, and there was only the sound of the next piece being carried in. Nell thought she must have imagined that glimpse of eerie movement. But as she sat back in her seat, she could feel people looking at her. William Lee, she thought, what on earth is the legacy you've left behind you?

The rosewood table came up shortly before three o'clock, and bidding went briskly up to £2,000, with Nell and three other dealers competing. At £2,250 one of the dealers dropped out, and at £2,500 another went. Nell was within £250 of Liz Harper's budget, but she kept her nerve and in the end got the table with £50 to spare. Making out the cheque, she thought it had been a very good afternoon's work.

Liz and Jack Harper had authorized the solicitors to lend Nell the keys of Charect House, but she had not yet needed to borrow them. She did not really need to do so now. Yes, she did, she wanted to make sure the rosewood table and the clock had reached their destination safely and undamaged.

The solicitor's secretary confirmed that Cranston & Maltravers' delivery men had been out to the house that morning and had returned the keys. She handed them over and asked if Nell needed directions.

'I think I'll find it,' said Nell. 'I know more or less where it is.'

'It's a weird old place. Right in the middle of nowhere. There're a good few stories about it, if you take my meaning.'

'I'll pack the bell, book and candle,' said Nell, and she went out to collect her car from the square of waste ground next to her shop.

Probably, Charect House would look very pleasant and welcoming in sunshine, Nell thought when she arrived, but seen through a curtain of rain, with moisture dripping from the branches, it was depressing in the extreme. The garden was a tangled mass – nodding seed heads of rosebay willow-herb, rose hips from ragged-headed wild roses, and immense bushes of lilac and lavender. In summer the lilac would scent the air for miles around. On the other side was surely the remains of a herb garden: was that rosemary there? Rosemary, that's for remembrance. Nell and Beth had planted a rosemary bush on Brad's grave, Beth's small face solemn and absorbed in the task. Had Charect's rosemary bush been planted in memory of someone? A former owner? Presumably not William Lee though; from the way the local people shied away from his memory, deadly nightshade would be likelier.

Nell parked the car and went inside. There was a large hall with a staircase – at some time the boards would have resembled new-run honey with the sun on it, but they were dull with scratch marks where the auctioneers' men had dragged the packing cases. Nell followed the scratches into a room on the right. The rosewood table had been placed under the window, and the clock was against the far wall. She stood in front of it for a moment, wondering whether to wind it up and set the elaborate pendulum going. Better not. Something might be delicately balanced in the mechanism, and she might damage it.

This was a beautiful room, although it needed furniture – deep, squashy armchairs and sofas, books lining the alcoves that flanked the fireplace, and a fire crackling in the hearth . . . She and Brad had had a tall, old house in North London; it was a bit battered, always needing more work done to it than they could afford, but they had loved it.

It was at this point Nell realized she was not alone in the house. Someone was walking around upstairs.

She was not immediately concerned, although she was slightly startled, because she had thought the only set of keys was the one she had borrowed half an hour earlier. But it was most likely someone preparing an estimate for the Harpers or the friend they had mentioned. Whoever it was, she had better call out to say she was here. She crossed to the hall and stood at the foot of the stairs. Yes, there was certainly someone there – it sounded as if something was being dragged across the floor.

'Hello!' called Nell, her voice echoing in the empty house.

The sounds stopped at once, and absolute silence followed. Perhaps all she had heard was something on the roof. A bird? If it was, it was a very large one.

'Who's there?' Nell said and was instantly annoyed with herself because this was the classic bleat of every person in an empty house with a ghost legend.

She went cautiously up the first few stairs, her footsteps ringing out, uneasily aware of Charect's isolation. At the top of the stairs was an L-shaped landing, with doors opening off it. All the doors were closed and, at the far end, a small, secondary staircase wound upwards. Had the sounds come from up there? The attics? Or was someone hiding behind one of those closed doors?

Except they were not all closed after all – the second one on the left was ajar. Someone's standing behind it, thought

Nell, her heart bumping. Someone's watching me through the narrow crack in the door frame. No, I'm wrong, it's just the shadows. But I'm damned if I'm going to investigate.

She turned to go back downstairs, and her heart leapt into her throat, because there had been a whisk of movement from above – as if something had darted back into the concealment of the shadows. There was a brief heart-stopping image of a figure with a large, pallid face and staring black eyes . . . Nell froze, one hand clutching the banisters, then drew in a shaky breath of relief. The plaster and paper on the wall opposite the window was badly damp-stained, and from this angle the marks formed themselves into the hunched-over figure of a thickset man. Optical illusion, nothing more. Like seeing faces in the clouds or in melting butter on toast.

She went back downstairs and headed for the long room to collect her bag. Probably the sounds had some equally innocent explanation – timbers expanding in the roof, maybe. But as she pushed open the door, she heard a different sound.

The ticking of a clock.

For several minutes Nell tried to convince herself the auctioneers' men had set the long-case clock going after delivering it, but she knew they had not. The clock had not been going when she first came into the house.

The mechanism had a gritty, teeth-wincing sound which she hated. It sounded as if long, fleshless fingers were tapping a tattoo against a windowpane in the depths of a frozen winter. The pendulum swung from side to side, not quite aligned with the sounds, the bronze disc catching the light like a monstrous glistening eye.

Nell forced herself to think logically. Was it possible there had been some vibration in the house that had set the mechanism going? The sounds she had heard earlier might have been erratic plumbing – the scullery taps had looked pretty ancient, and there might be elderly pipes under the floors that had shuddered and sent a vibration up through the clock's spine.

She reached out to turn the gilt hasp of the door to see if there was anything in the clock's innards to account for the movement. A faint drift of old wood and something scented and sad came out, but as far as she could see there was nothing unusual. After a moment she grasped the pendulum to halt it, and the ticking faltered into silence. Nell was not sure if the ensuing silence was worse. She tapped the sides of the casing, hoping the slight vibration would start the pendulum going again, but it did not. How about the base? She tried tapping on the floor of the clock and this time felt something move uneasily. Was part of the casing loose? Nell peered into the narrow darkness. In one corner was a tiny triangle of something pale – a paper? Yes, it was the corner of some paper protruding through the oak strips. It was probably nothing more than the auctioneer's ticket that had slid down between the oak strips, but it might as well be removed.

But the fragment resisted being pulled free, and when Nell investigated further she discovered that a small section of the oak was loose. Working with extreme care, so as not to damage anything, she finally managed to lever up a tiny section of the oak strips. It was not nailed or glued down; it dovetailed with the other timbers, but the fit had loosened slightly with the years. Thrust into the narrow recess of the clock's base was a sheaf of brittle yellowing pages. As Nell lifted them out her hand brushed against the pendulum and the old mechanism struggled back into life. The ticking began again, but this time she barely noticed it, because her entire attention was on the retrieved pages.

She spread them out on the floor – there were ten or twelve of them, all handwritten, and, Nell had the sensation of a hand reaching out of the past. The feeling was so vivid that for a moment she could almost feel fingers curl around hers.

It was not unknown to her, this impression of the past taking her hand – she had encountered it several times during searches for particularly old pieces of furniture or china. It was a feeling she had always rather liked, finding it friendly and reassuring.

But as she began to read, sitting cross-legged on the bare, dusty floor, she knew there was nothing reassuring about the hand that was reaching out of this particular fragment of Charect House's past.

FOUR

A rrived in Marston Lacy this morning. It's a fragment of a village, a tiny place that slipped between a crack in the industrial revolution and got forgotten.

To the south are grey-roofed factories, with iron and steel foundries silhouetted against the skies. It's like stepping into a painting by Lowry, with the poor ant-workers scurrying in at eight a.m. and out again at five. But on the east and north, the rolling meadows and farmhouses are like something from a Van Gogh landscape.

That man from the Council, J. Lloyd, is a fool, but at least he has arranged for me to stay in reasonable comfort at the Black Boar. It's pretty ancient. The floors all slope, and the ceilings are so low that you have to walk about like Groucho Marx. But I shan't be there very much; I'll be camped out in Charect House. It's an odd feeling to think I'm finally going to see it.

3 p.m.

Unpacked and had a wash and brush-up (a very brisk process these days; I lost any vanity I had years ago). Then I drove out to inspect Charect House. I'll admit to feeling nervous. I must have seen more sinister houses than most people do in a lifetime, but this one is special.

It's a remarkable old place. Romantically-inclined folk would sigh poetically, and think it beautiful and sad, but I didn't think it was either of those things. I thought it was in a shocking state of dereliction and that it was a crying shame nobody had found money from somewhere to mend the gutters or shore up the sagging roof. I'll bet that cheapskate, Joseph Lloyd, and his committee tried to duck responsibility for it for years.

There are Victorian cobwebs in the corners of all the rooms, and under one window ledge is an anonymous insect that looks as if it reached the chrysalis stage, died, and became petrified. I can't say I'm surprised. It's as cold as a fridge in here, and if I have to spend any length of time here I'm likely to end up petrified myself by breakfast-time. (*Note to self*: don't forget to take along the whisky tonight).

There's mould growth around the windows and great swathes of damp on some of the walls – in fact when I went upstairs I had quite a bad moment because I thought someone was standing at the head, watching me. But it turned out to be the formation of the damp patches, and my heart returned to its normal rate. It wouldn't surprise me if that particular damp patch isn't one of the things that's given this house its reputation, because just for a moment the illusion was alarmingly vivid – a thickset man, his head turned towards me in a listening attitude . . .

Where there's no damp, there's graffiti. It's remarkable how most of today's wall-writers seem unable to spell even the most basic Anglo-Saxon epithets. There are piles of distasteful rubbish in corners, as well: greasy papers that once enclosed hamburgers, and foil trays of curry, and smashed beer bottles and used contraceptives. You could make a good case for the things the human race regard as necessary to survive by studying the detritus in a derelict building. Shelter, food, drink, and sex.

Still, Charect House hasn't fared too badly. I'm pleased about that, although its condition isn't my concern. What is my concern is whether there's a genuine presence here. That's why the council contacted the society and why I'm here. (It was a considerable feather in my cap to be given this assignment, because investigations for local authorities usually go to one of the directors. The fact that I intrigued a bit – well, more than a bit – to get it, is neither here nor there.)

Still, it's very unlikely there's anything in the least paranormal or supernatural here. It's my belief that all but a tiny percentage of so-called ghosts are due to one of three causes, and I'll set those three causes down here, just for the record.

The first and most common cause of 'hauntings' is man-made: spoofs done for money or malice or to gain a rather shallow fame. If I sat down to make a list of all the fraudsters the society has uncovered— Well, life's too short.

The second biggest cause of ghost-sightings is self-delusion or self-mesmerism – not necessarily conscious, but often infectious. 'I see a white figure,' cries someone, with such conviction that everyone else in the room instantly sees a white figure as well.

My third belief is contentious, but, put simply, I think strong emotions can leave an imprint on a place. Like entering a room and knowing that, despite the polite manner of the occupants, minutes earlier a vicious, cat-spitting row was in progress.

I've posited that last theory many times when I've lectured, and every time I do so, I remember how it's said that in Hiroshima the white-hot radiation of the atom bomb pasted the shapes of men's shadows on to walls, so that you could still see those shapes in the ruins years afterwards. When I think about that, I remember the young army captain with the slow smile who was stationed in Hiroshima, and how, if he had come back, we would have been married. Is his shadow imprinted on some shattered wall, I wonder? It's absurdly sentimental to think that, but there are times when I do, even now, nearly twenty years on. (And if anyone reads this and thinks the smudge on the page is due to a tear, let me state categorically that it isn't. It's whisky from the flask in my suitcase. There's nothing wrong with a little tot of whisky on these expeditions, although it's not advisable to get roaring drunk, of course.)

Anyhow, to conclude, what I do *not* believe is all that stuff about the fabric of time wearing thin, and it being possible to sometimes look through to other ages. (Except that if it were possible, Charect House would be the one place where I'd be able to do it.)

8 p.m.

Supper an hour ago in the Black Boar's minuscule dining room. Plain cut off the joint and vegetables. Perfectly adequate. I'm not one for fussed-up food.

I had a glass of beer in the bar afterwards. The local stuff is so fierce that it would peel varnish from wood, but I wanted to get into conversation with one or two of the locals. That's always useful for picking up fragments of gossip. If ghosts are likely to walk anywhere, they'll generally walk in a public house where the drink's flowing. They'll often take up permanent residence at the bar if you aren't careful.

I was ready to insert a carefully-prepared mention of Charect House into the casual bar-room conversation. Unfortunately, I didn't get the chance. It seems a local child is missing, and the men were assembling in the bar to help with the search.

'Evie Blythe,' said one of them when I asked. 'Only seven, poor little mite. Been gone since yesterday afternoon.'

'How dreadful. Do they think she's been taken by someone?'

'That's the concern. Don't seem very likely, though. We don't get much crime in Marston Lacy. Bit of drunk driving, the occasional housebreaking. Not many kidnappings. Still, there're peculiar folk around these days.'

An extremely elderly gentleman seated in a corner, mumbling beer and crisps through an overgrown beard, was understood to say there was evil everywhere in the world and always had been, you had only to read your Bible to know that. Sin and lipstick and modern music, that was where all the blame lay. He showed signs of becoming loquacious until somebody took another pint of beer over to him.

A couple of policemen came in and spread out maps of the area. They divided the terrain and assigned two men to search each section. Torches were distributed, and the Black Boar's manager came in with flasks of coffee for the searchers to take with them. I would have offered my help if it had been likely to do any good – appalling to think of a small child lost and helpless somewhere in the dark, or, God forbid, at the mercy of some pervert. But I had no knowledge of the area, and they weren't likely to trust a complete stranger.

But when the sergeant started telling the men to be sure to investigate all empty houses, I thought it advisable to enter the conversation and explain my presence. The customary reaction is usually derision or contempt. Men mostly laugh patronizingly, and women either shriek with pretended fear or want to involve you in intense conversations so they can relate their own encounters with the paranormal.

Marston Lacy behaved slightly differently. At mention of the house's name, an unmistakable stir of unease went through the listeners – exactly like one of those hammy horror films where the traveller enters the wayside tavern and innocently asks for directions to Castle Dracula. I wouldn't have been surprised if the Black Boar's inhabitants had pelted me with garlic or started drawing pentacles on the floor.

The sergeant was made of stern stuff, however. He merely said, 'Ah yes, Charect House. Got a bad reputation, that old place.'

'So I believe.'

'I'd better have a note of your address, if I may, miss. Just routine, you know.'

I supplied my name and address and added, perhaps slightly maliciously, that Mr Joseph Lloyd at the council offices would vouch for me. (He'll hate it if the police do contact him and he has to admit the local authority called in a ghost-hunter! That's a thought that gives me immense pleasure.)

'And you're actually going to spend the night at Charect House, are you, miss – uh, Dr Wilson?'

'That's the idea.'

'They say William Lee's been seen at Charect a time or two,' put in the much younger police constable rather hesitantly.

'More than a time or two from all I ever heard,' observed somebody else.

'Rot,' said the police sergeant with determination. 'William Lee's dead and under the ground and been there more than seventy years, so let's have no more nonsense about dead folks walking around. It'll be clanking chains and creaking gibbets next,' he said with an air of good-humoured exasperation.

The young constable volunteered the information that they had, in fact, checked Charect House earlier in the day. 'We went right through it, cellar to attic,' he said.

I heard one of the men from behind him mutter, 'Rather you than me.'

'Well, it was done to proper police procedure, and there was nothing to be found,' said the sergeant, raising his voice as if to make sure no one missed the statement. 'Nothing at all. Not William Lee, nor anyone else. It's a bleak old place, though, I'll say that for it.' He looked back at me. 'Best be on your guard.'

'I will.'

'And if you see anything suspicious, send for us.'
'Of course.'

10 p.m.

As is often the way, Charect House's personality is entirely
different by night. From being a rather forlorn old place, with
sagging timbers and rotting floors, it's become deeply forbidding. Even from the track leading up to it, it looked as if it
was leaning forward to take a look at whoever was brave or
foolhardy enough to approach it. But I've seen more glaring-
visaged houses than you can shake a stick at, and I know it's
simply an illusion: the effect of shadows and clouds behind
an erratic roofline. Prop up a sagging roof joist and nail a few
tiles into their proper place, and everything's rose-tinted.

I bounced the estate car up to the front door and set about
unloading the cameras and tape recorders. And now I'm inside
the haunted house and night has fallen. That looks dramatic,
written down, but when you get down to it, haunted houses
are seldom very dramatic. They're generally chilly, and the
worst part of the vigil is boredom. That's why I keep a journal
to help pass the time.

10.45 p.m.

I've positioned the cameras and tape recorders all over the
house – in the long drawing-room, in the dining room, and in
the hall, where there's a view of the stairs. There's a smaller
room, probably once used as a morning room, but I haven't
bothered with that. I haven't bothered with the kitchens, either.
But I've put cameras in the two main bedrooms. They all have
light-sensitive settings, so that any movement within their
range will trigger the shutter. I've got a Polaroid camera in
here with me.

There's no power on, of course, but I've got a good supply
of batteries for the recorders, which I'll have to replace at
regular intervals. For my own light I've got two electric torches
and a couple of oil lamps – what used to be called bullseyes.
I will do a good deal for the furtherance of the Society's work,
but I'm blowed if I'm going to sit all night in the pitch dark.

There's quite a lot of furniture in the house. I hadn't expected
that, and it means I can make myself reasonably snug – although

I do draw the line at actually lying down in one of the sarcophagus-sized beds upstairs. I may be a cynic and a sceptic, but I've read all those gothic ghost tales about ravished marriage beds and spectral bridegrooms. Not that I ever got as far as a marriage bed or a bridegroom, spectral or otherwise, and I shouldn't think I ever will, not now. Still, they say what you've never had you never miss, and I'm having a very full and interesting life without all that bouncing around in beds and having to put up with a man's moods and wash his socks. (Although in the privacy of these pages, I'll admit I wish my army captain and I had done some bed-bouncing before he went off to be frizzled to death by that wretched bomb. That's what you get for trying to stay virtuous when all around you are flinging virginity to the winds. Ah well. Can't be helped now.)

More to the point, I've rigged up a makeshift desk in the drawing room – I suspect it was once a library, with all the shelves that are still in place, so I think I'll refer to it as that for the rest of this report. I've beaten about three pounds of dust out of an old wing chair, and I'll be perfectly cosy.

I've put a large truncheon on the side of the chair – and never mind how I acquired it! If there's a child-stealer prowling around and he lights on Charect as a likely lair, he'll get very short shrift from me. On the other hand, if William Lee, dead for over seventy years, turns up, he'll have to be given quite different treatment.

Note to self: interesting to hear those references to William Lee in the Black Boar. I do know the house was built in the late 1700s by a John Lee of Shrewsbury, so William must have been a descendant. If the house passed down through the Lee family that would explain why I didn't find any land transfers or transfers of title when I searched – at least, until after WWII, when the place seems to have been passed from one government department to another until it ended up with J. Lloyd's council committee.

11 p.m.

I think one of the police searchers must have wound up the old grandfather clock while they were searching the house for the missing girl. It seems slightly whimsical of them, but you can never tell.

The clock stands in the corner, and it's ticking wheezily to itself as I write this. It's a florid, quite ugly, piece of Victoriana, but the ticking is rather a companionable sound.

It was at this point Nell knew she could not read Alice's diaries here, not in this room with the clock ticking scratchily to itself, and not in this house at all.

With extreme care she folded the papers into her bag, got up from the dusty floor, and went out.

FIVE

It was several hours before she was able to read the diaries. Beth was home from school at four o'clock and wanted to do her homework before her permitted television time. At some stage in the next few years she would no doubt become recalcitrant, listening to incomprehensible music and rebelling against every kind of authority, but at the moment she was seven years old and diligently bent over a page of sums. Nell supervised the sums, agreed they were boring, but explained they could come in useful, then sat with Beth to read the allotted chapter of a book for next day's reading class.

It was eight o'clock before Beth was finally in bed, with the array of fuzzy animals who kept her company and the curtains left slightly open.

'So I can watch the moon go over that tree before I go to sleep,' she explained. 'Then I can say goodnight to the moon an' he can say goodnight to me, then everything's safe.'

'You're safe anyway,' said Nell, wanting to hug the small figure tightly to her, but knowing Beth would shy away as she nearly always did from any physical demonstration.

Tonight though, Beth did not immediately lie down. She looked at Nell from the corners of her eyes and said, 'I s'pose nobody can get in here? While I'm asleep?'

'No, of course not.' This sounded slightly worrying. Nell sat on the edge of the bed, prepared to talk about it as much as Beth wanted. 'We're absolutely safe. All the doors are locked.'

'What about that, um, thing. The rhyme?'

'What rhyme?'

'The one about the dead man knocking on the door.'

Something cold and extremely unpleasant prickled across Nell's skin, but she said, as lightly as she could, 'Darling, that sounds horrid. Where did you hear that?'

'I can't remember. But the dead man knocks on the door an' there's a spell that means all the locks open, on account of it being a dead hand that's knocking.' Beth was huddled against the pillows, hugging her knees, not looking at Nell. In a small, scared voice, she said, 'I thought – s'posing Dad tried to do that? I'd want him to come back, but not – um, not as a dead person knocking to come in.'

Nell thought, oh God, if he came back I wouldn't care what he was – just half an hour with him would be enough . . .

She said, 'Beth, darling, dead people never come back. *Never.* And if Dad ever did, he wouldn't come in a scary way. I promise you he wouldn't. What he might do is be in a really nice dream, where he'd tell you he loved you and missed you.'

'I'd like that,' said Beth, having considered it. 'I think I'll go to sleep, in case he does that tonight, shall I?'

'That's a really good idea. Don't forget to say goodnight to the moon.'

'I'll wait until he's over that tree,' said Beth. 'G'night, Mum.'

Nell left the low landing light on for Beth and went down to the sitting room. The house was a shop in the main street, with a large flat on the first and second floors. She liked it very much; she had looked at a number of different areas to find the exact right property. She needed to go on working – partly for the money, but also for her own sanity – but she also wanted to be at home when Beth finished school each day. Living over the shop solved that.

The ground floor had two deep bow windows for displays, with the shop behind it and a tiny office. Upstairs was a long L-shaped living room, part of which overlooked the main street, with a kitchen behind. The second floor had three bedrooms and a bathroom.

Nell washed up the supper things, thinking about what Beth had said. The dead man knocking on the door. That was an eerie concept, however you looked at it, and whatever your beliefs. She might have a word with Beth's teacher tomorrow, to make sure there was no macabre local rhyme doing the rounds in the playground. Older children sometimes deliberately scared younger ones.

For now, though, she would light a fire and curl up with Alice Wilson's diaries. It was still a delight to have an old-fashioned fire, although it was a bit of a nuisance to have to sweep out the ashes next morning. But tonight she would enjoy the crackling flames. She poured a glass of wine, curled up in the deep sofa, and reached for the yellowing pages.

Alice Wilson's diary: Charect House, 10.30 p.m.

The old clock's ticking quietly away to itself in the corner, and I'm not sure that it's quite as companionable as I thought. In fact, a couple of times I've felt like hurling something at its smug, swollen face to shut it up. But here's a curious thing – twenty minutes ago I approached it with the intention of stuffing my scarf into the works to stop the mechanism, but when it came to it I couldn't. I can't explain it – but when I bent down and unlatched the door and saw the pendulum swinging to and fro, I was seized by such a violent aversion that I couldn't even touch it.

Now that it's night the house feels colder than it did this afternoon, but before leaving the Black Boar I put on a couple of extra sweaters and a fleece-lined jacket, together with thick flannel trousers and woollen socks. I've caught more colds than I can count over the years by spending the night in icily-cold houses, waiting for ghosts who never turn up, so now I swathe myself in layers of wool. I look like a roly-poly Mrs Noah, but there's nobody to see me except the occasional spook.

11.55 p.m.

I have a feeling that something's starting to happen. It's not anything I can easily describe on paper, but it's as if something's disturbed the atmosphere. As if Charect House is enclosed in a glass bubble, and something outside is chiselling silently at the glass's surface, to find a way in. Or even as if the tape recorders might be picking up sounds that humans aren't supposed to hear. Like the singing of mermaids or the sonar shrieks of bats. Or the hopeless sobbing of tormented souls, unable to leave a beloved home . . .

(This last sentence was barely legible, having been impatiently scored through, as if the writer had been exasperated at her sudden display of nerves, or perhaps even embarrassed by it. The next section was written clearly and decisively, as if the pen had been firmly pressed down on the page with the aim of dispelling any weakness.)

12.15 a.m.

We've passed the witching hour – although it always amuses me that people set such store by midnight, as if ghosts have wristwatches and check them worriedly to make sure they aren't missing an appointment to haunt somewhere. 'Dear me, I see it's five to twelve already, I'd better be off or I'll be late for the moated grange . . .'

What I will admit is that there can sometimes be a vague eeriness about the crossing of one day to the next, or one year to the next, as if something invisible's being handed from one pair of hands to another. And I have to say that when the old clock in here chimed twelve a short time ago, it startled me considerably. (It's somehow not a very nice chime either, although that's probably due to rust in the mechanism.)

It was shortly after the chiming of the clock that something happened.

I'd been reading (J.D. Salinger's *Catcher in the Rye*, just for the record) with my notebook and pen on the chair arm. Actually, I was almost falling asleep: what with the sweaters and the two oil lamps, I was comfortably warm and feeling drowsy. Also, I'd had a slug of whisky to help keep out the cold.

I must have been on the edge of sleep when something jerked me back to consciousness, and I sat up sharply, trying to identify what it was. I waited, listening. Sounds outside? Yes. Someone was walking very quietly and very stealthily around the outside of the house.

The chances were that it was a curious local skulking around, or teenagers playing a trick: 'There's a ghost-hunter up at Charect – let's give her a real scare.' At any minute a garishly-painted mask might thrust itself against the French window, or a white-sheeted figure, wringing its hands and moaning, would prance across the gardens.

But for all that, I was slightly unnerved. I flatter myself that if ever I met a real spook I'd cope with it, but prowlers and housebreakers are a different pair of shoes entirely. And there was that business of the missing child to take into account.

After a moment I quenched the oil lamp. Its light died, but

it hissed to itself in the shadows, like a coiled serpent. There was a pale blur from the French windows, where the faded curtains were partly open. The footsteps came again, and a flickering light showed in the monochrome tangle of the gardens. It was a smeary kind of light that didn't look like an ordinary electric torch, and I reached cautiously for the Polaroid. If there were any spooks that would show up on film, J. Lloyd and his council might as well have their money's worth. And if it did turn out to be some sick-minded child-stealer, then his features would be recorded and his capture made easier.

The light was coming closer, and the steps crunched on the gravel, but it was only when the footsteps stepped off the gravel on to grass that I heard the other sounds, and as God's my judge, they're going to give me nightmares for years.

A soft hoarse voice was weaving itself in and out of the greasy shadows. It was slightly blurred, but the words were dreadfully clear: I heard them as clearly as if they were being burned through my eyes straight into my brain.

'Open lock to the dead man's knock . . .
Fly bolt, and bar, and band . . .
Nor move, nor swerve, joint, muscle or nerve,
At the spell of the dead man's hand.'

I have heard some macabre things in my years with the Psychic Research Society, but I have never heard anything so chillingly terrifying as that soft chanting that dribbled across the dark garden of Charect House.

The sullen light came closer, and the footsteps were louder. I fumbled for the Polaroid, although to be honest, I'm not sure if I could even have found the shutter, never mind pressed it. The dreadful voice began its chant again:

'Open lock to the dead man's knock,
Fly bolt, and bar, and band.
Sleep all who sleep – wake all who wake.
But be as the dead for the dead man's sake.'

It was a minute or so before I recognized the words, but when I did, a chill traced its way down my spine. I knew what the rhyme was, and I knew what it meant. It sprang from a dark and very ancient belief embedded deep in the conscious-ness of Man – a belief and a desire stretching all the way back to Old Testament times. It's the desire to be invisible, soundless, to possess the ability to render an enemy helpless. But underlying that – perhaps even underpinning it – is a deeper, more visceral need, and that's the need for power over the dead.

You find the belief in the world's most ancient legends – some of them so old that Time has frayed them to cobwebs. But the belief has its genesis (and that's *not* meant as a pun!) in the biblical accounts of how Solomon caused temples to be raised in utter silence and without the use of any heavy tool – most of all without the use of iron, since iron, the substance used for weapons, shortens men's lives. It's a belief that's in Icelandic myths as well: tales of magic-laden stones that will break bolts and bars and also raise the dead. The Persians and Arabians had it, too: they believed a single enchanted word had power to roll back stone doors and open mountains. The story of Ali Baba and the Forty Thieves, and the *Open Sesame* spell, isn't just a Christmas pantomime.

And here in England is the belief in the Hand of Glory – the light fashioned from the fist of a hanged murderer and lit by graveyard fat and dead men's hair. The burning hand whose light bursts locks and lulls a house's occupants into sorcerous sleep.

I don't believe a syllable of it, of course. But whoever was outside believed. And if this was a gang of Marston Lacy teenagers pretending to be ghosts, they were the most literate and deeply-read ghost-fakes I had ever encountered.

The chanting came again:
'Open lock to the dead man's knock . . .
Fly bolt, and bar, and band.
Sleep all who sleep – wake all who wake.
But be as the dead for the dead man's sake . . .'

I can't tell how long I sat there, listening to that dreadful voice, hearing the footsteps going round the outside of the house. I believe I managed to scribble a few words in this notebook, although I dare say they won't make any sense later.

It was the sly chiming of the old clock that roused me to action. A single chime – one o'clock – and it was as if that wizened sound released something and the atmosphere of Charect House shifted again.

And as if the chime was a cue, on the outer door came three loud knocks.

My heart came up into my throat. Sensibly, it could have been an enterprising burglar making sure the house was empty, or the child-stealer looking for a hiding place. It might even have been a gypsy or a tramp looking for somewhere to spend the night.

But I knew it was neither of those things. I knew what it was. The dead man's knock.

The knock came again, louder and more peremptory this time. I sat absolutely still, hardly even breathing. Because the last – the very last thing – I was going to do was go out into the dark house to investigate the caller's identity. If he (it would be a "he" of course) was an ordinary living person, it would be the height of folly to open the door at one in the morning. If he wasn't an ordinary living person, it would be folly of a different kind to open the door.

I stayed where I was, forcing myself to remember how I had gone round the house earlier, systematically locking and bolting every door, then putting the bunch of keys safely in my bag. The bag stood on the hearth in this room, within reach. The house was secure. I was safe. It was all right.

It was not all right, though, and I was not safe at all. Into the silence came a new sound – a slow, stealthy creaking. A door was being opened, and it was opening very slowly and almost unwillingly, as if something was leaning heavily against it.

For anyone reading this, I do *know* it sounds like classic ghost story stuff, but it was the most frightening thing I've ever heard. Then the door banged against a wall, and with a new lurch of fear, I thought – he's got in. The owner of that dreadful hoarse voice, that figure who carried the bleared light, has got into the house. The lock has opened to the dead man's knock.

1.15 a.m.

There's been no further sound, but he's out there – I can feel that he is. And I'm sitting here, summoning up my courage to go out of this room and search for him. I don't believe what I saw was a manifestation, I *don't*, but I can no longer ignore

what's happened. And the thought of J. Lloyd's disgust if I
have to tell him I ducked out of the investigation because
I was frightened is spurring me on. J. Lloyd, if you ever read
this, you'll know if anything did happen to me tonight, it was
your fault.

The Polaroid's still round my neck on its strap, and I'll
take pictures of everything that moves. I'll check the light-
sensitive cameras in each room as well and the tape recorders.
What if that grisly chanting has been recorded? But what if
it hasn't . . . ? Because there are sounds humans aren't meant
to hear, remember? The murmuring of demons, the secret
whispering of wolves. And the chanting of a dark charm to
open doors and cast slumber over human brains . . .

I'll take the heavy torch with me, too. Its light will be a
comfort, and it'll also be a good weapon if this turns out to
be a flesh and blood prowler. Oh God, if only it's a living
human intruder, after nothing more sinister than money.

1.30 a.m.

As I went out of the library, my nerves were jangling like
piano wires. The camera clanked against the torch as I opened
the door. In that listening silence it was loud enough to waken
the dead, although it was starting to seem as if the dead needed
no waking – they were already rampaging around the house.

As I stood in the hall, everywhere was silent and cold
moonlight trickled through the narrow windows, lying across
the dusty oak floor like flecks of silver.

I looked into each of the rooms in turn. The dining room
was silent and still, but when I opened the door of the morning
room, something reached down to brush soft, light fingers
across my face. I gave a half-scream and nearly dropped the
torch, but then I realized it was simply the long cobwebs
drifting down from above, disturbed by the current of air
from the open door. I brushed them away, shone the torch
on an empty room, and went along to the scullery. It seemed
unlikely that with the whole house at its disposal, a ghost
would choose to hide in extreme discomfort in a dank, evil-
smelling scullery, but I still checked. But nothing was moving
in the kitchens, unless you count the presence of several
healthy-looking black beetles in the copper washtub and some

lively mould working its way across the windows. I shone the torch on it with distaste and wished myself back in my flat in Peckham, with everything clean and organized and unthreatening. Actually, I wished to be anywhere in the world other than in this house.

Eventually, I stood at the foot of the stairs. They were in semi-darkness, but some light came in from a tall window on the half-landing. A hundred years ago, ladies would have sat there to recover their energy after the effort of rising and dressing each morning, or to rest on the way up the stairs in the evening. No one was there now, of course. Or was there? My heart began to bang against my ribs, and I peered through the gloom, hesitant to advertise my presence by shining the torch. But, of course, there was no one there. It was the large, damp stain on the upper wall that was creating the illusion of a figure again – the stain that earlier on had looked so much like a thickset man.

But it was not the discoloured patch at all. Someone *was* there. A man – his features in deep shadow – was standing at the head of the stairs, his head bowed as if looking down into the stairwell.

I bolted back into the library and slammed the door shut. It resounded like the crack of doom, and plaster showered down from the ceiling. A ridiculous thing to do, of course, for when did a closed door ever keep out a ghost . . . ? Particularly one with the spell to open doors . . . *Open lock to the dead man's knock . . .*

It's a few minutes before two a.m. and I'm sitting here with my eyes on the closed door, trying to make some order of my tumbling thoughts. There's no doubt in my mind that I really did see that figure at the top of the stairs.

I'll finish this sentence, then I'll tear these pages out of the notebook and fold them inside the old clock – the oak floor inside the case is slightly loose, and a section tips up like an insecure floorboard. I'll wait until the clock has chimed the hour though. For some reason I flinch from touching it while it's chiming.

It's not at all like me to do something so whimsical as hide a diary, but I'd like to leave a record of sorts for people to find. Just in case something happens to me tonight . . .

* * *

Nell's skin was prickling with horror. It's Beth's rhyme, she thought. The rhyme about the dead man knocking on the door, and the spell that opened all the locks.

Open lock to the dead man's knock . . .

She was just reaching out for the glass of wine at her hand when screams rang out from Beth's room.

SIX

Beth was huddled against the wall in the bedroom, clutching the pillow against her as if to shield herself from something, and staring in wild-eyed terror at the far corner.

Nell was across the bedroom in two strides, scooping up the small, frightened figure and hugging it to her.

'Darling, it's all right, whatever it is, you're absolutely safe. I'm here, you're safe, you're safe.'

Beth was shaking so violently that Nell was afraid for a moment she was having some kind of fit, and she seemed scarcely to recognize her mother. Nell sent an uneasy glance to the corner, where Beth was still staring. Was there something there that had frightened her? A spider? But Beth would not scream and shiver like this for a spider. She held on to the small figure, repeating the words about being safe, praying the reassurance would get through, and at last Beth drew a deep shuddering breath and clutched her mother's hands so tightly that Nell nearly cried out.

In a faltering voice, Beth said, 'There was a man in the room.'

Nell's pulse skipped a beat or two, then she said, 'Bethy, there's no one here. You had a nightmare.'

'He was here,' said Beth. 'I woke up and he was standing there, watching me.'

'There's no one here, sweetheart. You're safe and no one can get in, and I'm here.'

The fear was gradually fading from Beth's eyes. She sat up a bit straighter and looked about her. 'There's nobody here, is there?'

'No, nobody at all.'

'He couldn't be – um – hiding anywhere, could he?'

'No, but we'll look so you know for sure,' said Nell. She opened the door of the wardrobe and then the cupboard built into one side of the old, blocked-up chimney breast. 'All right?'

'Um, yes.'

Nell said, 'How about if we put your dressing gown on and

you come downstairs and I'll make some hot milk.' Beth liked
it if she ever had to be downstairs after her bedtime. She said
it was being allowed into the grown-ups' world.

But tonight she hesitated.

'I could bring the milk up to you, and we'll read a bit of
your book together,' said Nell. 'You can tell me about the
nightmare if you like. Telling a thing makes it go away.'

This seemed to help. Beth said, 'He *really* isn't here now?'

'No one's here,' said Nell. 'He was in the dream.'

'No, he was in the room,' said Beth, and Nell felt her shudder
again. 'He got in 'cos he knocked on the window. The dead
man's knock, like in the rhyme.'

Nell glanced involuntarily to the window, which was closed.

'An' he stood in the corner an' that's when I woke up,' said
Beth. 'He was looking for me.' She was making a valiant
effort not to cry, and Nell's heart contracted. 'Could I come
downstairs after all, Mum?'

'Of course you can.' Nell reached for the dressing gown
and wrapped it round the small, shivering figure. She would
crush a junior paracetamol in the hot milk. That would calm
Beth down and help her to go back to sleep.

'The bad thing,' said Beth as they went down the stairs.
'The really *bad* thing—'

'Yes?'

'It's frightening to say it.' Her lower lip trembled. 'It makes
it real if you say it.'

'No, it doesn't. Saying a thing shoos the fright away. Sit
by the fire and tell me.'

'He had no eyes,' said Beth, thrusting a clenched fist into
her mouth. 'That man who got into my room. He was trying
to find me, but he couldn't because he had no eyes.'

No eyes. How had Beth known something so macabre and so
deeply distressing? Because when Brad was killed, skidding
on that patch of ice so that the tanker smashed into his car,
the impact had driven one of the tanker's splintered wheel
arches straight through the car's side. His eyes had been shattered – Brad's dear lovely eyes that smiled with such love and
life. . . . His brain had bled out through the eye sockets while
the ambulances tried to get to him through the motorway
pile-up.

Beth had never known about the injuries, of course. Somehow Nell had managed to make Brad's death sound smooth and clean to her. They had discussed what might happen when somebody died; Nell, who had never really sorted out her own beliefs in that direction, had tried to give Beth a child's outlook on reincarnation, which seemed to her one of the happier theories, and which, for Beth, could be likened to plants that died in the autumn, but came up again the following spring, bright and new.

But the only people who had known what the tanker's huge metal struts had done to Brad were Nell herself, their GP in London, and the coroner's office.

And no one in the world knew about Nell's own nightmares, in which Brad, his face shredded, his eyes torn away, tried to fumble his blind way back to find her.

The photograph of Charect House showing the woman at the attic window had bothered Michael in a low-key way for several days, but he managed to push it to the back of his mind. He also managed to ignore the nagging memory of the shadowy figure he had glimpsed on the stairs.

Michaelmas term went amiably along its well-worn tracks, enlivened here and there by various college activities. Michael gave a paper to the Tolkien Society, which seemed to be well received, and was guest speaker at a Students' Union debate – the topic was the relevance of romanticism in the modern world, which made for some lively discussion. Afterwards, some of his students bore him off to the Turf Tavern, where inordinate quantities of beer were drunk and huge platters of seafood risotto circulated. Michael finally managed to extricate himself on the grounds that he had a faculty meeting at nine next morning and should get an early night. This was received with derisive hoots, and somebody started a limerick on the subject of faculties. Michael grinned, waited until the second verse was boozily completed, joined in the applause, then dropped an extra twenty-pound note into the drinks kitty before making good his exit. He reached his rooms shortly before midnight to find that Wilberforce had left a dead mouse on the step, which had to be disposed of in the incinerator in the basement. By the time he had dealt with this it was a quarter to one when he finally got to bed. Still, it had been a good evening, and it was nice that the students were so friendly.

It was during the first week of November when Jack Harper emailed again about the Shropshire house.

Michael—

Can you possibly find time to drag yourself away from your ivory tower again and make another journey to Marston Lacy? We need a reliable account of what's actually been done to Charect House so far. The builders went in three weeks ago, but they keep sending terrifying letters and faxes about planning restrictions, and admonitory notices relating to Listed Buildings, and asking if we know the true condition of the windows and the roof. If the surveyor's report can be trusted, the Georgian windows are infested with *coniophora puteana*, and the roof has *merulius lacrymans*. That's wet rot and dry rot respectively to the likes of you and me.

But we're staying with the plan to spend Christmas in the house – Liz has ordered camp beds and oil lamps and says it will be the greatest fun to eat picnic meals and dine by candlelight and we won't even notice the rubble and the mess. Also, it will be a good reason not to spend the holiday with the cousins. Personally, I'd rather have the cousins or even Liz's godmother for the winter solstice than camp out in an English ruin, however elegant it might be.

So you'd better let me have the phone number of that place you stayed (Capering Cow? Prancing Bullock?) because I'm blowed if I'll eat sandwiches on Christmas Day.

Still, the efficient Ms West emailed to say she bought the long-case clock and the rosewood table at the auction, so at least we'll be able to tell what time of day it is.

Anyway, here's the thing. I dare say you're knee-deep in students – do they still ask you to their parties, and if so, do you *know* how rare that is? My students here would be dismembered in slow stages before they'd ask me to have so much as a cup of coffee, but then I'm a slightly balding, becoming paunchy, married man, and even in my youth I never looked like Keats, preparing to starve with romantic intensity in his garret.

So if you could abandon the students again I'd be forever in your debt. (I'm in everybody else's, so one more won't make much difference.) I need to be sure they aren't wiring the electricity into the septic tank just for the fun of it, or installing the heating plant in the roof so it crashes through the ceilings one night like the falling mountain in Gilgamesh's nightmare. Talking of nightmares, Ellie is still having those God-awful dreams, poor little scrap. One of the things that helps her, though, are your stories about Wilberforce. Last night she fell asleep smiling after Liz read the latest episode of how Wilberforce went on his holidays, but the mice sabotaged his luggage and towed the train off the track so he ended up in Oswaldtwistle instead of Devon, and with no swimming trunks. Where the hell is Oswaldtwistle, by the way? And did you ever try writing kids' books? I bet Wilberforce would outsell Harry Potter.

But most nights Ellie wakes in a sobbing panic, apparently frantic with anxiety for 'Elvira'. From which you'll see we haven't been able to get rid of Elvira yet. Two nights ago Ellie told Liz someone was trying to find Elvira, and when Liz asked to know a bit more – sort of going along with the fantasy in case she could find a way to dispel it – Ellie said it was the man with holes where his eyes should be. I don't know about you, but that was enough to give me the creeps, never mind a seven-year-old.

Let me know about Charect. Liz sends love.

Jack

Michael did not really want to leave Oxford, which at that time of the year was rain-scented and chrysanthemum-tinted, but he could probably steal twenty-four hours.

Before he left, he sent Ellie a new episode of Wilberforce's tribulations, in which the mice put on a display of street-dance, wearing baseball caps back to front, and thwarting Wilberforce's attempts to disrupt the performance by tying him up with the strings from the cello and upending the tuba horn on his head.

Then he sent a second email to Jack, saying he would drive to Marston Lacy on Friday. He might as well stay overnight again.

Michael reached Marston Lacy shortly before eleven on Friday morning, checked in at the Black Boar, and asked about the availability of rooms for Jack and Liz's Christmas sojourn.

It appeared there would be no problem; the Black Boar prided itself on providing a really good family Christmas, said the manager. A proper turkey dinner at two o'clock, and a festive supper in the evening with mulled wine and carol singing. A lot of local people came in for the evening – they made quite an event of it. This Dickensian prospect might not entirely live up to its promise, but Michael knew it would delight Liz, so he booked a double room there and then, with a small adjoining one for Ellie. On impulse, he booked a third room for himself. Jack had been fairly insistent about joining forces for Christmas, and Michael remembered that his rooms at Oriel were due to be repainted during the holidays.

Blackberry Lane, when he reached it, was drenched in gentle autumn rain and still felt as if it was caught in its own tiny shard of the past. But there were a number of large tyre tracks, which had not been there on his first visit and which presumably belonged to builders' lorries. Michael wondered if the lane was to be resurfaced or even widened. It would be a pity to lose the feeling of having stepped backwards – of having wandered by chance into an England where there were quiet lanes with dappled sunlight, and where the cuckoo called in spring and blackberries were picked by children in autumn. (And where three-quarters of the population had no inside lavatory or piped water, and at least half of the people earned wages so low they could scarcely feed their families, and children were sent into the mines and up chimneys, said his mind.) On the other hand, it would make life easier to be able to drive to the house without getting stuck in a ditch halfway.

At first sight, the only thing different about Charect House was the large skip, which appeared to be filled with a embarrassment of riches in the form of yards of lead piping, sections of uprooted bathroom fittings, and an assortment of rotting window frames. Two lorries were parked alongside the house, and a man wearing several sweaters and a hat with ear flaps was crawling, spider-like, across the roof, doing something with a large hammer to the tiles.

Michael called out a good morning and received a wave and an invitation to go into the house, on account of it was cold enough to freeze the balls off a brass monkey out here, pardon the French.

As he stepped through the half-open door, there was a moment when the hammering from the roof fell into the rhythm he had heard on his first visit: that grim tattoo somewhere within the house, that let-me-out tapping. He frowned and pushed the memory away. If Charect House had ever contained ghosts or even down-to-earth intruders, they would all certainly have fled in exasperation days ago to escape the hammering and drilling, and the thudding music coming from the small stereo in the hall.

Michael negotiated the builders' debris with care and, encountering a rotund gentleman who appeared to be in some sort of overall authority, introduced himself and explained about being a friend of the owners.

'They asked me if I could look in to see how things were going.' He did not say he had made a two-hour drive from Oxford for this looking-in, in case the builder thought he was being spied on.

But the builder apparently saw nothing wrong and accompanied Michael on a tour of the house, explaining, in largely incomprehensible terms, what was being done, cheerfully pointing out such mysteries as RSJs in the drawing room, new lath and plaster ceilings in the bedrooms, and insulated bonding for the electrical circuit, which, he said, you had to have in a place like this, because you were so far from your substation.

'Ah,' said Michael, blankly.

'I reckon your friends have taken on quite a task with this place,' said the builder.

Michael reckoned so as well. 'I think they inherited it out of the blue,' he said. 'They had no idea it was even in their family.'

'So I hear. It's being said those scoundrelly old solicitors lost the deeds for the best part of forty years. Grimley and Shrike they were called. They had offices on the edge of the High Street. It's a health food shop now, but I remember it being Grimley and Shrike when I was a boy. Like something out of Dickens they were.'

'I did hear something about the deeds being mislaid,' said Michael.

'That's putting it politely,' said the builder cheerfully. 'If you ask me, it's surprising old man Shrike didn't mislay himself along with the deeds. I never knew him, of course, but my father did a job at the offices – thirty years ago it must be. He said old Shrike used to wear one of those old-fashioned high wing collars, and you could hardly see his desk for all the files. Deed boxes stacked halfway up to the ceiling, cobwebs in every corner, and cigarette ash over everything. He died at his desk one day, just fell down while he was drafting somebody's will and stayed there until the office boy found him. Great old character, by all accounts. Rotten solicitor though, so they say. Ah well. Come and see what we're doing upstairs.'

'Dr Harper mentioned something about turning part of the attics into one large room,' said Michael as they stood at the foot of the stairs. Jack had thought, from the layout plans supplied by the surveyor, that the attics might be made into a combined bedroom and playroom for Ellie.

'We're starting on that tomorrow,' said the builder. 'Wait a bit, I'll show you the plans if you like.' He fished a sheaf of papers from an inner pocket and spread them out on a window sill.

'See that line of wall there?' He jabbed at the plans with a pencil. 'Well, unless the surveyor got the layout wrong – and I've known that happen more than once, trust me! – Dr Harper's idea is that if we knock that out it'll make for one big L-shaped room.'

'Yes, I see,' said Michael, to whom the plans were almost entirely incomprehensible, but understanding the general principle, which was that Ellie would have a rooftop hideaway. She would love it; she would have shelves of books under the windows and brightly-coloured pictures on the walls, and Liz would probably find a jazzy bedspread and curtains. When Michael stayed here, he and Ellie would sit in her rooftop room and discuss what further adventures Wilberforce might have.

'And we'll run the wiring up there and put in a radiator, although it'll be snug enough with being immediately under the roof.'

'You seem to be getting on well.'

'Interesting old place,' said the builder, pocketing his pencil and rolling up the plans. 'Wouldn't be everybody's choice, of course.'

He sent Michael a sideways look, and Michael said, 'I expect there are a few local ghost stories about it.'

'Always are with an old empty house,' said the builder, matter-of-factly. 'And this one's been empty ever since I can remember. But they tell how William Lee, who died more than a hundred years ago, haunts the place.' He grinned. 'Folk used to say he'd walk through the rooms and what used to be the orchard, although nobody seems to know why.'

Almost against his will, Michael said, 'Have you ever seen anything?'

'I have not. My brother, though, he reckons he saw William once. But then my brother sees pink elephants dancing with elves when he's been at the sauce.' He lifted his elbow in a descriptive gesture. 'Lot of rubbish, ghosts,' he said roundly. 'But any old empty house has to have a few tales told about it, don't it, squire?'

Michael agreed it did and went out into the timeless rain.

SEVEN

The rain had stopped by the time he got back to the little town, and as he negotiated the narrow main street he saw a sign over one of the shops saying Nell West Antiques. Michael slowed down, remembering that Nell West was the antique dealer Jack and Liz had commissioned to find Charect's original furniture. Should he go into the shop? Yes, why not? Liz in particular would like to know a bit about the person who was scouring the county for Charect's furniture, and it would be nice to report that he had made friendly contact on her and Jack's behalf. He found a parking space and walked back.

The shop was on the ground floor of a nice old building, which looked as if it had recently been painted. Michael went inside. No one seemed to be in attendance, but the interior was invitingly arranged and there was a pleasing scent of good polish and lavender. He wandered around, wondering if any of the items were destined for Charect or had been part of Charect. In one corner was a Victorian sampler with a date of 1878. It depicted a house and garden. Near to it stood a pair of decanters with silver labels, and Michael paused to examine these, wondering if they would make a good house-warming present for Jack and Liz. Liz would like the idea of elegant decanters, and Jack would humour her. The figure on the price tag was high, but not exorbitant.

'Sorry I kept you,' said a slightly breathless voice behind him. 'I was upstairs. Can I help with anything, or do you prefer to trundle round on your own?'

She was slightly-built and had short brown hair that looked as if she might thrust her fingers through it when she was concentrating. She had on what looked like working clothes – cords and trainers and a loose shirt. Michael said tentatively, 'I wondered if I could have a word with Nell West.'

'I'm Nell West.' She regarded him quizzically. 'Are you a buyer or a seller?'

'Probably a buyer. But we have mutual friends. I'm Michael Flint—'

'Oh, you're Liz Harper's friend from Oxford,' she said at once and smiled. Her eyes lit up with the smile, and her whole face changed. 'Liz said you might call when you were here. Have you been looking at the house?'

'I have. Jack wanted a progress report, although I think the only thing I can report is that builders are crawling all over the place and it's ringing with the sound of thudding rock music.'

'Well, that ought to rout the ghosts at any rate,' she said.

So she had sensed the ghosts as well. Or perhaps it was just a throwaway remark. Michael said, 'I was admiring these decanters.'

'They're nice, aren't they?' she said. 'Quite unusual designs. I found them in a sale in a big old house on the Welsh border. They're early nineteenth-century – just about pre-Victoria, I think. 1830-ish.'

'Which makes them a bit younger than Charect House,' said Michael. 'I think Liz and Jack would appreciate them, though. Could we—'

He broke off. From overhead came the sound of a child's terrified, desperate screaming. Nell's eyes widened in horror, and she said, in a smothered voice, 'My daughter— She's upstairs— I'm sorry, I'll have to go—'

She ran to the back of the shop, and Michael heard her footsteps going swiftly up a flight of stairs. He hesitated, not wanting to intrude on a stranger's problems, but the screams came again, filled with real panic, then the words, 'Help me . . .'

Clearly, this was more than a child's tantrums, and Michael realized this shop was a place burglars might target, creeping in through a rear door, frightening a small child. And if Nell West was here on her own—

He went through to the back of the shop and ran part-way up the stairs. 'Nell – it's Michael. What's happening?' With relief he heard her call back. 'Up here. Come up. Second stairway.'

At least it did not seem to be a burglar. Michael went up the second stairway and saw Nell through a half-open door at the far end. She was sitting on a bed, hugging a small girl to her. The child was sobbing and clutching her mother, almost distraught with terror. Her hair was the same autumn-leaf colour as Nell's.

He paused, suddenly aware that the sight of a strange man might frighten the child even further. So he stopped at the head of the stairs and said, 'Are you all right?' which was an outstandingly ridiculous thing to say because clearly neither of them was all right at all. 'Is there something I can do to help? Phone anyone for you?'

'No, it's fine, she'll be all right soon. It's just – she's been having nightmares. Beth, darling, it was just the bad old dream again, truly it was.'

Through hiccuping sobs, the child said, 'It wasn't a dream. He was *here*. The man. He was in my room – I saw him. He was standing in the corner again.'

Michael looked involuntarily towards the corner. There was no one there, of course.

Over Beth's head, Nell said, 'She's been having a series of nightmares – really vicious ones. Last night was particularly grim, so she was going to have a bit of a sleep this afternoon, to catch up. I'm sorry to have alarmed you—'

'I'll go,' said Michael, feeling inadequate. 'We'll sort out the decanters another day.'

'There's no need. She really will be all right in a minute. Beth, darling, stop crying, I promise you're absolutely safe. There's no one here – only Mr Flint who's a friend of— Sorry, I think that should be "Dr", shouldn't it?'

'Hello, Beth. I'm Michael.'

'You gave him quite a shock shouting like that,' said Nell. 'He's a friend of the American people with the little girl who's going to live here. I told you about her.'

'Yes.'

Michael said, 'I'll go downstairs and check everywhere. Just in case there really is anyone prowling around. Would that make you feel better, Beth?' The two figures on the bed seemed to him dreadfully vulnerable and fragile.

'Um, yes, thank you.'

'Had I better lock the shop door while I'm there? Just for the moment?'

'Would you?' said Nell. 'Drop the catch and turn the sign to "Closed".'

The shop and the rooms above it were innocent of any

passing burglars, and the back door, which appeared to open on to a small courtyard with outbuildings, was firmly locked and bolted. Michael went back into the shop, intending to make a tactful exit, but Nell came down to meet him.

'Can you stay for a cup of tea? I'm just making it.'

'Well, that would be welcome, but I don't want to—'

'If you were going to say "impose", you aren't,' she said. 'I'd like to thank you properly. You can tell Beth about Liz Harper's little girl. Beth's looking forward to meeting her. Come up to the sitting room.'

Beth was huddled into a chair near the fire. She had a bright rug wrapped round her, and she was hugging a large, furry bear. The marks of tears were still on her face, and she looked so small and white that Michael forgot about being a stranger or intruding and sat down opposite her.

'Hello, Beth,' he said. 'The American girl your mum talked about is my god-daughter. I think she's about the same age as you.'

'I'm seven,' said Beth rather shakily.

'Exactly the same, then. My god-daughter's called Ellie, and she's coming over here for Christmas. She doesn't know anyone in England, so I think she'd like to meet you and have a friend here.'

Beth said, 'I didn't know any people when I came here either. Is she nice?'

'Yes, very.'

'What does she like to do?' It was said a bit dubiously.

'All kinds of things. She likes animals.'

'I like animals.'

'Cats? Ellie loves cats. She likes hearing about my cat,' said Michael. 'His name's Wilberforce, and he's always getting into trouble.' Without realizing he was going to do so, he started to relate one of the adventures he made up for Ellie – the one where Wilberforce got mixed up with the mice's redecoration of their home.

Beth's small face was instantly absorbed, and she laughed when Wilberforce ended up sitting in the paint pot, very indignant, with scarlet paint on his whiskers.

'I'll send you a photograph of him, shall I?'

'Can it be on the computer? I'm allowed to use it after homework.'

'Yes, certainly.' He could send Beth one of the photos he had sent to Ellie. He would tell Ellie about this possible British friend waiting to meet her, as well. He finished the cup of tea, then got up and said, firmly, he would leave them to it.

'I'm so grateful to you,' said Nell as they went down to the shop. 'I loved the story of your cat, by the way. Beth did, as well.'

Choosing his words carefully, Michael said, 'That nightmare . . . For a child to think there's someone in her room – someone standing there watching her while she's asleep – would be terrifying. It would spook me, never mind a child.'

'It's the recurrent theme,' said Nell. 'I don't know if it indicates a lack of security – whether I should get medical advice. Whether it's something to do with her father dying last year—' She broke off, and Michael saw her eyes flinch as if from a too-bright light. She said, 'Beth insists the man who comes into her room has no eyes.'

Michael had been reaching for the door, but at these words he felt as if something cold had clutched at his throat. He turned back. 'What did you say?'

'The man in the nightmare has no eyes.' She had half-turned away, and without looking at him, she said, 'Last year my – Beth's father was killed in a car crash. It – the impact of the crash – penetrated his eyes. Tore them out completely.'

'Oh no,' said Michael, appalled. 'Nell, I'm so sorry. And you think that's what's triggering Beth's nightmares?'

'She doesn't know any of the details of Brad's death,' said Nell.

'Are you sure? Could she have overheard somebody talking?'

'Well, I'm as sure as I can be. The only other people who knew were the coroner and our GP in London and they certainly didn't tell her.'

'Could it be a form of telepathy?' said Michael after a moment. 'Could she have picked it up from you?'

'I suppose it's just about possible. It's the only explanation, isn't it?' She finally turned round to look at him.

'Yes,' said Michael very firmly. 'It's the only explanation.'

He left for Oxford late next morning, calling in at the shop on his way to see if Beth had recovered.

'Entirely,' said Nell. 'She went to bed talking about Wilberforce and the mice, and she slept all the way through till breakfast, then got up and ate a huge bowl of porridge and honey.'

Michael smiled at the thought of the small, grave Beth, diligently eating an A.A. Milne breakfast. He said, 'That's great. I'll send the photo later today. Have you got a card or something with your email— Thanks. I'll email Liz as well and tell her I've met you and that I might have found a friend for Ellie.'

'Beth's pleased at the thought of meeting Ellie,' said Nell. 'It's taken her mind away from the nightmare. You're very good with children. Have you any of your own?'

'No,' said Michael. 'I haven't got a wife either, so it's just as well about the children.' He grinned at her.

'You were looking at those decanters for Liz and Jack,' said Nell. 'If you do decide to get them as a house-warming present, I'd let you have them for what I paid. I don't mean that to sound like a hard sell.'

'It's not much of a hard sell if you're offering them at cost,' said Michael. 'I'd already decided to get them, but I'll pay full price.'

'I mean it. There wasn't much of a markup anyway.'

He saw she was not going to change her mind, so he said, 'All right. But on condition I buy the sampler at its full price, as well.'

'That's supposed to be local work,' said Nell. 'It'd be nice to think it's from Charect, but I don't think it is.'

'No, but there's a cat worked into it – in one corner. So I'd like to get it for Ellie's room.'

'Wilberforce,' said Nell and smiled. 'OK, that's a deal. D'you want to take them now? I can wrap them up fairly quickly.'

To his own surprise, Michael said, 'I thought about coming back next weekend to check progress for Jack. Can you keep them until then? I could call around lunchtime.'

The smile came again. 'Yes,' she said. 'Yes, do that.'

Michael had no idea why he had made that tentative arrangement to see Nell West again. He could easily have taken the decanters and the sampler with him. He had, in fact, meant to remain firmly in Oxford for the rest of the Michaelmas term, but as he drove back he found he was looking forward to seeing Nell and the small Beth again.

It was curious that Beth seemed to be having the same nightmare as Ellie. A man with no eyes, Beth had said. And Ellie, thousands of miles away, had talked about a man with holes where his eyes should be. Michael had only just stopped himself from blurting it out to Nell West. It was just a macabre coincidence, of course. Something to do with insecurity, maybe – Beth had lost her father a short time ago, and despite Nell's conviction that she had not known about the injuries in the car crash, children had a way of picking up things their parents did not realize.

But Ellie, suffering what sounded to be the same nightmare, had not lost her father. Ellie was surrounded by love and stability, and she had two eminently sane parents who had a happy marriage. She was probably one of the best-adjusted children on the planet. Or was she? Who knew what darknesses existed in any child's mind?

He reached Oriel College on Saturday evening to find that Wilberforce had got into the buttery and eaten an entire cream trifle intended for the weekend visit of a second-year's parents, after which Wilberforce had apparently been sick on a pile of essays about Swinburne. Michael apologized to everyone he could think of, told the second-year to buy another trifle from the pastry shop in the High at his expense, and cleaned up the Swinburne essays as well as he could. After this he sat down to send the photos of the unrepentant Wilberforce to Beth West, with an email for Nell saying he would see her next weekend.

He surveyed the Swinburne essays with distaste and, instead of reading them, sat down at the computer to record Wilberforce's adventures in the buttery before he forgot it. He would send it to Ellie later. He might send it to Beth as well.

Nell hoped she had not been too pushy with Michael Flint over the decanters, but he had definitely said he was intending to buy them. He had been great with Beth. She and Beth had talked about Wilberforce over their supper, and Beth had asked if they could invite Ellie Harper to tea one day, did Mum think that was a good idea?

'Terrific,' said Nell, so grateful for Beth's apparent return to

normality that she would have agreed to the entire population
of Marston Lacy coming to tea.

They spent most of Sunday in the workshop at the back of
the shop. Nell was currently stripping a small oak table that
had been semi-vandalized by several applications of dark
brown varnish at some stage in its life. The work was slow,
but it was immensely satisfying, and she was uncovering an
inlay on the top – squares of African blackwood and pale
beautiful beech, immaculately dovetailed into a chessboard.
Beth pottered around, fetching rags and cloths, singing to the
radio.

After they'd had supper and Beth was in bed, Nell tidied
the sitting room, coming across Alice Wilson's journal, which
she had thrust on top of a bookshelf. It was annoying that it
ended so abruptly. Alice had hidden the pages in the clock
and then seemed to vanish. What had happened to her? It was
a good forty years ago, and the trail – if there was a trail –
would be very fragile by this time.

Next morning she dropped Beth off at school, relieved there
had been no more nightmares. She generally opened the shop
at ten, but Mondays were always quiet, so she finished work
on the oak table. She enjoyed being in the workshop: it was
a large, one-storey outbuilding, and it was exactly right for
storage of furniture not currently on display and for renovation
projects. There was electricity and even an old Victorian stove,
although Nell was not inclined to trust its efficiency and she
had fitted modern convector heaters.

She was hoping she could hold antique weekends next
spring, booking small groups of people into the Black Boar
and providing practical workshop sessions on restoration,
interspersed with trips to one or two nearby National Trust
properties to study furniture and tapestries. It would be an
interesting project, and Nell was enjoying working out the
details.

She locked up the outbuilding around eleven, washed the
cobwebs and dust away and put on a clean shirt and cords,
then opened the shop, flipping her mobile on, which she had
switched off while she was sanding the table.

There were two messages. The first was from Beth's school
asking her please to telephone them as a matter of some
urgency.

The other message was from the local police station requesting her, in even more urgent terms, to call them without delay. There was no immediate cause for panic, said the fatherly voice on the voicemail, but there was a strong possibility that her daughter was missing.

EIGHT

Nell drove to the police station as if the denizens of hell were chasing her and was taken straight to an interview room, where the owner of the fatherly voice, who introduced himself as Detective Inspector Brent, explained there was no immediate cause for concern. The thing was that Beth's school had phoned them when Beth had failed to appear for class at nine o'clock.

Nell, fighting to keep panic down, said, 'But I dropped her off at the gates. It was ten to nine – I didn't watch her go in, but the gates were open and I saw her wave to a couple of friends and walk towards them.' She frowned, then said, 'Why did the school phone you so quickly? Oh God, is there something you haven't told me? Was she seen getting into a strange car or—'

'Nothing like that at all,' said Inspector Brent at once. 'At first they thought Beth was sick and not coming in. As there didn't seem to have been a note sent in or a phone call, her teacher asked if anyone knew where she was. A couple of her classmates said they had seen her get out of your car and walk towards the school gates.' He spread his hands.

Nell said with horror, 'But she didn't turn up in the classroom?'

'No.'

'She disappeared between getting out of my car and her classroom.' It was bizarre and impossible and terrifying.

But Brent said, 'I'm afraid that's what seems to have happened. After the teachers realized she had been on her way through the gates, they were a bit concerned. They searched the school – thinking, you know, she might have fallen down and sprained an ankle or something of that kind. The search didn't take long – it's only a small place.'

'Yes.'

'It's possible, of course, that she's bunked off for the morning,' said DI Brent. 'She's a bit young for that – it's usually teenagers – but it's not out of the question.'

'No,' said Nell at once. 'No, it won't be that.' Beth liked the
small, friendly school. She said it was much nicer than the big
modern one she had attended in North London, and she had
made a number of friends.

'She's happy there,' she said to the inspector. 'I know she
is. And she was looking forward to this morning because they
were having a spelling test, and she likes spelling. She's good
at it.' She gripped the sides of the chair. It was important not
to remember Beth's bright eyes and pleased anticipation of
the morning, or how the two of them had gone through a list
of words last night in preparation, laughing when Nell
pretended not to know how to spell cat or dog.

'Can I ask about her father—?'

'He died eighteen months ago,' said Nell, seeing that
Inspector Brent was wondering if this was a modern case of
a split-up family and the child running off to be with the absent
parent. 'But she's adjusted fairly well.' Except for the nightmares, said her mind, and a small alarm bell sounded in her
mind. Could this have anything to do with the nightmares?
What if Beth had run away because of them? To get away
from the man she thought stood in a corner of her bedroom
– the man who had no eyes . . . ? But that did not seem to
make any sense. She brought her attention back to the inspector,
who was saying he was sure there was no cause for real worry.

'I've sent uniform out to look, of course,' he said. 'Mark
my words, though, she'll have gone off somewhere with a
friend. Maybe they were dared to do it, something of that
kind.'

'Is anyone else missing from the school?'

'Well, no,' he said reluctantly.

Nell suddenly wanted Brad more than at any time since
his death. He had loved Beth so much; he had cried with
emotion on the night she was born, wrapping his arms around
Nell and Beth together as if he wanted to shield them from
every bad thing the world held. After he had been killed it
had been agony to know he would never see her grow up.
He would never be there to frown in pretended disapproval
at the outrageous clothes she would wear and the music she
would listen to, or the boys she would go out with. But what
if Beth never grew up – what if she was in the hands of some
warped creature who would hurt her beyond bearing?

'We'll take you home,' said DI Brent. 'I'll get someone
to drive your car – you're in no fit state – and we'll come
in to check the house in case there are any clues.' As an
apparent afterthought, he said, 'I dare say there'll be a recent
photograph we can have, will there?' and Nell understood the
photograph would be circulated and maybe even displayed
on regional television, with the heartbreaking question: 'Have
you seen this girl?' She had always felt deeply sorry for
parents of missing children, who had to have their private
lives broadcast half across the country. Now, she did not care
if they beamed Beth's photograph around the world if it meant
finding her.

DI Brent and a woman police officer followed her through
the shop and upstairs to the flat. Rain slid relentlessly down
the windowpanes, like tears, as if the sky was weeping because
Beth was lost. Nell took the recent photo of her daughter from
the mantelpiece and removed it from the frame.

'Will that do?'

'Yes, certainly. What a lovely girl,' said the female PC, studying it. 'I'm sure she'll be found very soon, Mrs West. I'll just
make a note of what she was wearing this morning if you'll
describe it.'

Nell forced herself to think. Beth had on her ordinary school
uniform of grey skirt, white blouse and red pullover. Black
shoes and white socks. Asked if Beth's room could be searched,
she said they could ransack the whole building if they wanted.

She sat on the settee, trying to sip the cup of tea the PC
had made. If Beth was dead, the world would no longer hold
anything, anywhere. She was just about managing to cope
with not having Brad, but she would never cope with losing
Beth.

While the PC was in Beth's room, the inspector walked
round the sitting room. He paused by the laptop, which was
in the shorter part of the L-shaped sittingroom.

'Does Beth have access to the Internet, Mrs West?'

'Limited access,' said Nell. 'I've got the various safeguards
on, and I keep an eye on what she does. She doesn't go in chat
rooms or on Facebook.'

'Can we look?'

'Yes, certainly.' It was helpful to have something to do, even
something as small as booting up the laptop.

'She has her own email box?' he said, opening the email programme.

'Yes.'

'Mobile phone?'

'No. I've promised her one for her next birthday though.'

'They text and email one another even at that age, don't they?' he said, with a brief smile, and then scrolled down the few blameless emails. Friends at Beth's school, some cousins in Scotland on Brad's side of the family who sometimes sent emails. He paused, and a small frown creased his brow.

'What's this one? It's sent by a Dr Flint, and there's an attachment.'

For a couple of seconds Nell could not think who Dr Flint was, and then she said, 'Oh, that's Michael Flint. I met him at the weekend – he's a friend of the Americans who've just bought Charect House. He was here to check the work that's being done. He told Beth a story about his cat which made her laugh, and he sent her a photo of the cat when he got home.'

'Do you know where he lives?'

'He's a lecturer at Oxford. Oriel College, I think.' She saw Inspector Brent make a note and said, 'He won't have anything to do with this, though.'

'We'll just check with him, however.' He shut his notebook.

'But surely you don't think—' Nell stopped, understanding the police would see the sudden entrance into Beth's life of a single man as potentially suspicious. So she only said, 'I'm sure he hasn't got anything to do with this.'

'We will just check, though.'

'Have there been any other cases of – of missing children in the area?' It felt like a betrayal to use the expression – it felt as if she had already given up on Beth. But the curious thing was that as she said it, a faint memory stirred at the back of Nell's mind – something she had heard or read very recently. She tried to pin down the memory, but her mind was filled up with Beth and it eluded her.

'No. And that's good,' said the inspector.

The search of Beth's room was over, and it seemed nothing had been found that was likely to be of any help.

'Is there anyone we can call who'd come to be with you?' asked the PC. 'Family – close friend?'

Nell tried to think. Her own parents were dead, and there were only some cousins in the north. Brad had family in Scotland, but they had never been very close. There were friends in London, but she did not want to drag people up here unnecessarily. 'There's not really anyone who could come up here at a moment's notice.'

'All right. Now listen, if there's anything you think of that might help us – even the tiniest detail, even if you think it sounds ridiculous – tell us at once.'

He paused, as if allowing her time to consider this, and Nell said, 'There's nothing I can think of. Only—'

'Yes?'

'She's been having one or two quite bad nightmares,' said Nell slowly. 'She's been really terrified of them.'

He did not move but there was the impression that he sat up a bit straighter. 'Can you describe the nightmares?'

'She said someone was in her room,' said Nell. 'Just – standing in a corner of her bedroom, watching her. Oh, but – that couldn't be actually true, could it? There couldn't have been someone getting into her room—' She broke off, hearing the escalating note of panic in her voice, frightened that she might lose control altogether.

'No,' he said, so definitely that Nell relaxed. 'We'd have found signs, and you'd certainly have known if anyone was getting in and hiding somewhere.'

'Yes, of course. And the only access to Beth's room is through the window.'

'Which is two storeys up. Did she describe this figure, though?'

'She said—' Nell forced herself to use Beth's own words. 'She said he was trying to find her, but he couldn't because he had no eyes.'

'Nasty,' said DI Brent, non-committally. 'But that could give us a bit of a lead. It's possible that she saw someone outside the school this morning who looked like her nightmare man. A blind chap, perhaps, or a cripple of some kind.'

'And ran away from him?' said Nell, torn between panic all over again and half-guilty hope, because if this was the solution it might not be so bad.

'It's not beyond possibility,' said Brent. 'I'll pass it on to uniform right away.'

'I'll stay here,' said the policewoman as the inspector got up to leave. 'That's all right, is it, Mrs West?'

'Nell.'

'OK. I'm Lisa. We like to be at hand in this kind of situation, just to help out and relay any news.'

Nell did not know whether she wanted this or not. She was not keen on the idea of a stranger, however kind and efficient, being in the flat, offering cups of tea and reassurance every five minutes. But sitting on her own would be even worse, and probably it was police procedure to have an officer there. It would not be for long, of course. Beth would turn up at any minute. She looked at the clock and saw, incredulously, that it was only a quarter past twelve. Only just over three hours since she had dropped Beth off at the school gates.

It was at this point her eyes lit on the old diaries, on the top of the bookshelves, and the vagrant memory clicked into place. Alice had recorded details of a missing child – a child who had been seven years old. She went into the kitchen where Lisa was washing up the teacups.

'This is most likely of no help, but the inspector said even the smallest thing—'

'You've remembered something?'

'I think another seven-year-old girl went missing from Marston Lacy in the nineteen sixties,' said Nell. 'And I know that's over forty years ago, but—'

'But there are such things as copycat crimes,' said Lisa at once, and Nell was grateful for her quick understanding. 'And there are weird people in the world nowadays. I'll call the DI and let him know.' She reached in a pocket for her phone. 'There probably won't be a connection, but let's not ignore anything. How on earth did you know about it?'

'It was in some old diaries I found,' said Nell.

When the voice on the phone announced itself as being Detective Inspector Brent from Marston Lacy CID, Michael assumed it was something to do with Charect House. Perhaps the builders had blown the place up, or maybe there had been a break-in.

But it was nothing to do with Charect House at all. DI Brent wanted to talk to him about Mrs Nell West and her daughter.

'Beth?' said Michael, puzzled. 'Is anything wrong?' He listened with mounting horror as the inspector explained that Beth West had apparently vanished that morning.

'That being so, sir, we're just checking on recent visitors to the antique shop.'

'Well, I was there at the weekend,' said Michael. 'I called in to introduce myself to Nell West. She's helping some American friends of mine find furniture for a house they've just acquired in the area. Charect House. I expect you know it.'

'I do indeed, Dr Flint. What time would that be? When you called in?'

'Late afternoon on Friday. I can't remember the exact time. Oh, and I was there next morning, on the way back to Oxford. Just very briefly, though. About eleven-ish, that was.'

'Any particular reason for that second call, sir?'

'Not specially. There was an idea that Beth might become friendly with the daughter of my American friends – they're the same age – so I thought I'd take the acquaintanceship a bit further. Inspector, what d'you think's happened to Beth?'

'We don't know yet, but I'm sure we'll find her,' said the inspector in what Michael thought was an automatically reassuring voice. 'Tell me, Dr Flint, is there anyone who can vouch for your movements from around eight thirty this morning?'

'What?' said Michael, stunned. 'Are you wondering if I've got anything to do with—' He broke off, fighting the sudden anger. 'I'm sorry. It's understandable that you should ask. A stranger befriending Nell West and her daughter – a single man. And two days later the daughter disappears.'

'I'm grateful you see it that way, sir. It's purely for elimination, you know.'

'I had breakfast in my rooms here at seven thirty,' said Michael. 'I can't back that up – oh wait, though, the porter brought up the milk, he'd remember. After that I had a meeting with my faculty head – eight forty-five. That's a regular Monday morning event. There were four others there – you can have their names, but they're all senior members of the college. At ten I had a tutorial with four of my second-year students – we had a cup of coffee together at eleven. Any more?'

'That's absolutely fine, Dr Flint,' said Inspector Brent warmly.

'If there's anything that occurs to you that might help us, I'd be glad if you'd give me a call. Here's the number.' Michael foraged on his desk for a pen and scribbled the number down. 'Anything at all that you might have noticed while you were in the shop.'

'I do remember Beth having a vicious nightmare,' said Michael. 'I'm no psychologist, but I suppose that might indicate some deep-seated fear. I wouldn't have thought it would cause her to run away, though.'

'We know about the nightmares,' said the inspector. 'Thank you, Dr Flint.'

Clearly, he was preparing to ring off. Michael said quickly, 'Inspector – is there anything I could do to help? Is Nell – Mrs West – coping?'

'Just about,' said Inspector Brent. 'The parents usually manage to stay in control until there's a – well, some definite news.'

'I see. Thank you.' This time he did ring off. Michael sat wrapped in thought for a few moments, then hunted out the card Nell had given him and, before he could think too much about it, dialled her number.

She answered at once, with a breathless eagerness that brought home to him how she must be sitting next to the phone, willing it to ring, willing there to be good news.

He said, quickly, 'Nell, it's Michael Flint. I've just had a call from Inspector Brent. This is dreadful. Is there any news?'

'Oh, Michael— No, nothing yet. It's nice of you to phone, though.'

'Would you let me know when she's found?' he said.

'Yes, of course. Thank you for saying "when".'

'No clues as to what happened? Where she might be?'

'No, except—'

'The nightmares?' said Michael.

'Yes.' He heard the relief in her voice, as if she was grateful to him for identifying the nightmares as a possible clue. 'And there's one other thing – it's only very small, but I discovered that another seven-year-old girl vanished in Marston Lacy in the nineteen sixties. I know it's too far back to have any real connection, but still.'

'But people sometimes try to reproduce old crimes,' he said. 'Does Brent think that's possible?'

'He's going to check the files. He said it might take a few hours because he'll have to get them from a central division or something.'

'I'll ring off,' said Michael. 'In case Brent tries to get through. But here's my number, Nell – I mean it about letting me know.'

'Thank you.'

He hesitated, wondering if he should offer to go up there, but then thought the acquaintance was too slight. She would have other people she would prefer to be with – family, her husband's people.

As he hung up, a number of thoughts were arranging themselves in layers inside his mind, like the striations of the earth.

There was the memory of Beth, sobbing and insisting a man had been in her room – a man with no eyes.

Beneath that was the thought of Jack's emails about Ellie, exactly the same age, also sobbing with terror that there was a man in her room – a man with holes where his eyes should be.

These two thoughts bound themselves together, to create a single curious fact – two seven-year-old girls, living thousands of miles apart, had both been having what sounded to be an identical nightmare.

On top of this was Nell's mention of a girl having vanished forty years ago. This was a thin, insubstantial layer, probably of little account. But overlying all of this was a very solid and insistent thought, and it was the memory of that first afternoon at Charect House – the afternoon Michael had seen a man crouching on the stair. A man whose eyes had been so deeply shadowed they had looked like black pits.

He considered the memory for a moment, then reached for the phone and dialled DI Brent's number.

Brent listened intently to Michael's story of the intruder at Charect House.

'I didn't make the connection when you phoned,' said Michael. 'And I'd have to say I only glimpsed the man. I was there on my own at the time, and I didn't feel inclined to confront him. So I dialled the police and waited in my car until someone came out. We searched the house, but he'd gone. Probably scrambled out of a window at the back and down a drainpipe or something.'

'Your description of him sounds very like Beth West's night-mare,' said Brent thoughtfully.

'Is it possible he's been watching her, and that she was half-aware of it and it caused the nightmares?' But that did not explain Ellie having the same nightmare.

'It not impossible. Dr Flint, I don't suppose there's any chance you could—'

'Drive back up there?'

'Could you?' said Brent. 'To look at photos – maybe spend an hour or so with a police artist to see if we can put together a computer image? It could be done via email, but it wouldn't give the best result. Say tomorrow morning? It wouldn't take more than a couple of hours. We could arrange transport if that's a problem.'

'No need,' said Michael. 'I'll set off first thing in the morning.'

NINE

He reached the police station around lunchtime.

'There's no news,' said Inspector Brent, taking him into an interview room and introducing a young tousled-looking man who was apparently trained in creating computerized facial images. 'So I don't need to tell you how serious the situation now is.'

'Oh God, no, you don't. Can I go to see Nell West after we've done this? Not if it would hassle her.'

'I'll call and ask,' said Brent and went out, leaving Michael to attempt a description of the figure he had seen on the stairs at Charect House. It was a difficult task, but in the end between them they came up with a reasonable image.

'I'd have to say my memory isn't very exact, though,' said Michael, critically surveying the screen. 'And if a man looking like that has been prowling around Marston Lacy, I'd have thought he'd be noticed.' A doughy-looking face with sunken eyes and a heavy jowl looked out of the computer screen.

'So would I,' said the artist. 'Still, it's worth a shot.'

DI Brent thought it was worth a shot as well. 'If that's what Beth West saw, I'm not surprised it gave her nightmares,' he said. 'But we'll get copies made right away and do another house-to-house. That'll take a long time, unfortunately – there are a lot of outlying districts in this part of the world. Odd cottages scattered along lanes. It's not like a town where you just walk along a street, knocking at each door.'

Michael said, 'Did you find out any more about that other girl who vanished in the nineteen sixties? Nell told me about her.'

'Oh, that girl turned up. Wait a bit, I've still got the report somewhere – yes, here it is. Just the basic details were on file, but they're quite clear. She was reported missing around half-past four – hadn't come home from school, and a search was mounted later that evening. Apparently, they didn't find her for nearly two days, but she was safe and well when they did.'

'Where was she?'

'Doesn't say.' A wry half-smile lit his seamed face. 'Report-keeping wasn't so good in those days. They've just recorded the "missing" incident and the outcome.'

'Pity,' said Michael. 'Did you phone Nell? Would it be all right for me to call?'

'She says you're very welcome. My advice, though, is if you do, don't stay too long. She's all right for short spells, but that's about all.'

'I will call,' said Michael. 'But I'll bear your advice in mind. In the meantime, Inspector, does Marston Lacy have a newspaper? Ah, good. Can you give me directions? And d'you know if it keeps archives?'

The newspaper offices turned out to be part of a large group, with a chain of papers covering two counties, which Michael thought augured well for an archive department.

The head office was on the other side of the county. He followed Inspector Brent's directions carefully, realizing he was heading due west, and that he was close to, if not actually crossing, the border into Wales. Village names started to begin with two LLs and end with *rhy* or *og*, and most of the signs were in Welsh without the English translation. He rather liked this; he liked the feeling that this was where England crossed over into Wales and where the lyrical Welsh language still lived.

The newspaper said it did indeed have almost all the back issues for the Marston Lacy and Bryn Marston Advertiser, as far back as 1915.

'We started as a news-sheet to inform people about the Great War,' said the receptionist. 'There's no problem whatever about access to back issues. We get a lot of people wanting to trace odds and ends of local history. And it's what news-papers are for, isn't it? To inform people. What years were you interested in?'

'The nineteen sixties, please.'

As he sat down at the microfiche screen, he thought this was where and how history was stored nowadays. It no longer preserved itself in carefully folded tissue paper, with lavender or camphor or magic charms scattered in the creases, nor was it set down in crabbed writing on curling brown paper, or stored in leather-bound books or pipe rolls or tax chronicles.

The modern age packed its history away on microchips and SIM cards and within the electronic and Ethernet mysteries deep inside computers. Michael considered this, and he wondered what would happen to the present age's history if the language of computers were to be lost. Would this present civilization become lost for all time, or would the people of the far future be able to decipher the fragments that survived, in the way Egyptologists deciphered tomb writings?

The sixties, as experienced in this part of the British Isles, looked to be a slightly gentler version of what was going on elsewhere. This quiet part of England-going-on-Wales did not seem to have succumbed to flower power or free love, although people in the photographs wore miniskirts and boots, and the girls had long, straight hair and Cleopatra-style eye make-up. The men sported Beatles' hairstyles and narrow trousers.

At first he thought he was not going to find what he wanted – that the brief disappearance of a seven-year-old girl would have been too slight an incident to warrant a newspaper report. And then, quite suddenly, it was there. Three columns of a news story, with a photo of a small girl with long hair and a slightly turned-up nose that gave her an impish, rather attractive, look.

MISSING GIRL FOUND SAFE AND WELL IN CHURCHYARD

Local girl Evie Blythe was last night found alive and well in St Paul's Churchyard, after being missing from her home for almost forty-eight hours. Local residents helped look for her after she failed to return home from school on Tuesday after a sports' afternoon – searching all night and most of the following day.

At first it was feared Evie, 7, had been abducted, and fears grew for her safety. However, she was found by searchers near an old grave in the disused part of the churchyard, apparently suffering a temporary loss of memory.

Older inhabitants of Marston Lacy recalled a similar case before the war, when a small girl vanished for several days and was later found in the same churchyard, apparently with no notion of how she got there. But police

have quashed speculation that there could be some form
of copycat crime at work.

Superintendent Halden told our reporter that not only
were the two cases a good thirty years apart, but in neither
case did there appear to be any sinister motive. 'We can
only conclude that Evie was overcome by tiredness after
the school sports' event,' he said. 'And that she succumbed
to a bout of temporary amnesia. We're delighted to have
found her safe and well.'

It is known that short-term amnesia can sometimes
strike at random, more often after some form of trauma.
It is unusual in so young a child, but not entirely unknown.

Evie told our reporter that she can't remember how
she came to be in the churchyard. 'It's a fusty old place,'
she said. 'I'm not going there again.'

St Paul's Church, thought Michael, leaning back from the screen
and turning his head from side to side to ease the tension that
had built up in his neck and shoulders. She was found in the
churchyard near an old grave. So was another girl thirty years
before that. He hesitated about searching for the earlier story,
but it was more important to locate St Paul's Church and get
out there as soon as possible.

He went out to request a printout of the article and, while
he waited for it, asked the helpful receptionist if there was a
local phone book he could consult.

There was one church dedicated to St Paul in the phone
book. It was listed as St Paul the Apostle, and it was on the
edge of Marston Lacy. Michael got back into the car, turned
it round, and headed back.

This was so wild a shot, a bow drawn at such an unlikely
venture, that he did not think he could phone Inspector Brent
yet. It might take up police time and resources better used
elsewhere, and it might raise Nell's hopes only to dash them.
But was it so wild a shot? Two girls, both found in the same
churchyard? Yes, but one was over sixty years ago, said his
mind.

It was just after two o'clock. If he could find St Paul's he
would search it himself. How difficult could it be to find a
church in a tiny place like this?

Marston Lacy did not quite lie in a valley, but it was certainly in a slight dip in the countryside, and the road wound sharply downwards. Michael saw the church spire as he drove down this road – it jutted up into the slate-coloured sky like a skeletal finger, iron-coloured and stark. Good. He turned off the main road and, keeping his eye on the spire, reached it within ten minutes. It was a rather gloomy place, grey stone with lichen speckling the roof, and there was a hopeless air about it, as if it had long since stopped expecting people to attend any of its services. As Michael parked on the narrow grass verge, a thin rain began to fall. He turned up his coat collar, remembered to put the phone in his pocket, and went through the old lychgate. The cemetery was on one side, and narrow, poorly-tended paths wound between the graves. His footsteps crunched on wet gravel, and the trees dipped their boughs, their leaves dark and dripping with moisture. This would be a terrible place for a child, and if Beth had been out here all night . . .

As he walked around the graves, the patter of the rain sounded like mocking voices, and the pitted stone faces of angels peered at him from elaborate tombstones. Several times Michael had the eerie impression that the blank, blind eyes were watching him. Ahead of him were much older graves, some marked by ancient Saxon crosses that thrust starkly upwards into the misty afternoon. Several of the stone crosses were leaning to one side, presumably from ground subsidence, but it gave a nightmare sense of distortion to the place. But the newspaper article about that other little girl had referred to an old grave in the disused part of the cemetery, and Michael went towards these older headstones. A flash of colour against one sent his heart leaping with hope, but when he got nearer it was a torn paper bag, probably blown here from the road.

Four graves were set on a little rise of ground near the edge of the churchyard. They were shaded by one of the ancient cedars, and two of them had large, elaborate headstones. One, more badly affected by ground slip than the others, leaned drunkenly sideways, and as Michael got closer he saw a patch of scarlet and a black lace-up shoe lying by this grave. She's here! he thought. Oh God, but is she still alive . . . ?

He supposed, afterwards, that he ran the rest of the way across the overgrown grass, but he only remembered kneeling at Beth's side, reaching for her hands, seeing that her eyes were closed, and her hair damp from the rain. With a shaking hand he felt for a pulse. Was it there? Yes! It was like a fluttering bird under her wrist and at her neck, but it was there. He was about to lift her up, then thought she might be injured and to move her might make matters worse, so he dragged off his coat to throw it over her. Only then did he reach for the mobile phone. One call to Inspector Brent would bring out everything that was needed – ambulance, police. And Nell.

Nell had just about managed not to break down during the long agonizing wait for news, and she managed not to do so when Lisa's phone rang and she came running up to Beth's room, where Nell was sitting, hugging Beth's beloved furry animals.

'She's all right – Nell, she's safe and well – a bit confused, but absolutely all right!'

There were tears running down Lisa's face – Nell would always remember that, and she would always remember being deeply grateful to Lisa for spilling the emotion she herself seemed unable to.

Her mind could not take in all the details – something about Beth being found in an old churchyard, and about Michael Flint having discovered some sort of clue. She would find out about that later, though.

When she tried to put together a few things to take to the hospital, her hands were shaking so badly she could not do it, and it was Lisa who folded pyjamas and slippers for Beth, and fetched sponge and toothbrush from the bathroom.

'It's only routine checks they're doing,' Lisa said. 'She's fine – the inspector was very clear about that. They might keep her overnight, just to be sure.'

Lisa drove them to the hospital, which was small enough to warrant the term cottage, and it was the sight of Beth obediently lying in the narrow bed in the children's ward that finally broke through Nell's defences. Tears streamed down her face, and she wanted to snatch Beth out of bed and never let her go.

'Sweetheart, you had me so worried. What happened?'

'I 'spect you thought you'd lost me,' said Beth, uncertainly.

'No, I'll never lose you, never ever. Wherever you are, I'll always find you.'

'Promise?'

'Promise absolutely.' Beth seemed content with this. She submitted to her mother's hug for a moment longer, then wriggled free and lay back on the pillows.

'What happened?' said Nell, sitting on the edge of the bed, holding her hands.

Beth seemed reassured by this practical approach. She sat up. 'I'm not ezzackerly sure,' she said. 'I went to school, only I think I sort of fell asleep because it was – um – like the nightmare.' Her pupils contracted, and a shiver went through her small body. 'I didn't know you could fall asleep and not know,' she said.

'It hardly ever happens. It can't happen again,' said Nell at once. 'And you don't have to talk about it if you don't want to.'

'I don't remember it much,' said Beth. 'Except it was the nightmare sort of starting while I was awake. Nightmares aren't supposed to do that, are they?' She looked at Nell for reassurance.

'They don't, and they won't again,' said Nell.

'Oh, you've brought the animal people,' said Beth. 'Can I have them in bed with me? Thanks.' She wrapped her arms round the furry creatures Nell had asked Lisa to pack, then, not looking at Nell, said, '*He* was there, that was the really bad thing.'

'The – man from the nightmare?' Nell said this cautiously. She had no idea if she should let Beth talk or if it would be better to let her think it really had been a form of nightmare.

'Um, yes. I didn't look at his face, but I know there weren't any eyes in it – just black holes.' The shudder came again. 'And he sings as he walks along.'

'Sings?'

'The rhyme about the hand and the dead man – I told you about that.'

Nell thought: oh God, the Hand of Glory. That's what she means. Alice's rhyme.

'Open lock to the dead man's knock . . .

Fly bolt, and bar, and band.

Sleep all who sleep – wake all who wake.

But be as the dead for the dead man's sake . . .'

In as down-to-earth a voice as she could manage, she said, 'Some people do sing to themselves. It does sound a bit odd though, doesn't it? And I think that's a local rhyme – a bit like a nursery rhyme.'

'It was pretty spooky, actually. But what was really odd is that I sort of had to go after the music to find out about it. I *know* I'm not s'posed to talk to strangers and stuff,' said Beth earnestly, 'but I couldn't help it, honestly, Mum. It sort of pulled me along, an' it's not even as if it was *nice* music,' she said, indignantly.

'Some music can do that,' said Nell carefully. 'It's pretty rare, though.'

'I thought,' said Beth, 'that if I ever met him properly, that man from the nightmare, it'd be really frightening. But it wasn't. He's very sad, and you can't be frightened of a sad person,' said Beth, suddenly sounding much older than her seven years. She paused, frowning. 'But there was something else, Mum, an' that's why I wasn't absolutely all-time frightened.'

'Yes?'

Beth was studiedly picking at a thread in the sheet, no longer looking at Nell. In a low voice, she said, 'It wasn't me he wanted.'

'Well – well, that's good,' said Nell.

'Yes. I don't 'spect he'll come to see me again, do you?'

'Definitely not,' said Nell. 'Beth, why did you say you weren't the one he wanted? That man?'

'I don't know, not ezzackerly,' said Beth, frowning. 'Might he have told me?'

'He might. Yes, that's very likely. Perhaps you look a bit like somebody else and he got mixed up.'

'He really wanted Elvira,' said Beth, and Nell looked at her sharply.

'Who's Elvira? Darling, who's Elvira?' Because if there was another girl somewhere, a girl called Elvira who might be in danger . . .

Beth hunched her shoulders. 'Don't know,' she said. 'There's no one at school called that. It's a silly name, I think. Oh, did I tell you I'm having fruit trifle for supper? The nurse said it was today's pudding. And scrambled eggs first. They won't be as nice as the ones you make, of course,' she said, confidingly. 'But I'm 'strordinarily hungry.'

Nell smiled for the first time in twenty-four hours. That had
been one of Brad's expressions. 'I'm extraordinarily hungry,' he
used to say. Beth had picked it up, and Nell liked hearing her
say it. It's all right, Brad, she said in her mind. We've got her
back. She's safe.

'She's checking out fine on all scores, Mrs West,' said the
young Indian doctor while Beth was tackling the scrambled
eggs with reassuring enthusiasm. 'We'll keep her here overnight, just to be sure, but we can't see any real cause for
concern.' He frowned slightly. 'As to what happened – who
can say? Temporary amnesia is a possibility. The trauma of
her father's death . . .'

'I thought she was coping with that,' said Nell quickly.

'Again, who can say? One thing we are fairly sure of though,
and it's that she wasn't in that churchyard very long. There
was no hypothermia, no slowing of the body's metabolism. If
she was abducted, she was kept somewhere. Oh, and there were
no traces of any kind of drugs,' he said, clearly anticipating
Nell's next question.

'The police are going on the assumption that she really was
abducted.'

He spread his hands. 'Police deal in facts. My belief is that
this is something of the mind. Your daughter was somewhere
during those hours, but you might never know where. She
might not know, either. But she may have instinctively gone
somewhere she felt safe. Even into the church. Are you a
churchgoer? Was your husband?'

'Not especially.'

'I've talked to the on-duty psychiatrist – just in general terms.
But we can book an appointment for Beth to see her properly
if you wish.'

Nell had no idea if this would be a good thing or not. She
said, carefully, that she would think about it.

'My advice – also that of the psychiatrist – is that it would
be better to let this episode fade gradually and naturally,' he
said.

'I think so, too.'

'If it happened again, that might be different, of course. But
the mind heals itself in odd ways. We can do deeper tests later
– for epilepsy, for disorders of the brain . . .' Nell flinched,

and he put out a reassuring hand to her shoulder. 'There are no indications at all of anything wrong there,' he said. 'But I suggest we make an outpatient appointment for her – two weeks ahead, let's say – and if we think it necessary then, we can arrange some scans. But I don't think it will be,' he said quickly.

Nell stayed with Beth until visiting hours ended, then hugged her goodnight, promising to be back early in the morning when they would go home. Beth was apparently content with this. She was a self-contained, self-sufficient child. As far as Nell could tell, the experience had bewildered her, but not unduly. She was interested in being in hospital, she had eaten the scrambled eggs and trifle, and she would have an adventure to tell when she went back to school. Above all, she seemed definite that the man she called the nightmare man had got her mixed up with someone else.

'I'm sure he did,' said Nell. 'Go to sleep now, and when you wake up it'll be tomorrow, and I'll be here to take you home.'

TEN

As Nell went through the hospital's small reception area, Michael Flint came in. It looked as if he had been waiting for her, because he came up at once and said, 'She's all right?'

'Quite all right,' said Nell. 'And I'm so pleased to see you. I haven't had a chance yet to thank you. Inspector Brent said you were the one who found her.'

'Well, I did, but it was just luck, really.'

Nell said, 'I don't care what it was. I'm so grateful I don't think I can put it into words. And if I do I might start crying.'

'You're entitled to cry for hours, I should think. But Brent's men would have found her before much longer, you know.'

'Yes, but— I don't know all the details yet, but I do know you drove all the way here to help the police artist, and you found out about the church, and you went out there—' This time her voice did wobble, and she broke off, because she would not cry again, certainly not in front of someone she hardly knew.

Michael appeared not to notice the wobble. He said, 'Has she been able to talk about any of it? To tell you what happened?'

'She doesn't seem to remember anything,' said Nell, grateful to switch to practicalities. 'I don't know whether to be relieved by that or terrified. She's seeing it as a kind of extension of the nightmares.'

'What do the doctors say?'

'I don't think they really know. They've talked about some sort of temporary amnesia— What have I said?'

'Nothing. Go on. Temporary amnesia?'

'Perhaps connected to her father's death, they said. The inspector's still following up the theory that it was a genuine abduction, of course, but I think he's a bit unsure. He's going to get the church checked by his forensic people tomorrow – the inside of the church, I mean.'

'To see if she had been in there all night?'

'Yes.'

Michael said, 'When I found her – she looked almost as if she had been laid down quite carefully. She looked perfectly comfortable. I honestly don't think she could have been out there in the churchyard all night.'

'I think that's a comfort,' said Nell. 'Although I'd rather know where she was all those hours.'

'Yes.' They were outside the hospital by now. 'Is your car here?' said Michael.

'No, Inspector Brent said to ring when I was going back and he'd arrange a lift.'

'I can drive you home,' he said.

'Don't you have to get back to Oxford?'

'Not tonight. I'd booked at the Black Boar again. I didn't know how long this might all take.' He looked round the car park. 'I'd probably be quicker than calling the inspector,' he said.

'Yes, you probably would. Thanks very much,' said Nell gratefully.

As they pulled up outside the shop front, Michael said, 'I'm sure you're exhausted and you just want to go home and go to bed. But in case you haven't eaten, the Black Boar do a reasonable bar meal.'

He said this diffidently, as if he was not at all sure it was the right thing to say, and certainly as if he was not sure of her reply.

Nell started to say she would go straight in, then realized two things. One was that she still did not know what had sent him out to the old churchyard and it was important to find out as much about that as possible. She could let Inspector Brent and the hospital know where she would be for the next hour or so, and in any case, she would have her phone to hand.

The other thing was that, as Brad would have said, she was suddenly extraordinarily hungry. So she smiled and said, 'D'you know, that's a very welcome suggestion.'

The Black Boar's dining room was small and had the air of being an extension of the bar with a few knives and forks dropped casually on a couple of the tables. Even so, it felt odd to be facing a man across a dining table after so long.

Michael ordered the food, then took from his pocket a folded A4 sheet. 'This is what sent me to that church,' he said, handing it to her. 'It's a printout from an article in one of the local newspapers.'

Nell looked at the headline. '"Missing girl found in church-yard". She glanced at the date then read the article through, frowning slightly. 'How on earth did you know about this?' she said, looking up at him.

'You mentioned it to me on the phone.'

'Did I? Oh yes, so I did.'

'And you told the inspector as well,' said Michael.

'I do remember that,' said Nell. 'He managed to get the case notes, but he said they were very brief. That there was nothing to link it to Beth's disappearance.'

'There wasn't. I saw the file. But I had something else to go on,' said Michael. 'Two things, in fact.'

'What?' For the first time she felt a faint suspicion.

'The first is that when I was at Charect House a few weeks ago I saw – or thought I saw – a man who fits Beth's nightmare.'

'A real prowler after all?' Nell felt a bump of fear. 'Not just a nightmare or amnesia?' But I don't want him to be real, she thought. I don't want Beth to have been threatened by someone who might still be around, still watching her. The man with holes where his eyes should be, the man who sings that macabre rhyme . . .

'I'm not sure if he was a prowler at all,' said Michael. 'I'm not really sure what he was.' He paused as their food was brought and set down. 'I told you there were two things,' he said, after the waitress had gone. 'And it's the other thing that's worrying me.' He frowned, as if searching for the right words, then said, 'My god-daughter, Ellie, has been having nightmares that sound identical to Beth's.'

'The man with holes where his eyes should be.' It felt even worse to say the words aloud than it had to have them inside her mind. Nell wanted to gather Beth up and move as far away as possible from Marston Lacy and forget all this had ever happened. But if another child was having the same terrors as Beth . . . 'That's really disturbing,' she said, after a moment.

'Yes, but what if it's just a fairly common manifestation of

a child's secret fears?' said Michael. 'I have no way of knowing
that. It would need a psychiatrist specializing in the problems
of children.' He made an impatient gesture with one hand.
'But I don't know very much about children.'

'I'm beginning to wonder if I do. Children can have quite
severe nightmares, though. Tell me about Ellie's. There might
be all kinds of differences.'

'There is one difference,' said Michael. 'Ellie has another
character in the nightmare. She says the man is trying to find
someone.'

Nell stopped with a forkful of lasagne halfway to her mouth.
'Elvira,' she said. 'Is it Elvira he's trying to find?'

'Yes. How on earth did you know that?'

'Because earlier this evening, Beth said she hadn't been as
frightened of the man as she might have been, because she
wasn't the one he wanted. He wanted Elvira.' The lasagne,
which was beautifully cooked and served with crisp warm
Italian bread, and which Nell had been enjoying, suddenly
tasted of nothing.

At last Michael said, 'Does Beth know anyone called Elvira?'

'No. Nor do I. I'll bet you'd have to go a long way to find
anyone called Elvira these days. Michael, what is all this?'

'I don't know,' he said. 'But I think we need to find out who
– or what Elvira is. The first thing to do, is for me to ask Jack
a bit more about Ellie's dreams.'

'Don't alarm them unnecessarily,' said Nell. She liked the
sound of Liz Harper and her family, and it would be terrible
to put needless fears in their minds.

'I won't,' said Michael. 'I'll email them as soon as I get
back to Oxford.' Then, as the waitress hovered, 'Would you
like anything else to eat? No? A cup of coffee?'

Nell shook her head. When the waitress had gone, she said,
'I was thinking you could email from the flat if you like.
You're welcome to use my computer – I've got Liz Harper's
email address on it.'

'It's a bit late to do that now,' he said slowly.

'It needn't take long. And if you send something tonight
there might be a reply as soon as tomorrow.'

'That's true,' he said. 'But I'll use my own laptop – I brought
it with me thinking I might do some work and thinking the
Black Boar would have Internet connection, but it doesn't,

at least not for customers. There might be an email from Jack to pick up, as well. Wait here, will you, and I'll get it from my room.'

If it had felt odd to dine with a man again, it felt even odder to be unlocking her own door and going up to the sitting room with him. There was a moment when Nell wondered if she was being stupid, inviting this near-stranger into her home late at night. But it was not so very late – barely ten o'clock – and in a way this was a semi-business arrangement. The trouble was that she was out of practice at dealing with a situation involving herself and a single man. On the heels of this thought came another one: that Michael Flint was actually quite attractive – the dark hair and eyes, and the diffidence mingled with undoubted intelligence. And the vague impression that in certain situations he might be very far from diffident . . .

She was instantly horrified and sickeningly aware of disloyalty to Brad. It would be gratitude to Michael she was feeling, nothing more. Relief that Beth was safe. There was some German phrase about immense emotion being churned up towards people with whom one shared a danger or a difficult situation – this would be an example of that.

She pointed out the Internet connection so he could plug in the laptop and, as he sat down at the desk, headed for the kitchen to make coffee. As the percolator hissed and bubbled, Nell's thoughts strayed again and she found herself wondering if he was linked up with anyone. He had said he was not married, but he would be sure to have some incredibly learned female don eagerly waiting for him at Oxford. Someone who was fluent in five or six languages, or wrote papers on ancient Sanskrit or obscure corners of medicine, and who lectured to immensely scholarly societies. One of those women who wore infuriatingly-flattering glasses and scooped their hair into loose chignons with apparent carelessness, but looked fantastic. Thinking man's crumpet. Was it Joan Bakewell who had originally inspired that phrase? The coffee blew a series of loud raspberries, and Nell reached hastily for the jug and poured the steaming brew into mugs.

Michael had tangled up the laptop's power lead with the Internet cable and was half lying under the desk, frowningly trying to sort them out.

He looked up as she came in. 'I don't think this is right, do you? I'm not actually terribly good at mechanical things or electronic things.' He looked so perplexed that Nell laughed properly for the first time in twenty-four hours and said, 'It looks as if you've been trying to plug the phone cable into the mains. Come out of the way and let me do it. If the battery's sufficiently charged, you don't really need to connect to the mains, not for the few minutes it'll take to type an email.'

'I can generally get somebody else to do this kind of thing,' he said apologetically as Nell crawled under the desk and connected the laptop's USB cable to the phone line. 'Thanks, Nell. I'm fine from here on.'

As soon as the laptop came on and the email programme opened, Nell saw the email with the name Jack Harper on the 'From' line at once. Her heart leapt, even though she told herself it would contain an ordinary message, something to do with Charect House's renovations. She sat in the deep armchair, her hands curled round her mug of coffee, trying not to watch as Michael read the email. But when he said, 'Oh God,' a voice within her said: something *is* wrong.

'Come and see this,' he said, getting up from the desk.

Nell, her heart racing, sat down and began to read.

Michael—

We're thinking we might have to get Ellie away from Maryland for a time to see if it will cure these nightmares. Last night was by far the worst ever, and in the end we took her to ER. They checked just about everything that could be checked – all absolutely fine. All they could do in the end was hold her down and sedate her. If you've ever seen a seven-year-old girl restrained by two nurses and given chlorpromazine – well, I shouldn't think you have, but it's killing to see it. Liz was devastated, and so was I, although I didn't show it as much as she did. Maybe I absorbed some British reserve at Oxford.

They're waving the prospect of psychs at us, of course. It's this business of 'Elvira' they're worried about, and we understand that because we're agonizingly worried about Elvira as well. I don't know very much about schizophrenia or whatever it's correctly called nowadays, but what I do know is that last night Ellie screamed Elvira's name over and over again. Most of what she said was unintelligible – hysterical sobbing – but at one stage she said, very clearly, "He's going to get her very soon. Only he mustn't, he really *really* mustn't . . ." She clung to me, shouting, "Daddy, don't let him get her – promise you won't let him . . . She's so frightened of him . . ."

I promised I wouldn't let anyone get Elvira – wouldn't you have done the same? I said she was safe and Elvira was safe – Michael, I'd have promised her the moon and the universe to reassure her. But then I said, "In any case, hon, that man can't ever get at anyone – he's safely locked out."

Ellie started sobbing again then. She said, between anger and panic, "But that's just it, Daddy. You're so stupid, you don't understand. He can get in anywhere, he *can*. Because he can do the dead man's knock on the door. When he does that, the doors open for him. All locks open to the dead man's knock."

Truly, Michael, I've never heard anything so all-out chilling in my life. Ellie believes all this – she believes this man is trying to find 'Elvira' – that he can get inside houses by means of a dead man's knock, and I *know* that sounds like a macabre party game, but it's what she said and I've no idea where she got hold of such a grisly idea.

What I do know is that Ellie believes when this man finds Elvira he'll harm her in some appalling way she can't explain.

The medics think Ellie's had some sort of traumatic experience at the hands of an adult – something we don't know about – and that she's transferring the bad experience on to an alter ego. And it's true the names are similar – Ellie and Elvira. But Liz and I would know if Ellie had been hurt or frightened or – oh God – abused. I can't believe I wrote that last word. I'm sure we'd know, though. Ellie's in school all day, and Liz takes and collects her along with a bunch of other kids. She and three neighbors take turns. So we know where she is all the time. We know her friends and their families. And listen, I *know* that's what all parents of abused kids say, but I'm absolutely convinced nothing's happened to her. And it *can't* be right to put a seven-year-old into analysis.

Sorry for the long and (I'm afraid) emotional rant – but it feels like talking to you to write it all down. Like all those nights we used to thrash out the world's problems and our own into the small hours and I used to drink too much, because most of the problems were generally mine. You hardly ever got drunk, did you, and on the rare occasions when you did go over the top, all that happened was that you had a look of soulful decadence next morning – like a romantically-inclined monk who went on the loose and found it so good that he was wondering if he should do it again.

Anyhow, here's the thing. If Charect House is anywhere near habitable, we think we really will come over for Christmas. It would do Ellie – and Liz – so much good. Different places, different people.

Talking of people, we're looking forward to meeting the cool-sounding Nell West. Also your mystery lady who looked out of Charect's window that day. Or are they one and the same?

Till soon,
        Jack

As Nell finished reading and sat back in the chair, Michael said, a bit awkwardly, 'That last bit – Jack thought there was someone in one of the photos I sent him of Charect. It looked as if someone was peering out of an upstairs window, and he thought . . . There wasn't anyone, of course, it was a trick of the light.'

Nell did not care, at that minute, whether Michael had imported an entire bed-full of females to Marston Lacy or whether he had been presiding over a modern-day harem in Charect House. She was still drained from so nearly losing Beth, and she was horrified at what Jack Harper had written.

She said, 'That poor little girl. But that stuff about the dead man's knock . . .'

'Horror films? TV?' He said it tentatively.

'I don't think it's either of those,' said Nell. 'Beth mentioned it, almost in the same words as Ellie.' She frowned, then said, 'We can't very well email to ask for information about Ellie, can we? Not now.'

'No.'

Nell paused, then said, 'But – there's this, as well.' She reached for Alice Wilson's journal, which she had left on top

of the bookshelf. She had taken a photocopy of the pages, and
she had known, since they had sat down to eat at the Black
Boar, that she was going to let Michael see the original.

'What is it?' He was already scanning the first few lines.

'Diaries from a haunted house is probably the best
description,' said Nell. 'It makes strange reading. It's got
the same reference in it – the dead man's hand. Let me find
it for you.'

She flipped through the pages, and Michael read the grisly
chant aloud:

'"Open lock to the dead man's knock . . .

Fly bolt, and bar, and band . . .

Sleep all who sleep – wake all who wake.

But be as the dead for the dead man's sake . . .'

He looked up from the journal. 'That's pretty chilling,' he
said. 'What on earth is it?'

'It's from something called the *Ingoldsby Legends*. I'd never
heard of it, but I looked it up after I read that journal – and
after Beth talked about the rhyme. One of the legends used
in it is called the Hand of Glory. It's about a grisly old country
belief that the hand of a murderer can cast an enchanted sleep
and cause all doors to become unlocked – I can't believe I've
just said that.'

'I can't believe you've just said it, either. I've heard of the
Ingoldsby Legends,' said Michael thoughtfully, 'but I've never
read them. It's a Victorian collection of myths and legends.
Some of them quite comical – almost parodies. But it's fiction,
surely?'

'Sort of fiction. It's based on genuine old superstitions,
seemingly. And this Hand of Glory thing is apparently a very
old belief indeed.'

'The power of the dead over the living,' he said thoughtfully,
and Nell was grateful for his instant comprehension. 'Yes,
that'll go back thousands of years.'

'Beth said she had a – an absolute compulsion to go after
the music,' said Nell. 'She was quite upset about that – she
knows she mustn't talk to strangers or go off with them, but
she said it was as if the music pulled her along.'

'That's quite creepy,' said Michael. 'It's almost taking us
into Pied Piper territory. But I can't see, at the moment, how
it fits in to all the other things.'

'Nor can I. But I'm not sure it's a good idea for Liz and Jack to bring Ellie to Marston Lacy.'

'Because of Elvira,' said Michael.

'Yes. Only, I don't know how you'd put them off without telling them the truth.'

'And the truth is so off the wall, they'd probably think I was losing all grip on sanity,' said Michael. 'I suppose I could tell them to delay the trip because the house doesn't look as if it'll be ready by Christmas.'

'Would that work?'

'I don't know, but I'll do my best,' said Michael, opening a new email message and starting to type. 'I think that's strong enough,' he said after a couple of minutes. 'I've implied it's unlikely there'll be any electricity or hot water.'

'That would certainly put me off,' said Nell. 'If Liz happens to email me again – about the clock or anything else for the house – d'you want me to say anything to her? I don't mean about what's happening to Ellie or Beth, but just an offhand remark about the renovations seeming to take a long time.'

'I think it's probably better not.'

'All right. Michael, is it possible that Ellie has read the *Ingoldsby Legends*?'

'I shouldn't think so.'

'I'm as sure as I can be that Beth hasn't.' Nell drank the remains of her coffee, then said, 'That grave where you found her. Whose grave was it?'

'I didn't notice. It was quite an old one, though.'

For a moment Nell wanted to believe it did not matter whose grave it had been. But those two other girls had been found in that churchyard, and supposing they had been on the same grave . . . ?

She looked at Michael, willing him to follow her thoughts. It seemed he did, because he said, 'What time are you collecting Beth tomorrow?'

'They said any time after ten. Ward rounds and discharge procedure have to be dealt with first, I think. So I was going to get there for about quarter past.'

'It's only three or four miles to St Paul's Church. Shall I pick you up at half past eight tomorrow morning?'

'I could do it on my own,' began Nell.

'Wouldn't it be easier if you had someone with you?'

'I suppose so. Yes, of course it would. Thank you.'

'In the meantime,' he said, picking up Alice Wilson's journal and reaching for the laptop, 'I'll take the ghosts back to the Black Boar.'

ELEVEN

Afffter Michael had gone, Nell rinsed the coffee things, then fell into bed and went instantly into a deep, more or less dreamless, sleep. She woke at seven to the sound of birdsong, and remembered that Beth was all right and in just over three hours she would be home. She smiled, planning how she would make all Beth's favourite things for lunch, then remembered about meeting Michael and leapt out of bed and headed for the shower.

Michael phoned shortly after eight, to say he would pick her up in twenty minutes if that was all right.

'Fine. I'll look out for you and come straight down.'

'Did you sleep? And is Beth all right this morning?'

'Bright as a button.' Nell had phoned the hospital at twenty to eight and the staff nurse had said Beth was about to eat breakfast and was looking forward to coming home.

As they drove down the High Street, Michael said, 'I read Alice Wilson's journal. It's extraordinary, isn't it? Once I started I had to read all the way through to the end – it was nearly one a.m. before I finished it. It's classic ghost stuff, of course – those three knocks on the door. In fact—'

'What?'

'Only that I thought I heard someone knocking the first time I was there,' he said. 'It was probably something outside, but it was very macabre.'

Nell said, 'It was the part where she talked about hearing things not meant for human ears I found so chilling.'

'The whispering of wolves and of demons,' he said, half to himself. 'Alice wrote very vividly, didn't she?'

'You think it might all be a form of fiction?'

'I'd have to have known her before judging that,' he said. 'But if it was fiction, it was a peculiar way of writing it.'

'And let's remember she hid it in the clock,' said Nell. 'If you were writing fiction, surely you wouldn't do that?'

'It might have been part of the plan,' he said.

'But she put it there forty-odd years ago,' pointed out Nell.

'That'd be a very long-term plan. I do take your point, though. An intriguing old manuscript coming to light in an empty house . . . And clocks are often in ghost stories. They're like cats and mirrors and mountains. They have a secret life of their own.'

'Alice didn't sound as if she'd be devious in that way, did she?' said Michael. 'If she wanted to write a ghost story, I have the feeling she'd have bombarded publishers.'

'I rather liked the sound of her,' said Nell. 'I'd like to know what happened to her. It's a pity Wilson is a fairly common surname – it might be difficult to trace. I wondered if it might be possible to find out more about the society she belonged to.'

'Psychic investigation,' said Michael, thoughtfully.

'She called it the Society for Psychic Research,' said Nell. 'Which might have been its exact name or just her own short-hand. And there must have been dozens of psychic research set-ups around then – well, there're probably dozens now.'

'If the local council called her in, there might be correspondence with an address in their files,' said Michael thoughtfully.

'I wouldn't bank on it. I found a few letters when I was trying to trace Charect House's previous owners for Liz Harper,' said Nell. 'I was looking through land registration documents and transfer of titles, and there were three or four letters written to Alice by someone from the council – asking her to come to Marston Lacy to investigate the house. I think they'd got into the file by mistake. There was a note of exasperation in them, as if the council was only doing it as a last resort. I don't think there was an address.'

'I'll bet the council destroyed anything official and missed those,' said Michael. 'Can you imagine any local authority admitting it employed a ghost-hunter?'

'The society might not exist any longer,' said Nell.

'No. And even if we did find Alice, she'd be pretty elderly now. That journal was written in the nineteen sixties, and she mentioned a boyfriend who was killed at Hiroshima.'

'Nineteen forty-five,' said Nell, nodding. 'That means she'd have to be at least forty when she was at Charect.'

'Yes, and in that case— Hold on, I think this is the turning for St Paul's Church. Or is it?' He slowed down, peering doubtfully at the road.

Nell found this uncertainty rather endearing. She said, 'I think it's right – I can see the church spire from here.'

'That's how I found the place yesterday,' he said, turning the car into the lane. 'I just looked for a spire and drove towards it. If I got lost I was going to phone Inspector Brent and call out the cavalry.'

'But you weren't sure, not at that point, that Beth would be there.'

'No, but I'd rather have looked stupid in front of the police than take the chance of missing her,' he said, and Nell was so deeply grateful to him she could not speak for several minutes.

St Paul's was, Nell supposed, a fairly typical country church: not very big, not particularly attractive or graceful, just a mass of grey stones that had been put here so the local people could worship. Once it would have been the centre of the small community, but now it did not look as if anyone had been here for years. The thought of Beth out here alone, in the dark coldness, twisted painfully around Nell's heart again. We *will* leave here as soon as we can, she thought. Once I know Beth's completely recovered, I'll sell the shop and we'll go. But then she remembered that other little girl, sobbing with terror at what might happen to Elvira, having to be forcibly sedated, and she realized that leaving Marston Lacy would feel like abandoning Ellie Harper.

Michael led the way through the old lychgate. As they went along the uneven path it began to rain – the same relentless rain as yesterday. Nell shivered and turned up her coat collar. Seeing this, Michael paused under an ancient cedar. 'We should have brought an umbrella,' he said. 'I've got one in the car, I think. Stay here and I'll dash back to get it.'

He was gone before Nell could say anything, and for a moment she watched him half-run between the trees, towards the road, then she turned back to look round the churchyard. The headstones jutted up out of the ground like black teeth, but the actual graves were covered with thick, soft grass; in spring and summer there might be the hazy colours of bluebells beneath the trees or primroses. And there was a serenity about the place which Nell had not expected. The thought of Beth being out here on her own would still give her nightmares, but it was not quite as macabre as she had feared. And you survived, Beth, thought Nell. I got you back.

Little clouds of mist rose from the grass, and the rain drained any colour the church might have possessed. Nell quite liked rain if she was indoors; she liked watching it beating against the windows. But this rain was thin and spiteful, and if you listened intently you could almost believe spiky little voices chattered inside it. The murmuring of demons, Alice had written. Nell shivered and peered through the dripping trees, hoping to see Michael returning, but it was difficult to see or hear anything in this rainstorm. No, it was all right, he was coming back now, she could hear footsteps.

And then, between one heartbeat and the next, she suddenly knew it was not Michael, and apprehension scudded across her skin like the prickle of electricity before a thunderstorm. Nell pressed back against the tree trunk, not wanting to be seen, knowing this to be ridiculous because even if it was not Michael it would be some perfectly innocent visitor to the church – a tourist or even one of Inspector Brent's men: he had said something about the forensic team checking the place.

But apprehension was still clutching her because tourists did not usually walk through pouring rain at nine o'clock in the morning to view undistinguished, semi-derelict churches, and forensic experts would be noisy, lugging along cases and cameras. And neither tourists nor policemen would walk slowly and uncertainly, as if making a blind fumbling way towards the graves . . .

As this last thought formed, Nell became aware that something was disturbing the lonely serenity of the church and its surroundings – a sound so fragile it could barely be heard by human ears.

Dead souls sobbing, wolves whispering . . .

She stood very still, listening intently. The sounds came and went, like a bad radio or TV signal. She was about to call out or make a dash for the lychgate when something moved on the edge of her vision, something that was not quite substantial enough to be a figure but that was more than the curtain of rain. A figure moving between the trees, was it? For pity's sake, this was turning into every classic ghost scenario ever written! But there *had* been something, she was sure of it.

The sounds were forming a definite pattern – forming words, a faint rhythm.

'At the midnight hour, beneath the gallows tree . . .
Hand in hand the Murderers stand . . .
By one, by two, by three . . .
Open lock to the dead man's knock . . .'

Horror closed around Nell's throat. It was the rhyme – the rhyme Alice had heard that night, the rhyme Beth talked about and Ellie had known. She waited, but the eerie chanting had stopped and she could only hear the rain pattering on the leaves and against the walls of the church. And then footsteps, blessedly ordinary footsteps, came towards her, and there was the bright colour of an umbrella and Michael's voice calling that he was sorry to have been so long, but he had dropped the car keys and they had rolled into the ditch and nearly been washed down a roadside grid, and he was covered in mud from retrieving the wretched things. This small, ordinary thing was somehow so reassuring that Nell smiled. Because, of course, those sounds had been simply the rain and the dripping trees mixed up with her own nervous tension. Anyone would be jumpy and a bit over-imaginative in a deserted old grave-yard, for goodness' sake.

But some perversity made her say to Michael, 'Did you see anyone on your way back?'

'No. Why?'

'I thought Inspector Brent said something about sending his forensic people in to see if Beth had been taken inside the church.'

'I shouldn't think they'd come here in all this rain,' said Michael. 'Are you alright to look at the grave? I mean, it isn't going to upset you?'

'I'm tougher than that. Let's do it before one of us gets pneumonia.'

'Well, stay under the umbrella.'

They went as quickly as possible towards the old gravestones. The umbrella was a large golfing one, but it was still necessary to huddle quite close together. It brought back the rainy after-noons when Nell and Brad used to take long walks on the heath, their arms round one another under an umbrella, and how they would come back to the tall, old house where Brad would wrap her in a huge bath towel and make love to her in front of the fire while her hair was still wet . . .

The headstone Michael indicated was very weathered. Moss

and lichen covered parts of it, but most of the lettering was legible. Michael read it out: "'Elizabeth Lee, wife of William Lee. Tragically taken from the world in October 1888.'"

'William Lee,' said Nell, staring down at it. 'Charect House again. That's a curious coincidence.'

'Yes.' Michael knelt down, heedless of the sodden bracken piled around the grave, and began to scrape the moss from the lower part of the stone. 'Look,' he said, and something in his voice sent Nell's nerve-endings shivering again. Brushing off the moss had uncovered the rest of the lettering. Beneath the wording about Elizabeth Lee, wife of William, was another line.

Dearly loved mother of Elvira.

Elvira.

Michael sat back on his heels, staring at the carved words. 'Elvira,' he said softly, and the name seemed to hiss through the trees.

Elvira . . .

Nell found she was gripping the umbrella handle so tightly that it was scoring marks into her palms. Elvira, the name that had haunted Ellie Harper's nightmares. Elvira, for whom Beth believed the eyeless man searched.

Michael stood up, brushing the wet bracken from his cords. Half to himself, he said, 'So she existed. And she must have lived at Charect House – grown up there. That's extraordinary. D'you know, I didn't believe in her until now.'

Nell had not believed in Elvira either. She had thought Elvira was a nightmare figure, a phantom of a child's imagination. But she was real, she had been the daughter of William Lee, the man who, according to Alice Wilson's journal, was said to be still seen in Marston Lacy, seventy years after his death.

'I suppose,' said Michael slowly, 'it would be possible to trace Elvira. Probably, it would be fairly easy, in fact.'

'I'm not sure if I want to trace her.'

'I'm not sure if I want to, either.'

They looked at one another. 'But,' said Nell, at last, 'we must. It might lay the ghost for Beth and Ellie.'

'Yes.' He looked back at the headstone. 'Does anything strike you about this grave?'

'I don't think so— Oh,' said Nell. 'Oh yes, it does. In those days, they'd have buried husband and wife together, wouldn't they? Or at the very least side by side in adjoining graves.'

'Exactly. And there's plenty of room in this part of the churchyard. But William isn't here.'

'No. So where,' said Nell, 'is his grave?'

'There might be any number of quite ordinary explanations,' said Michael as they drove away.

'He might have left the area after Elizabeth died,' said Nell. 'He could have gone to live anywhere in the world, couldn't he? Or he might simply have been travelling and died abroad. Or been killed in the Great War – no, he'd have been a bit too old, wouldn't he?'

'There were other wars,' said Michael. 'But somehow I don't see him as a soldier, do you?'

'No. And there's the legend that he's still sometimes seen in Marston Lacy,' said Nell. 'That doesn't quite square with a peaceful death in Biarritz or a heroic one in the Dardanelles, does it?'

'No.' Michael turned the car into the main street and drew up outside Nell's shop. The rain was stopping at last, and a thin shaft of sunlight was breaking through the greyness. Nell thought it was nice that Beth would be coming home in sunshine.

'Let me know about Beth,' said Michael.

'Of course I will.' Nell thought: do I ask him to call at the flat later? She glanced at him and saw he had the hesitant look again, as if he, too, was not sure what to say. Before she could think too much about it, she said, 'If you want to bring the laptop back later, we could check if there's another email from Jack Harper.'

He looked pleased. 'We ought to do that, oughtn't we?' he said at once. 'This afternoon I'll go out to Charect House to see how the work's getting on. It'd be ironic if I've told Jack it won't be ready for Christmas, then find the roof's fallen in or something. Would around five be a good time?'

'You can have a cup of tea and tell Beth some more about Wilberforce,' said Nell.

TWELVE

Charect House, when Michael got there, did not look very habitable; in fact, it did not look as if it was likely to be habitable for another ten years. Window frames were hanging off their moorings like teeth torn from the roots, and it looked as if there was a gaping hole in part of the roof. But the skip parked on the lawn on his last visit seemed to have vanished, which presumably was progress.

He went cautiously inside. The skip had not vanished at all; it, or a smaller version of it, was blocking most of the hall. Michael stepped carefully round it and went into the long drawing-room. This was a daunting sight, but probably it would not take very long to sort out the bare electricity wires spilling riotously out of the wall. He went across the hall to the room Liz had designated as a dining room – 'Although we'll mostly eat in the kitchen,' Jack had said, sending Liz's enthusiastic sketches for the kitchen's comprehensive refurbishment. 'Except when we have classy Oxford dons to stay . . .'

The dining room was not much better than the drawing room. Michael sat on a low window-sill and saw he had told nothing but the truth to Jack and Liz about the house not being habitable in time for Christmas. But as he had booked them into the Black Boar, they might still decide to come, just for a short stay. The idea of asking Nell and Beth to join them there for Christmas dinner flickered in his mind, but probably Nell would be spending Christmas with her own family or her husband's. Still, they might all meet for a drink.

The rotund builder he had met last time came trundling down the stairs and hailed Michael with cheerful recognition. 'Taking another look round, Dr Flint?' he said.

'Yes. You've made a lot of progress,' said Michael, hoping this was the right thing to say and trying not to look too fixedly at the cascading electric wires.

'We've done a lot of the basic work,' said the builder. 'Plumbing and treating the rot. Those things don't show. The electricians are in this afternoon to finish off most of the wiring,' he added, clearly seeing Michael's doubtful look at the tangle of cables. 'And high time too, for I'm surprised the whole place didn't go up in smoke years ago. Matter of fact, we're about to make a start on opening up the attics – smashing down that dividing wall for the playroom Dr Harper wanted.'

'That sounds quite a major job.'

'No, we'll have it down in a trice. No sooner the word than the deed. Come and watch, why don't you?'

'Well, I don't think—' began Michael, but the builder was already going upstairs.

'I like seeing a wall come down,' he said, over his shoulder. 'Very satisfying it is. You see something happening for your efforts. There's always a lot of dust, though.'

Michael, who had spent ten minutes trying to brush the bracken of St Paul's Churchyard from his cords, supposed one more layer of dirt would not make much difference, and he followed the builder, grateful that the secondary stair, where he had seen the intruder that first day, was brightly lit by battery-powered lamps.

Access to the attic was by a low door, which the men had propped open. There was a slanting ceiling, and beneath the miasma of builders' rubble was a warm, powdery scent of age. Michael thought if you were here by yourself there would be a sense of having crossed from one world to another – of having come through a semi-magical portal. Wardrobes and railway stations, he thought, smiling inwardly.

Two tiny windows let in a small amount of light, softened by the thick dust on the panes, but when Michael walked across to the nearer one he saw there were views of Shropshire countryside stretching for miles. In one direction was a faint blue-grey smudge that might be the start of Welsh mountains. He looked down into the gardens directly below, and the memory of the photographs he had taken that first day came back to him – that faint but unmistakable figure of a dark-haired female pressed against an attic window, one hand raised in greeting or entreaty . . .

'These floors are pretty sound as far as we can tell,' said the builder, walking experimentally along the sides of the room. 'But we'll lay new boards where we think they're needed. Probably strengthen the roof joists as well, before we create a false ceiling.' He reached up to tap the rafters overhead and a shower of dust cascaded down. 'Clean dust though,' he said, happily, wiping his palms down the sides of his overalls. 'No bat droppings. Makes a difference, not finding bats in a house.'

'Protected species?' said Michael, eyeing the rafters with misgiving.

'Too true. Once you've got bats you can't do much to get them out. Personally, I'd poison the evil little bastards as soon as look at them, never mind if twenty Preservation Groups or fifty Dracula Societies marched round the place waving banners. Still, whatever else might live here, there's no bats.'

Michael, ignoring the oblique reference in this last sentence, said he was very glad to hear there was no evidence of bats and he thought his friends would agree. 'They're wondering about moving in for Christmas,' he said tentatively. 'Would the work be finished by then?'

'Bit tight,' said the builder. 'New Year, more like.' He walked along the wall due to be demolished, while two men, armed with fearsome-looking sledgehammers and pickaxes and wearing yellow site-helmets, awaited his verdict. When he tapped the wall, the sound, in the small space, was shockingly loud, and Michael jumped because it was exactly the sound he had heard on his first visit.

The builder produced a stub of pencil and drew esoteric-looking symbols on the far wall. 'All yours,' he said to the two men. Then, to Michael, 'Stand well clear, squire. In fact, you'd better stand on the stair outside.'

In the muted light from the two small windows the massive sledgehammer swished through the air and, with a boom of sound, landed squarely on the pencil marks. The whole of the wall shivered, and a myriad of spider-cracks appeared in its surface, as if a giant hand had crumpled a sheet of paper. The sledgehammer whirled a second time, and at the second blow, the thin cracks deepened and spread, and plaster dust showered everywhere. As the dust clouds billowed upwards, a small room, shut away for countless years, gradually became visible. At first look it did not seem as if it would add much to Ellie's playroom – it was barely six by eight – but at least it made the attics lighter, because a tiny window had been behind the wall, a small oblong of glass, framed by crumbling wood. The window was cracked and thick with the dirt of decades, but if you stood on tiptoe and leaned forward you would be able to see down into the gardens below. That's what she did, thought Michael. One day, a long, long time ago, she stood there, that dark-haired woman, and in some way I can't begin to understand, years later, the image came out on the photo I took.

But if anyone really had stood in this room and looked down from the window, there was no trace of that now. Michael was conscious of a stab of disappointment. But he stepped through the jagged pieces of wall and into the dusty space beyond. Was there a faint imprint of a hand on the grimed window, as if someone had pressed against it? But there seemed to be nothing except the encrusted dirt of years. He looked out, seeing the outlines of the old shrubbery below, then turned back into the room. The plaster and brick-dust was starting to settle, and the builder and his assistants had gone in search of implements to clean it up. Michael could hear them calling to one another as to the whereabouts of the heavy-duty vacuum cleaner, asking which daft bugger had used it last and not put it back in the hall.

He was about to go back downstairs when he saw that a small section of wall near the window had crumbled away. Fresh plaster dust had showered out, together with some kind of packing, which must have been thrust into the cavity of the partition wall.

It was not packing. It was a sheaf of yellowed papers, covered in writing. Michael's heart began to race. Even from here he could see that the writing was erratic, the ink faded to sepia, but it looked as if it was just about legible. Was this something more from Alice Wilson?

The men were coming back up the stairs, dragging the vacuum cleaner with them, grumbling good-humouredly about the narrowness of the attic stair.

Michael bent down, picked the papers up and slipped them into an inside pocket.

It was almost three o'clock when Michael got back to the Black Boar, and he suddenly realized he'd had nothing to eat or drink since breakfast at seven. Bar lunches had finished, it seemed, but some sandwiches and coffee could certainly be made up for him. What would he like?

'Anything,' said Michael, who wanted nothing more than to get to the privacy of his room and read the papers he had stolen from Charect House. No, stolen was too strong a word. He fully intended to give them to the house's owner. After he had read them. They would turn out to be just somebody's old laundry list, of course.

He put them on the bedside table and managed to make himself wait until the plate of sandwiches and pot of coffee had been brought. He was starting to feel slightly light-headed, although he had no idea if this was from ordinary hunger or nervous tension. Just in case it was hunger he gulped down some coffee and crammed a ham sandwich into his mouth, then reached for the papers.

He had more than half expected to see Alice Wilson's familiar writing at the top of the first page – his mind and his eyes were prepared to do so. But the writing was very different to Alice's impatient scribble. The date was a good thirty years before Alice had come to Charect House.

7th February 1939

This morning I received the letter for which I have waited almost my entire life.

That strange, tragic woman, who dwelled in a sad twilight world for so long, has died, and Charect House is finally mine.

Father always said it would be. 'One day, Harriet,' he used to say, 'one day, we shall be rich. We shall have a beautiful house in a wonderful party of the country. Remember that. Remember there's only one person who stands between us and our inheritance.'

When I was small I believed it, but over the years the story of the house we should one day own took on the flavour of a dream – another one of Father's many fantasies. Mother never believed it at all. She died telling me to look after Father because he was a dreamer and dreamers were notoriously impractical.

Sometimes Father tried to explain why we would one day inherit a house and to sketch out the line of descent, although I never really followed it. 'The Ansteys are an obscure branch of the Shropshire Lees,' he said. 'It's a complicated descent though.'

I don't know the complexities of the line of descent, but I do know any cousins I might have had – any children born to my father's generation – were all lost. The Great War took most of the men, leaving the ladies behind in a welter of jingoism and songs about it being a long way to Tipperary. It's scaldingly sad that thousands of those men never came back, and that an incredibly large number of the girls never found anyone else to love, but clung to letters and photographs of heartbreakingly young men.

I'm one of those girls. I have my own sepia photograph of someone who might have married me if he hadn't been killed on the Somme, and my own might-have-been daydreams. He still smiles out of the photograph at me, and I often smile back and say goodnight to him as I get into bed. Harry, that was his name. Harry Church. He used to say we were destined to be together because even our names fitted. Harry and Harriet.

But it's sentimentality to talk like that, and it's over twenty years ago since he died. And if I didn't meet anyone else I could care about, I've had a good life so far. Nor is it over by a long way, because I'm only just turned forty, and if this new war is coming, as everyone says, I dare say there will be ways in which I can be useful.

And now, after all these years, there's Charect House.

The solicitor's letter says, with an unmistakable note of apology, that the place is not in a very good condition, due to its having been empty for a very long time. That sends me into a whole new set of romantic daydreams, visualizing a grey grange or gloomy manor house, dripping with cobwebs, occupied by insubstantial wraiths or unhouseled souls, sobbing with loneliness . . .

It takes me back to that strange haunted woman inhabiting her own mist-shrouded half-world for so many years.

I make no apology for those last two paragraphs, since I feel I can be allowed an outbreak of romantic Gothicism on the occasion of inheriting the tumbledown home of my ancestors. When I finally walk up to it, I shall be like the heroine of that splendid book by Daphne du Maurier I read at Christmas – *Rebecca*. 'Last night I dreamed I went to Manderley again . . .'

On a more practical note, I have arranged to travel to Shropshire next week. The solicitor's letter requests me to provide suitable proof of my identity – birth certificate and passport were suggested as being acceptable. But I've never possessed a passport because I've never been outside England. I've always dearly wanted to see other lands and meet other races, but with that vulgar little man Adolf Hitler rampaging greedily across Europe, occupying Czechoslovakia as if he considers it his own back garden, it doesn't look as if I'm likely to get my wish for a good while.

So I'm taking my birth certificate as proof. It's a bit ragged at the edges because of being stored in a tin box all these years, but it states, quite clearly, that Harriet Anstey was born in the county of Cheshire on the 10th day of April, in the year 1898.

Harriet Anstey, thought Michael, lowering the papers for a moment. For a moment he could almost see her, bright-eyed and intelligent, walking along Blackberry Lane to the house. The lane would have looked much as it looked now, and she would have been excited and slightly amused at her own romantic expectations. 'Last night I dreamt I went to Manderley again . . .' But for Manderley read Charect House, thought Michael, and for Rebecca read Elvira.

He saw it was half-past four, and with extreme reluctance he put the papers carefully inside his suitcase, locked it, and prepared to go along to Nell's shop. He nearly forgot the laptop, which they had arranged he would bring to check on emails from Jack, but remembered in time and went back upstairs.

THIRTEEN

Nell was making a pot of tea when Michael arrived, and Beth was toasting teacakes with careful concentration. You could not, she explained seriously, burn teacakes or they would taste horrid.

'I love toasted teacakes,' said Michael, going over to help her watch the teacakes turn the required shade of golden brown. 'I expect you're glad to be home, aren't you?'

'I had trifle in hospital,' confided Beth. 'It was nice, but not as nice as Mum's.' A tiny frown creased her brow. 'I didn't like that man carrying me away,' she said.

Michael glanced at Nell and saw that although she was apparently concentrating on pouring milk into a jug, she was listening intently. He said, 'I should think it was pretty grim.'

'Yes, it was pretty grim.' She appeared to like the expression.

Michael said, 'Did you know who he was?'

'No. I don't know, akcherly, how he got me,' said Beth. 'On account of I know about not speaking to strangers or getting in cars and stuff like that, and I never do. I jus' remember him carrying me down a road and singing to himself.'

'I think it was a really bad dream,' said Nell. 'I think you were sleepwalking.'

'It sounds like it,' said Michael, following her lead.

'Sleepwalking's pretty important, isn't it?' said Beth hopefully.

'It is, rather.'

'I didn't much like it, however,' said Beth. 'I most of all didn't like it when he sang 'bout the dead man's hand.' She looked at Nell from the corners of her eyes. 'I don't s'pose there's any such thing, really, is there? I mean, you couldn't have a dead man's hand that opens doors that're locked?'

'Definitely not,' said Nell at once.

'Or that sends people to sleep? That's what he sang. "Sleep and be dead for the dead man's sake."'

She glanced nervously at Nell, and Michael, seeing Nell's

hesitation, said, 'It'll have been part of an old song. Country places like this have really old songs – people hand them down from their grandparents, and they've handed them down from *their* grandparents. Some of them are actually quite interesting. It lets us know what people sang hundreds of years ago. I quite like knowing what people used to sing.'

'I'd like knowing as well,' said Beth. 'Only, not when it's about dead men's hands and stuff. That's pretty grim, I think.'

'So do I. But I bet it really was just an old song you heard.'

Beth appeared to find this acceptable. She said, 'That man thought I was somebody else. He thought I was somebody called Elvira.'

Elvira . . . It whispered into the kitchen, leaving a snail's trail of fear through the homely scents of teacakes being toasted and the singing of the kettle as it came up to the boil. Elvira whose name was inscribed on a forgotten gravestone in a desolate churchyard. But where was Elvira's grave?

Nell said, 'Beth, that teacake's burning. How did you know that about Elvira?'

'Because he said so.' Beth rescued the teacake. '"You're not Elvira," that's what he said. "I must find her." Then he sort of cried a bit. It was sad when he did that.'

'Perhaps Elvira was somebody he had once known.'

'I think Elvira's a stupid name,' said Beth robustly. 'Can we have the teacakes now? And can I hear some more about Wilberforce?'

After the teacakes had been consumed, Beth went up to her room to tell the animal collection about a new exploit involving the mice's preparations for Christmas and a Christmas tree in which Wilberforce had become indignantly entangled.

Nell said, 'Sleepwalking was the most reassuring answer I could think of.'

For her or for you? Michael wondered, but he only said, 'It might even be true.' He studied her for a moment. 'D'you still think the nightmares are bound up with her father's death?' Damn, he thought, why can't I say "your husband". Or even use his name? Brad, that's what he's called.

'I'm not discounting it entirely,' said Nell slowly, and Michael looked at her and thought: you're not discounting it because you have nightmares of your own. 'It doesn't explain Elvira, though,' said Nell and, before Michael could say anything, she

said: 'It doesn't explain the Hand of Glory rhyme, either. That's
what Beth heard, isn't it? It's what Ellie hears, as well. "Sleep
all who sleep, wake all who wake, but be as the dead for the
dead man's sake." And Michael, the thing that terrifies me most
about that—'

'Is that it actually seems to have sent Beth to sleep,' said
Michael.

'Yes.'

It terrified Michael as well, but he only said, 'She seems to
have bounced back fairly quickly.'

'She does, doesn't she?' said Nell with a kind of eager
gratitude. 'She's astonishingly resilient, really. I think she could
go back to school in a couple of days. I think the normality of
that will help. She'll get absorbed in lessons and her friends,
and it will fade. At least, that's what I'm hoping. Would you
like another cup of tea? And d'you want to check your emails?'

'Yes to both questions, please,' said Michael, smiling at her.

He connected up the laptop, pleased to find he remembered
which socket plugged into the phone line, and switched on.

The email programme opened up and Jack's name seemed
to jump out at him.

Michael—

We've made a decision, and it's that Ellie absolutely must
have a complete change of scenery and people. Frankly, it's
the only thing left we can think of to try.

Last night she began crying around midnight – the most
despairing, heart-rending sobbing you can imagine, and
nothing we could do or say seemed to reach her.

"He's waiting for me," she kept saying. "He really is. Don't
let him get to me, please don't."

She wasn't asleep, and she was perfectly lucid – she knew
me, and she knew Liz, and she clutched at us, begging us to
keep 'him' away from her. We considered ER again, but they
couldn't help last time and all they could suggest was analysis.
But that will be our last, despairing resort for Ellie.

It's now six a.m. and she's finally fallen into an exhausted
sleep, but every so often we can hear her crying inside whatever dreams she's having.

I'm typing this very hastily because Liz is packing our
things and in about half an hour we're going to drive out to

her cousins at New Jersey. It's a five-hour drive, but I'm beyond caring. I'd drive round the entire globe if it would help Ellie. The cousins have one of those rambling old houses, and it's permanent open house to the world and his wife. They're noisy and cheerful and eminently sane and I defy anyone to have nightmares in the midst of that crowd – in fact, if Liz's godmother is there I defy a nightmare to come within gibbering distance. (First and probably only glimmer of humor from your usually flippant friend.)

If we can, we'll spend about a week at the cousins', then drive up to New York and get a flight from JFK to Heathrow around the 16th. All being well we'll have a few days in London – Liz can shop and we'll take Ellie to all the tourist places. Ellie's never been to London, and surely it will drive the ghosts away for her. Then, jet-lag permitting, we'll hire a car and come up to Marston Lacy for the 22nd or 23rd.

I'll put the laptop in the case, but it'll probably stay there for the next couple of weeks, so don't worry if you don't hear from me until we're actually in London. You've got my mobile number if you need to reach me – if Charect House blows up or falls down.

Liz is already yelling up to me to get a move on so I'll send this now. I'll phone when we reach London – I don't know yet where we'll stay.

But – you will spend Christmas with us in Marston Lacy, won't you?

Till then,
    Jack

'This was sent at seven a.m. their time,' said Michael, sitting back. 'That's about midday here. I'll send a reply, but I don't think they'll get it.'

'You've got his mobile number, though?' said Nell, who had come to stand by him and was reading the email over his shoulder. 'You can reach him on that?'

'I should have it somewhere. I don't think I've ever used it,' said Michael. He tried not to think that if he couldn't reach Jack, he would be arriving in Marston Lacy in two weeks' time, along with Liz and Ellie.

In disconcerting echo of this thought, Nell said, 'D'you think Ellie's in danger?'

'Oh God, I hope not,' said Michael. He thought for a moment, then said, 'I think I'll just repeat that Charect House won't be anywhere near ready for Christmas and ask him to phone so I can explain in more detail.'

'Shall you tell him about our side of things with Elvira? When you get to speak, I mean.'

'I think I'll have to.'

'It won't sound as peculiar to him as it would to anyone else,' said Nell. 'He's more than halfway there already.'

'That's true.' Michael drew breath to tell her about finding Harriet Anstey's journal, then changed his mind. He would keep Harriet to himself just a little longer.

He sent the email to Jack and closed the laptop. As he got up to leave, Nell said, 'Will you stay in touch?' And then, hastily: 'Because I do want to know what happens.'

There were still smudges of tiredness under her eyes, and she looked small and vulnerable, and Michael discovered he wanted to put his arms round her. He said, 'Of course I will. I'd stay in touch even without all this.'

'Oh good.' The words appeared to come out involuntarily.

Back at the Black Boar, Michael arranged to have an early breakfast and to check out afterwards, then went up to his room. He would probably reach Oxford around mid-morning tomorrow, and providing he could find Jack's mobile number he would phone him then. In the meantime, there was Harriet Anstey's journal.

He would not have been surprised if it had vanished like the chimera it probably was, but it lay as he had left it in the locked suitcase. Michael looked at the papers for a moment, trying to work out why he had not told anyone about them – in particular why he had not told Nell. He frowned, shook his head impatiently and took the papers out.

16th February 1939
7.00 p.m.

Tomorrow I shall finally see the house that lay at the heart of all father's stories. And – more to the point – that lay at the deepest point of my own nightmare. The nightmare Father and I shared and that we never repeated to Mother.

Charect House itself won't hold any nightmares – how could

it when I've never seen the place? But it feels remarkable to
know I'm about to see it, and that's why I've decided to keep
this journal. There are moments in one's life that one wants to
erase for ever, but there are also moments – whole experiences
– one wants to preserve. So that, a long way in the future, it
will be possible to unwrap the memories and the experiences,
and relive them and think – oh yes, that was the day I was
really happy. You can't preserve those things by coating them
in isinglass like eggs, or putting a glass case over them like
waxed fruit, but you can write them down while they're still
fresh. I wish I had done that on the night Harry asked me to
marry him. I wish even more I had done so after that night in
the old gardens with the air heavy with the scent of lilac and
the grass soft under us . . . I have no regrets about that night
– it was sweet and sinless and he was being sent to the front
the next day and we both knew he might not come back.

And if I had written it all down, that marvellous cascade of
astonished delight, I could occasionally reread it and recapture
fragments . . . How he looked and felt, and how, afterwards,
he propped himself up on one elbow and smiled down at me,
and traced the lines of my face with his fingertips as if he
wanted to absorb every detail of how I looked, not just with
his eyes, but with his skin and nerves and mind . . .

But I promised myself I would not become sentimental in this
journal and I won't! Instead I'll tidy myself for supper in the
Black Boar's dining room – and admit privately I'm a touch
nervous about walking in there by myself, because no matter
how emancipated we're supposed to be, ladies don't very often
stay in hotels by themselves. I wonder if the locals will be
curious – if they'll see me as a mysterious lone traveller, or
even think I'm an adventuress (ha!).

Adventuress or not, I've been given a very pleasant room.
Chintz curtains and matching counterpane, and a writing desk
in one corner. The window overlooks what I think might have
been the old coach yard – I can see the cobblestones and the
big wide doors. Beyond that are gardens, fringed by whispering
trees and with an old sundial half covered in moss at the centre
of a velvety lawn.

She stayed here, thought Michael, looking up from the slanting
writing. In this room? There was a writing desk in the corner

– had Harriet written these pages there? He went to the window and opened the curtains a little, and even in the darkness, he could see what was unmistakably the old tilt yard. The cobble-stones had been replaced by a patio with wrought-iron chairs, but beyond that were the whispering trees and the mossy sundial. He returned to the bed and began to read.

FOURTEEN

I thought I would remember everything about the Black Boar, but now I'm here I can only remember parts. But then it's more than thirty years since I came here as a wide-eyed child, clinging to Father's hand. One thing I do remember though is Mother saying to me beforehand: 'You'll be staying at an inn, Harriet. It's a very grown-up thing to do, so you must be well-behaved and polite to everyone, and make Father proud of you.'

She knew I would be well-behaved and polite, and so did Father. I was a polite child. Children were in those days. And I was wide-eyed with awe at the huge adventure of going on a train with Father, just the two of us.

At the little station was a trap drawn by a fat pony, which took us into Marston Lacy and the Black Boar. Eating our supper in the dining room was another adventure. We had Brown Windsor Soup and roast mutton, and I was given half portions. Father had a joke with the waiter about whether he would only have to pay half of the cost for me.

But what I do remember in clear detail is the trap returning next morning after breakfast to take us to the place we were here to visit.

There are some memories that with time become buried, almost painlessly, beneath thick layers of scar tissue. They only hurt occasionally, those memories, and they're natural and wholesome and part of the journey through life. The memories of Harry are like that.

But there are other memories, darker, deeper ones, that never quite heal, no matter how much they become overlaid with other experiences. They stay raw, those memories, and from time to time something will jab into them, making them bleed. My memory of that morning when I was seven years old, and Father, dear impractical Father, was in quest of his improbable inheritance, is one of those painful, unhealed memories.

I hadn't intended to write an account of that time, but there's more than an hour before I shall want to get into bed and I suddenly feel I would like to do so. Perhaps if I expose that deep, unhealed wound to the light, it will finally skin over and leave me.

That long-ago morning began happily enough with breakfast and then another ride in the trap. I was allowed to stroke the pony's velvety nose, and the driver showed me how to offer a lump of sugar to him, with my hand flattened.

The trap jolted us through the centre of Marston Lacy, which was yet another adventure for me who had never been in a pony trap. I had never been outside our own Cheshire village either, although Marston Lacy had the same kind of village street with shops displaying their goods. But there were what Father called workshops here, as well: places where people made cabinets and chairs and clocks, and a blacksmith's where a scent of hot iron gusted out into the street. I would have liked to see more of that, but the trap rattled its way on, all the way through the village and out the other side.

Father pointed out to me the smudgy mountains in the distance. 'That's Wales,' he said.

But I had never heard of Wales, so I just said, 'Oh, is it?'

As we went between hedges and fields, the sky seemed to grow darker. 'Rain,' said Father, glancing up. I believe that was the moment when I stopped being excited and inquisitive and when fear scratched at my mind, because the dark sky did not seem like the start of an ordinary rainstorm.

The trap turned into a narrow lane where the hedges gave way to high brick walls. I didn't like them – they were too high and dark and if you were trapped behind them you would not be able to climb out because there were little hard bits of glass on the very top. Then, directly ahead of us, a massive building reared up. It seemed that one minute it was not there and the next it appeared between the trees. It had flat, dark-grey walls and tiny, mean windows with iron bars at some of them. I hated it.

'Here we are,' said the driver, pulling the pony up before black gates. Without the cheerful clatter of the wheels and the clip-clop of the pony's hoofs it was suddenly and disturbingly quiet. There was lettering set into the gates, but although I leaned forward to try to read it, I could not.

'This is where you wanted, isn't it?' said the driver.

'I think so,' said Father. 'If this is—'

'Brank Asylum,' said the man.

I didn't know, not at seven years of age, what an asylum was. But the sound of the name frightened me – *Brank*. It made me think of iron and blackness, and it made me wonder why there had to be bars at all those windows.

Father was handing the driver some coins. 'You'll come back to collect us in one hour?' he said. 'I shall pay you the other half of the money then.'

'I will indeed,' said the man, touching his cap and turning the pony's head round.

'We shan't be as long as an hour, Harriet,' said Father, taking my hand firmly and leading me forward. 'But there's someone in here who wants to meet you.'

That sent the fear spiking even deeper. 'Someone who wants to meet you . . .' Like any child of the early part of the century, I had read the extraordinarily macabre fairy-tales deemed suitable then. It meant I knew what sort of people lived inside lonely forbidding houses and wanted to meet little girls. Witches who put children in cages and fattened them up for the ovens. Wolves who dressed up in human clothes and pretended to be human.

Father rang the bell outside the huge main doors. He kept a firm hold of my hand – perhaps he thought I might suddenly bolt and run back down that long drive to the lanes beyond. I wish I had. I wish I had never gone inside Brank Asylum, and I wish, above everything in the world, that I had not followed Father and a grey-clad, slab-faced woman to the small, mean room at the end of one of the corridors. They smelt of food cooked too long, those corridors – unappetizing food, boiled cabbage and onions. Beneath that was another smell I had never encountered. I could not, then, put a name to it, but it made me think of people drowning in the dark. It made me want to cry.

'In here,' said the granite-coloured woman, opening a door and standing back to let us go inside. I hung back, but Father said, quite gently, 'Come along, Harriet, it's all right,' and I had to go in.

The sad, drowning-in-the-dark smell was much stronger, and there was a horrid smeary darkness in the room. I had the feeling that things might be hiding inside that darkness – things that never went outside, things that had become covered with layers and layers of cobwebs until the cobwebs had formed thick ropes that tangled in hair and coiled around ankles and wrists . . .

But I stood obediently inside the door and waited to see what came next. At first I thought the room was empty, but then from the darkest corner came a voice – an ugly voice that made me think of a fingernail scraping across a slate surface.

'You are Anstey?'

'I am Frederick Anstey.'

There was a blur of movement, as if the cobwebs gathered themselves together. I flinched and glanced behind me, but the door was firmly shut.

'You have brought the child?'

'Harriet. Yes. She's here with me.'

Father glanced down at me, and I managed to say, 'How do you do,' directing the words towards the dark corner.

'They wrote to you?' said the voice, as if I had not spoken. 'They wrote asking you to come here?'

'Yes. The solicitor—'

'The details have no interest for me.' The movement came again. 'Tell the child to speak to me.'

Father bent down. 'Harriet, tell this lady how old you are and how you are good at lessons.' He gave me the smile that meant: everything is perfectly all right. It wasn't all right, of course, but I saw he wanted me to pretend.

So I said, as politely as I could, 'I'm seven. I like reading books.'

'She is well-mannered.'

'I hope so.'

'Her mother?'

'She is at our home in Cheshire.'

'Harriet Anstey,' said the terrible voice, suddenly addressing me directly, 'one day somewhere in the future, after I am dead, you will own a house – my house. If your father is still alive then it will be his first, but he is older than I am so he will most likely die before me. You may not understand all this now, but you will do so in time.' A pause. 'When you finally own that house, if you go to live in it, *he* will come looking

for you. That's what I want to warn you of, in case there is
no one to protect you by then. You must never – *never* – let
him find you. You understand that? For if he finds you—' The
voice stopped, and then went on again. 'You may lose your
sanity, as I did. At times it still deserts me. At those times I
am mad.' There was a movement within the darkness – the
impression of something shrivelled and brittle unfolding itself.
'It may desert me at any moment, that sanity, so I must know
quickly that you understand.'

I said, 'I will make sure he doesn't find me.'

The sounds came again – like the dry rustling of some
ancient winged insect – and a figure walked slowly into the
dim light at the centre of the room.

I cried out, and at my side I heard Father gasp. A tall, thin
woman, wearing – I don't know what she was wearing exactly,
but it was some sort of grey, shapeless garment that hung from
her bony frame. Her hair was grey as well, but it did not look
like hair, it looked like thick cobwebs.

Where her eyes should have been were two deep, dark pits,
which was fearsome enough in itself. But what was so much
worse, what had made me cry out and Father gasp, was that
both eye sockets were faintly crusted over with grey. As if
spiders had spun webs over them, and as if she had not known
or felt it happen.

As she moved, her hands reached out in front of her, feeling
her way towards me. I gasped again, and her head turned towards
me. This time I thrust my clenched fist into my mouth to stop
myself from making a sound. If she heard me she would know
exactly where I was standing. If she touched me I would not
be able to bear it.

She did not touch me. She had taken four steps when she
stopped and lifted her head as if listening.

'Hear him,' she said, and her voice was different – younger,
almost a child's voice. 'Hear him singing. He's coming along
the passageway outside – here he comes. Tappety-tap, feeling
his way . . . If you listen, you'll hear his singing. You oughtn't
to hear it, for there are some things human ears were never
meant to hear. But I hear it – oh God, I hear it every night,
just as I heard it the night he found me . . .'

In a cracked voice, she began to sing:

'Open lock to the dead man's knock . . .

Fly bolt, and bar, and band . . .
Nor move, nor swerve, joint, muscle or nerve,
At the spell of the dead man's hand.
And now with care, the five locks of hair,
From the skull of the murderer dangling there,
With the grease and the fat of a black tom cat . . .'

She stopped, and when she spoke, her voice had returned to the scratchy, ugly tone.

'That's not the real spell, of course,' she said. 'The real spell is far more ancient, far darker – it comes from the black marrow of the world's history – and the world has many such blacknesses. He learned the spell when his own mind touched one of those black cores.'

The terrible head tilted, as if trying to sense where we were standing, and Father seemed to understand this, for he said, 'I'm still here. Harriet is with me. Say whatever you wish.'

She nodded, as if grateful. 'He was once a cheerful man, so they say,' she said. 'An ordinary man – what they call Everyman. He enjoyed the company of his fellows – he would have a glass of ale with them at the end of his day's work. He would laugh at a joke. That is what is said of him. But something happened. Something warped him.' She paused again, and neither Father nor I spoke.

'I wonder, Anstey and Harriet, if you have ever had an old tree in your garden which will not bear fruit. We had one when I was very small. An apple tree. Its roots had gone into unwholesome ground, and the branches were withering and dying. So my father had the tree dug up. I remember the day it was done – a sharp, cold winter's day it was. I wore a scarlet scarf and hat. So vivid, that memory. I remember Father explaining it all to me – saying the roots were getting no nutrient from the soil, so we would replant it in better soil. Healthier soil. We made a little ceremony of it after the gardener had gone, just the two of us . . .' Her voice broke again, as if some disturbing memory had come to her, then she said, 'So it was with him. His heart went into unwholesome ground.'

Father said, 'I understand you. But that song you chanted . . .' I felt a shudder go through him.

'He likes to sing it.' The ugly voice was almost eager. 'But it is a – the child will not know the word parody, but you would know it.'

'Yes.'

'It is a parody of the real spell. The essence can be found within the Greek writings of Herodotus. In the *Petit Albert* and in the *Compendium Maleficarum*, also. The enchanter Mohareb used it to lull to sleep the giant Yohak, who guarded the caves of Babylon. It is referred to in the Bible – Solomon had the secret of it, and the servant of Elijah, when he told his master that he saw from the top of Mount Carmel a cloud rise up from the sea like a man's hand – he, too, spoke of it. That black cloud with flames issuing from it may have been the original of the dread and magical hand of glory.'

Her voice faltered, as if a string was fraying. Father said, 'You are extremely knowledgeable.'

'For one who has no sight? I have not read the books for myself, but when you have money it is possible to pay others to read them for you. I was taught most straitly never to discuss money,' she said. 'A sordid subject, it was always thought. But I ceased to care long ago about that.'

Without warning she began to chant again, crooning the lines about *open lock to the dead man's knock*. Her face seemed to change, as if a looking glass had splintered, and she sank to the floor, wrapping her arms around herself, sobbing pitifully, writhing and screaming and beating on the ground with her fists.

Father instinctively moved forward – I think to comfort her or prevent her from injuring herself – but before he could do so the door was flung open and the grey woman who had brought us here darted across the room. In her hands she held a thick leather strap, and before either of us could speak or move, she had it wrapped around the woman – not too unkindly, but firmly. I had backed away to a corner of the room by then, but I saw how the strap pinned her arms to her sides.

'He's not here,' said the grey woman. 'You're safe. He's not here.' She looked back over her shoulder. 'Best go now,' she said. 'This one won't be lucid for at least a day. And we know what to do for her. You had the speech with her you wanted, did you? The speech she wanted?'

Father began to say he had no idea, but the grey woman had already dismissed him, and so without saying anything we went out, and somehow – I cannot remember how – we found our way back down the stairs and out into the sweet fresh air.

We sat for a long time on the side of the road, not speaking. Then, finally, I summoned up enough courage to say: 'Who was she, that woman?'

He took a long time to reply, but at last he said, 'She owns the house that will one day be yours. She told you that, didn't she?'

'Why doesn't she live in it if it's her house?'

'Because she's – she's very poorly. Her mind is sick, Harriet. Always remember that it's possible for people's minds to become ill, as well as their bodies.'

'Who lives in her house now?'

'Nobody. It's looked after by people called solicitors. They keep it clean and tidy the garden and make sure it's all right.'

'Would she like to live in it if she could?'

'I don't know. She was there when she was a little girl. But she's lived in that place – Brank Asylum – for a very long time.'

'She has no eyes,' I said, and he shuddered.

'No. You heard her say she can pay for people to come in to read to her. She pays people to write letters as well. She asked her solicitor to write a letter to me.'

'Will she ever get better?'

'No. She'll have to live there for always. That's why she sent the letter – she wanted to meet the people who will inherit her house after she dies.'

'Is she going to die soon? Is she very old?'

'Oh, Harriet, she can't be much more than thirty. That's the great tragedy.'

Thirty was quite old, though. I said, 'Is she my aunt? What's her name?'

'I'm not sure of the precise degree of relationship,' said Father. 'She's a cousin to me – perhaps a third cousin. So she'd be a cousin to you, as well. Her name is Elvira Lee.'

Elvira Lee. The name seemed to jump out of the page and snatch Michael's throat. Elvira, who had been commemorated on an old, forgotten grave as a dearly loved daughter of Elizabeth. Elvira, who Ellie insisted was in danger, and Beth said was being sought by the man in her nightmare.

If Harriet's journal could be believed, Elvira had ended her life, blind and insane, in a place called Brank Asylum.

Michael suddenly wanted to talk to Nell about this, but saw it was after eleven already. He would phone her tomorrow. But he would read some more of Harriet's journal before going to bed.

FIFTEEN

S unlight is pouring into my room at the Black Boar, and
it's almost dispelled the ghosts. But not quite. I can't
stop remembering Elvira Lee, poor haunted creature,
incarcerated in Brank Asylum for all those years – thirty years
at least. How much of those thirty years did she spend inside
that dark madness?

She was fifty-eight when she died – I know that because
the solicitor sent me her birth and death certificates. She was
born in 1880 at Charect House, and she died in 1938 in Brank
Asylum of arterial embolism. I looked that up in Mother's old
Home Doctor reference book, and I think it's what we would
call a stroke.

Even all these years later I can remember how sane Elvira
sounded when she talked about her own madness. I can
remember her terror of the man she believed searched for her,
as well.

After breakfast, I asked at the reception desk for directions
to Charect House. The man gave me a slightly startled look,
but said it was easy enough to find.

'Out of the village, and along Blackberry Lane, past the old
carriageway to the manor – that's long since gone, of course –
and there you'll be. It's a fair old walk, though. I could telephone
the local taxi service. They'd be here in a matter of minutes,
well, always supposing they're free.'

A 'fair old walk' might mean anything from a mile to five
miles, so I've accepted the taxi offer, and I'm writing this in
my room while I wait for it to arrive. The romantic in me
would like to walk by myself to the home of my ancestors,
savouring every blade of grass and every breath of atmosphere,
but the pragmatist knows perfectly well I should get lost in
the bewilderment of lanes around here. So I shall approach

my inheritance, Father's cherished dream, in a cloud of exhaust
fumes.

3.15 p.m.

In the end I compromised. I asked the taxi driver to let me
down at the end of Blackberry Lane so I could walk the rest
of the way. With a faint echo of my childhood, I arranged for
him to collect me in an hour's time.

Blackberry Lane is like any other English country lane. It's
fringed with hedges, and at this time of year there's the promise
of cowslips in the fields and of May blossom and lilac to
come. As I walked, my spirits rose, and the lovely evocative
line that opens Rebecca was strongly with me.

Last night I dreamed I went to Manderley again . . . The
ruinous Manderley with its iron gates and blackened walls and
sad secrets would not be at the end of the lane. But whatever
was ahead, it was mine. I was coming home.

Everywhere was so quiet and still, I could almost have believed
I had stepped back to the days when Elvira Lee lived here. There
are places in England – I dare say all over the world – that have
that effect. As if, here and there, something has puckered the fabric
of time and tiny shards of the past can trickle out.

I went past the ruined carriageway, pausing to glance along
it and sparing a thought for a manor house no longer there. I
do know it's more important for ordinary people to have decent
houses and a bit of garden, but it's such a shame that so many
of England's great houses have been lost – to fire, to flood,
to improvidence or debt. If this war that's coming lasts as long
as the war that took my Harry and all those other young men,
I suppose even more of them will be lost.

I don't think Charect House will ever be lost, though. It has
such a stubborn air of survival. It stands well back from
Blackberry Lane behind overgrown gardens, and it's one of
those four-square red-brick houses built about a century and a
half ago. (Which means everywhere will be crumbling or
sagging or rotten, and it will probably cost far more money than
I shall ever possess to restore it . . .)

Tacked on to the gate was an oblong of wood with the
house's name and a rusting chain that snapped in two when I
lifted it. When I unlocked the door and pushed it open, there

was the most tremendous feeling of ownership. Again, I thought: *I am coming home*.

What did I expect from the inside of the house? Gothic gloom, shrouded rooms, dusty sunlight lying across oak floors . . . ? I got that, all right. But I also got the depressing, bad-smelling evidence of forty years of neglect and dereliction. The best ghost stories don't mention the smell you get from an old, deserted house. They don't mention the damp, dank stench – decades of ingrained grime and mouse droppings and rusting taps that drip into green-crusted sinks.

(Actually, there was a faint sound of water dripping all the time I was there – there's something so lonely about the sound of a tap dripping, and this was a particularly insistent, very nearly rhythmic dripping. It seemed to follow me into every room.)

I don't have very much knowledge of houses or what goes wrong with them, but anyone can recognize when age or rot has caused window frames to crumble, and sprawling grey-green patches of damp on walls. There was, in fact, a particularly unpleasant patch on the main landing wall. As I went up the main stairway I had quite a scare because it looked for all the world like the figure of a man, rather stocky, standing there watching me. I didn't quite scream, but it was several minutes before my heart resumed its normal rate.

But even with wallpaper peeling from the walls, and plaster mouldings fallen from the ceilings – even allowing for the army of invisible creatures undoubtedly nibbling industriously at the woodwork – the house is lovely. Someone has at least had the housewifely good sense to cover most of the furniture with dust sheets. I dragged them off because I wanted to see everything, and clouds of dust rose up nearly choking me. But when the dust settled it was worth it, because the furniture is beautiful. And valuable as well, I should think. If I really do need money (and it's looking as if I shall), I may be able to sell some of the better pieces. But I'd like to keep most of it: there are deep armchairs with faded rose-patterned fabric, a writing bureau, a round rosewood table, a long-case clock . . .

What daunted me far more than the elegant dereliction, though, were the boxes and trunks stuffed with papers and letters and fabrics and household miscellany. They'll all have to be opened and properly investigated. For all I know poor old Elvira might have murdered half a dozen people and secreted their remains in the two big cabin trunks. I don't really think she did, and I know that, just as anything of any value will have been destroyed or sold, every scrap of boring minutiae will have been diligently preserved. But there's always the faint chance that Great Uncle Somebody squirrelled a few Holbein sketches among the rubbish, or that great-grandmamma tucked a first-folio Shakespearean manuscript between the leaves of a cookery book.

All the time I was in the house I had the feeling of being watched. I do know that's quite common in empty houses though. It felt strongest in the library – that's a rather grand term for a house of that size, but the room is lined with books that nobody thought to pack away. There are rows upon rows of them, floor to ceiling. There's a big, leather-topped table and several deep chairs, and a long-case clock in a corner. It's long since stopped, of course, so winding it and setting the time is another task for me.

When my self-appointed hour was up, I locked the doors and went out to Blackberry Lane to meet the taxi.

I have no idea how much actual money (if any!) comes with this legacy or the likely cost of the work needed at the house, but tomorrow I shall ask the solicitor.

In the meantime, it's almost midnight and I've retired to bed. Charect House's atmosphere is somehow still with me though – and I don't mean the smell of damp or rot. It's that impression of being watched that's stayed with me – that, and that persistent dripping tap. And – let's be honest in these pages if nowhere else – it's Elvira's tale about a nameless man who sings that macabre song – it's from the *Ingoldsby Legends*, that rhyme, I found that out years ago – but whose mind touched a deep, unwholesome core, like the old apple tree's roots. On balance, I really could wish I had never heard that story, and I certainly wish I had never met Elvira herself.

18th February
Midday

Today I've brought my diary to Charect House with me. It will provide a welcome respite from all the sorting out, and it will be company in the silence of the place.

It isn't entirely silent, of course. No house ever is. And there's still the constant drip of water somewhere. It started to annoy me after a while, but although I've explored the sculleries – grim, badly-lit caverns – all the taps were dry. I hope it isn't something in the roof – I should think roofs cost the earth to mend – but if rain has got in and is leaking into the house somewhere, it will need to be dealt with.

I never realized before what a huge responsibility a house is! Harry and I used to talk about how we would have a cottage in the country after the war. We visualized log fires and latticed windows and chintz. We didn't get as far as leaking roofs and rusting taps, or crumbling window frames. If Harry was here now, he would laugh my fears away and probably trace the source of the lonely dripping tap or pipe quite easily, either mending it himself or arranging for a plumber to do so.

But it's an unsettling sound, that rhythmic drip-drip. I really do *not* like the thought of something dripping away somewhere in a dark, unreachable space . . . I don't like, either, how regular the sound is – it's almost like a small mechanism, or like someone lightly tapping a tattoo on the very tiny drum, or small, thick wings beating against a glass pane.

But whatever it is, I shall try to ignore it. I've made the library my headquarters. The Black Boar can provide a Thermos flask of coffee, together with a pack of sandwiches each day, so I shan't have to return there for lunch. It's bitterly cold in the house, of course – the cold of a house unheated and unlived-in for forty years – so I have arranged for a small delivery of logs (the taxi driver has a brother-in-law who can supply them). Providing it doesn't smoke out the entire house, I shall build a fire in the library hearth.

20th February
2.30 p.m.

I've had a very useful morning, and quite soon I shall lock everything up and go out to meet my friend the taxi driver who is going to pick me up here at four o'clock.

The logs duly arrived midway through the morning, and I've built a fire in the library hearth. It smoked furiously for about ten minutes, but now it's settled down to a very pleasant crackle and the room is nicely warm.

I've even set the old clock going. The hinges of the door

protested like a soul in torment, but they aren't rusted and the
pendulum with its weight turned out to be perfectly workable.
When I touched it, it moved at once, and (I know how fantas-
tical this sounds) it was as if a heart was struggling into life
after a long stillness. And then the rhythmic ticking began,
and I reached up to move the hands to the correct time and
closed the door.

I dare say a good deal of craft went into that clock, but I
don't much like it. To my eye it's Victorian workmanship at
its most florid. It has one of those vaguely macabre faces over
the main dial – a swollen moon-face, which I suppose marks
the passing of the moon's cycle. The sphere representing the
moon has been lightly marked to indicate features – like children's books with the Man in the Moon smiling benignly down
from the night sky. The face is half visible, which I suppose
means it was midway between moons when it stopped. Still,
at least the ticking seems to have smothered the dripping tap.
Perhaps it's ticking exactly simultaneously with it.

Regarded as a spyhole into the house's earlier occupants, the
contents of the boxes are fascinating. I'm trying to make notes
of it all as I go along. I've just found some letters from a Mrs
W. Lee, who had entered into a somewhat vituperative correspondence with the fishmonger over an order of herring that
appeared to have been dubious. I can't imagine why such letters
were preserved, but it's interesting to speculate who Mrs W.
Lee was. There are also a few old concert and theatre programmes
from performances at one or two local theatres, with notes made
in the margin by a neat, masculine-looking hand. The writer
compares one performance of *The Bells* unfavourably with
Henry Irving's appearance in the same piece, which he had
apparently seen in London a few years earlier. Personally, I
shouldn't have expected a small provincial theatre to even come
close to Sir Henry's incandescent acting, but it all makes
absorbing reading.

There's something soporific about a firelit room and a ticking
clock, and despite Sir Henry and the herring, I'm having to
fight the compulsion to drift into a half-doze . . .

It's so restful in here. Not entirely silent, but then no house
is ever entirely silent. As I make these notes, I'm hearing voices,
just very faintly. They're a long way off, though. Children,
perhaps, playing somewhere in a field. Or would children be

at school at this time on a weekday? Whatever it is, it sounds
as if they're singing . . .

It's rather a nice sound – it makes me think of peaceful,
soothing things. Warm honey running off the spoon into a
dish. Dappled sunlight coming through the trees on a green
and gold summer's afternoon, and bees humming among the
flowers. Soft rain in a forest in autumn, and the scent of
chrysanthemums . . .

I think someone tapped at the door a few moments ago,
but it was a soft, light tap and I was so comfortable and so
drowsy that I couldn't be bothered to wake up enough to see
if anyone was there. If it was important, whoever it was will
come back.

I don't think the singing I can hear is children. It's a single
voice – a man's voice . . . I can't quite hear the words, but it
sounds like one of those old-fashioned chants . . .

Black Boar: 6.30 p.m.

I'm not at all sure I shan't destroy these pages, but for the
moment it's calming to write down what happened at Charect
House this afternoon.

Sleep is a curious thing. It's a like an ocean. There are
shallow parts and very deep parts, and there are currents that
can pull you into very strange places indeed . . . The only
explanation I have for what happened to me this afternoon is
that one of those strange currents had me in its arms and took
me to a curious, none too comfortable, place.

At first I enjoyed the gentle undertow that tugged at my mind.
At one level I knew I was falling asleep, that I was on the
borderlands of dreaming, but it didn't seem to matter. I even
thought: perhaps Harry will be in the dream. He is, sometimes.
He comes walking towards me, smiling, holding out his hands,
and he looks so dashing in his uniform, and I'm so proud of
him and filled with such soaring delight at seeing him after so
many years . . .

At first I thought he *was* in the dream, and I think I smiled
as I lay back in the deep old chair. It felt as if he was closer
to me than ever before, and when I turned my head slightly,
I became aware of a hand moving lightly over my face, tracing
the features, exactly as he always did. If I opened my eyes he

would be there – this time he really would, and the bloodbath of the Somme would never have happened . . .

That was when I opened my eyes.

And oh God, oh God, standing over the chair, his face inches from my own, was a man I had never seen in my life – a man with a very pale face and black shadows half-concealing the upper part of his face. He was leaning over me, and his hands were crawling over my face like spiders . . .

I didn't scream, but it was a close thing. I gasped and started back though, and at once he flinched as if he had been burned. In that moment, I made to jump up from the chair, but it overturned and I fell backwards in an awkward jumble. By the time I scrambled to my feet, he had gone, but the door into the hall was swinging softly and slowly shut. Exactly as if someone had just gone through it and had pushed it closed.

I'm no braver and no more cowardly than anyone else, but I'm a modern female, and I refused, categorically and absolutely, to be frightened of something that had most likely been a dream. So I crossed the room and pulled the door open.

The hall was silent and still. Or was it? I glanced uneasily at the stair, then resolutely opened all the doors downstairs and looked inside. Nothing. So I went through to the back of the house, to the big stone-flagged scullery and the smaller scullery off it, which must have been a kind of laundry room. Lying across the cracked stones of the floor was a man shaped shadow, and as I stood there, frozen with fear, it moved slightly. My heart leapt into my throat, and I thought – he's here! He's standing behind the old copper. He's watching me – I can feel that he is . . .

And then a tiny breath of wind stirred the ragged curtains hanging at the small low window, and I saw that it was only the shadow of the copper itself, squat and thick, and that the movement I had seen had been the curtain.

I went back into the hall. The stair was wreathed in shadow, and as I hesitated, I heard a faint creak of sound above me. Someone stepping on a worn floorboard? Someone creeping across the landing? From where I stood I could see the huge damp stain on the far landing wall – the place where the wallpaper had blistered and formed the outline of a thickset man, his head slightly inclined forward. Tomorrow, in the bright daylight, I would tear that paper off. For now I would collect my bag from the library, lock the house up, and go back to the Black Boar. My friendly taxi was not due for another hour, but I no longer cared. I would walk back to the village.

I dived back into the library, slung my bag over one arm, and pulled on the jacket I had been wearing. The fire was burning quite low, but I dragged the old fireguard in front of it, although at that stage I believe I wouldn't have cared if the whole place had burned to a cinder.

As I locked the door and prepared to go down the overgrown drive towards the lane, it was raining – a soft, thin rain that would drench me within a dozen yards. I didn't care. I would rather catch a chill than remain in that house.

I reached the end of the drive and started along Blackberry Lane. Through the rain I heard, like a fading piece of music, the distant singing again. With the sound came the long-ago memory of Elvira in Brank Asylum, telling me there are some things human ears are never meant to hear.

Midnight

I've managed to eat a meal with reasonable normality at the Black Boar, and I've even made light conversation with one or two of the local people. It's a very friendly place, this. I wish I could live here, I really do. But I know I can't. Every time I entered that room I should feel those searching spider-fingers over my face, and I should see the man with the macabre shadowed face. Was he the one Elvira talked about all those years ago? The one she said had touched a black core of mankind's knowledge?

Whatever he was – whatever I saw or heard today – I've made a decision. I shall put the house into as good order as I can manage. Tomorrow I'll ask the solicitor to arrange for a local builder to inspect the place as soon as possible and tell me what needs doing and how much it will cost. Then, once the work is done, the house can be put up for sale. There's sure to be a firm of estate agents who can deal with it, and they will advise as to what price to ask.

I feel guilty when I think of Father, who had that lifetime

dream of owning this house, but I know I shall never be able to live in Charect House. I'm glad to think I need only stay here another two or three days before I return safely home to Cheshire.

SIXTEEN

Michael came up out of Harriet's story with the feeling that he was emerging from a deep lake. Harriet's story was absolutely classic ghost-tale material: it had every ingredient, right down to the ticking clock in the corner of the firelit room. Still, if you were going to discover a ghost, you might as well do so in the grand style.

It also struck him, very forcibly, that Alice and Harriet, both around the same age when they came to Charect, had each lost a lover to war – Alice's fiancé had died in Hiroshima, Harriet's in the Somme. Had that created some kind of bridge for whatever was in the house? And how about Nell, whose husband had been killed in a motorway pile-up? Did that put her in the same category?

It was twenty past two. Michael switched off the bedside light, hoping the images that had haunted Harriet all those years ago would not haunt him. But there were no troubling images or dreams, and he set off after breakfast next morning, reaching Oxford and his rooms just after eleven. He put Harriet's journal in a desk drawer where Wilberforce could not wreak havoc with it, then looked for Jack's mobile number. Now that he thought about it, he was not at all sure he actually had it, and an hour's search finally convinced him he did not, unless Wilberforce had eaten it in an absent-minded moment. Jack and Liz would have long since left for the cousins' house in New Jersey, but he dialled their home number anyway. It rang four times, then the voicemail cut in:

'Hi, this is Liz and Jack Harper's number. Sorry we can't take this call, but leave a message and we'll get back. Here's the cellphone number.'

Michael almost toppled backwards on to the floor trying to find a pen to write the number down, finally scribbling it on the back of an envelope. But when he called, it, too, went to voice-mail. He left a careful message saying he was sorry to hear about Ellie and hoped the stay in New Jersey would put things right.

He was just reinforcing an email sent last night, he said. Charect House had hit one or two unexpected problems, so it wasn't really going to be practical for anyone to live in it for a while.

'So please ring me as soon as you get this and I'll explain properly.' He added his direct number at Oriel College, in case Jack had not taken an address book with him, and remembered to add his own mobile as well.

Then it occurred to him it was possible to dial remotely into a phone to pick up messages and that Jack might do so, so he rang the home number again and left the same message there. It was annoying that he could not ring the cousins in New Jersey, but although he had met one or two of them at Jack and Liz's wedding – including Liz's redoubtable godmother – he had no idea of any surnames. But Jack and Liz were both efficient; one of them would ring him as soon as they picked up the message.

It was now one o'clock, and he phoned Nell at the shop. She sounded pleased to hear from him. She was fine, she said, and Beth had gone happily off to school that morning.

'Although I had to beat down the impulse to run after her to make sure she was safe. Shouldn't you be lecturing or studying or something at this time of day?'

'I've got a tutorial in half an hour,' said Michael, 'but I've found something out, and I think you might be able to track it to its source.'

'What have you found?'

He took a deep breath. 'I've found Elvira.'

Even over the phone he was strongly aware of her reaction. She said, 'Where? How?'

'I'll tell you properly later if that's all right. I'll have a bit more time this evening.'

'I'll be in all evening,' said Nell. 'What d'you want me to track down?'

'Have you ever heard of a place called Brank in that area? Brank Asylum it used to be. Maybe it's just known as Brank House now.'

'No. But I can look for it.'

'I can't tell you much about it, other than I don't think it was very far out of Marston Lacy, and it certainly existed around 1905.'

'Nineteen oh-five,' she said. 'All right, I've got that.' And

Michael had a sudden pleasing image of her in her shop or the sitting room on the first floor, her face serious as she wrote down the details. 'Was Elvira in an asylum?'

'It seems like it. I've even got her date of birth. She was born in 1880, and she died in Brank Asylum in 1937.'

'Fifty-seven. No age at all,' said Nell. 'The poor woman. And asylums were grim places then, weren't they? Well, they're grim places in any era. But it might make it easier to trace her. I'll see what I can turn up.'

'I'll phone around eight if that's all right.'

'Miracles might take a bit longer than that,' she said, and he heard the smile in her voice. 'But eight will be fine. Even if I haven't found anything out I'd like to know what's behind this.'

'I'm looking forward to telling you,' said Michael.

'I'm looking forward to hearing.'

As he put the phone down, it occurred to him that there could sometimes be a remarkable intimacy in a phone call. All physicality was absent, and everything became concentrated into your voice and the voice of the other person. And barriers were lowered.

He got through the tutorial, had a cup of tea with a colleague in the History Faculty, then thought he could allow himself a couple of hours with Harriet Anstey's journal. As he took the handwritten pages out of the desk, he found he was smiling at the prospect of discussing Harriet with Nell.

22nd February 1939
8.45 a.m.

Despite what I happened at Charect House, when I awoke this morning I found I was smiling at the prospect of returning there. And today is the day of the builder's visit, arranged by the solicitor. I've had breakfast – beautiful fresh eggs from some nearby farm – and I'm about to go downstairs to await the taxi.

2.00 p.m.

It took considerable resolve to go into the library, I have to admit that. It had to be done though, and eventually I drew a deep breath and opened the door. I have no idea what I expected to see, but there was nothing there. Whatever unquiet dream had surrounded me two days ago it had left no trace or taint. The library was bland and silent, save, of course, for the steady ticking of the old clock in its corner.

The builder arrived at eleven, trundling up the lane in a noisy and battered-looking lorry. He was a lugubrious person, given to gloomy silences as he surveyed a wall or a section of roof. He made copious notes in a small book, shaking his head dolefully, and my heart sank lower with each room we visited. I asked about the dripping tap or gutter I heard on my arrival, but he didn't seem to find anything to account for it. The plumbing would all have to be ripped out, though.

'Old soft-lead pipes, you see. Can't have those any longer.' The water tank, when he finally tracked it down, almost rendered him speechless, but he rallied and said it could be replaced with a nice modern one, sited in the roof or one of the attics.

We tramped up to inspect the attics on the crest of this idea, and that was when we found the worst of the neglect.

The attics are vast, and several roof joists seemed to have fallen in, so there were piles of rubble everywhere.

'Wattle and daub, these walls,' said the builder dolefully. 'Horsehair and lime in the main. I'm surprised to find such penny-pinching work in a house of this age and size.' He looked so disapproving, I wondered if I should apologize.

'Really, of course, the whole place should be pulled down and something built on the site. Couple of nice modern villas, that's what I'd have. Sell one at a very nice profit and live in the other.'

'It's certainly a thought. But I think I'd like to just put it into some kind of order and sell it in the ordinary way. I'm only here for another few days, so if you could let me have your estimate fairly soon I'd be very grateful. I'm staying at the Black Boar.'

'Tomorrow morning do you? I could work out some figures and bring them along first thing.'

'That would suit me very well.'

This time it was the ringing of a phone that jolted Michael out of Harriet's world and into the present. He swore, then remembered it might be Jack returning his call and snatched up the phone.

It was not Jack. It was the Dean's office, reminding him about the Dean's end of term lunch next week. Would he be attending – he had not yet let them know. Oh, he would? Excellent. They were promised they would be given a goose this year; it was nice to have a goose at Christmas, wasn't it?

This innocent remark upset Michael's gravity so much that he had to cover the receiver with his hand, and the voice on the phone had to repeat the next question, which was whether he would be bringing a guest.

'Probably not,' said Michael, repressing a sudden picture of himself walking into the Dean's lunch with Nell. It was an attractive idea, but it was not really practical. He could not ask her to drive all the way to Oxford just for a couple of hours, and then back again. She would have to leave her shop unattended, and she would have to make arrangements about Beth. No, it was not practical at all.

He rang off and picked up Harriet's journal again. The entry he had been reading looked as if it ended on the next page; he flipped over a couple of the remaining pages and saw with a sinking heart that they were badly faded and spotted with damp. Large sections looked as if they might be illegible. Damn.

But he would read to the end of the current entry.

22nd February, cont'd

The builder's visit has cheered me up, and I'm able to view the house with a friendlier eye. Also, if I'm to have work carried out, I ought to be on hand to supervise it. I shan't understand the technicalities, of course, and I dare say I'll be shockingly overcharged for some things. But I think I need to be here.

Can I face that? Another two or three weeks at the Black Boar? More of those friendly little journeys along Blackberry Lane? There'll nearly be wood anemones and primroses in the meadows by then.

After the builder went, I walked through the gardens. I might even start to put them into some order while they get on with the house. I looked for the apple tree Elvira talked about, but it's not there. It's possible to make out traces of

what might once have been a small orchard, but it's difficult
to be sure of anything. It's like stepping through a ghost world,
where nothing is quite alive, but nothing is entirely dead.
There's the remains of a huge mallow though, and also a lilac
bush, and I think with a little work the gardens could be made
beautiful.

I believe I can stay here a little longer, after all. I've listened
very hard, but there's no hint of the faraway singing I heard
last time. There's certainly no hint of any intruders, either.
I'm becoming more convinced than ever that my experience
that afternoon really was a dream. And I do like it here, I
really do.

So perhaps I shan't pack up and leave.

Nell had stopped thinking she would pack up and leave Marston
Lacy. This was nothing to do with having met Michael Flint,
although it had to be admitted she had enjoyed his company.
But it was important to remember that the two of them seemed
to have fallen into a very bizarre situation, and that people
thrown together in bizarre and unreal situations were apt to
become very close, very quickly. There were astonishing tales
of how people in hostage situations, or people trapped in lifts,
became lovers. Not that Nell was intending to become anyone's
lover, and certainly not Dr Flint's.

This absurd possibility having been put firmly in its
place, she commenced the search for Brank Asylum, so as
to have some information when Michael phoned. She
started with the local phone book, looking for Brank
Asylum in the business listings. Nothing. Fair enough,
thought Nell, who had not really expected the place to be
listed, and she turned to the classified section, for hospitals,
clinics and health authorities. Again nothing. What else?
Was it worth trying a Google search? She tried it anyway,
and again drew a blank.

This almost certainly meant Brank Asylum had long since
ceased to exist. It might also mean it never had existed at all
– that Michael had found a false trail. But Nell thought he
would be too accustomed to research not to tell fact from red
herring. She spent half an hour polishing up the inlaid table,
enjoying the scent of the beeswax polish. The table could stand
in the smaller of the two bow windows, where people could

see it from the street. She would try to pick up a really nice chess set to put on it. For the moment she placed a jar of sunflowers on it. It looked very good indeed. Nell tidied away the beeswax and polishing rags, and sat down to think about Brank Asylum again.

Presumably, it had been a very large, fairly important building, and large, important buildings in small rural areas do not, as a rule, vanish without leaving some imprint on their surroundings. Stories grow up about them – fragments of their histories become woven into the local folklore. If Brank had existed, its ghost – no, not that word! – its shadow-self should still lie on the air of Marston Lacy. Nell glanced at the clock, saw it was three o'clock and, remembering it was half-day closing, headed for the local library, which helpfully remained open until six each day.

There was a small section for Local History, and Nell opened one book after another, trying not to get sidetracked by the alluring photographs and fragments of information. Charect House was mentioned once or twice, but only briefly, and there did not seem to be any information Nell did not already know. The house had originally been known as Mallow House, it had been built by the prosperous Lee family of Shropshire, and it had not been used as a family residence since the death of William and Elizabeth Lee towards the end of the nineteenth century.

She finally found a reference to Brank Asylum in a small, rather insignificant-looking book at the very end of the shelf. It looked as if it had been printed locally and was intended purely for circulation in the surrounding area. But it had a number of photographs, and part of a chapter was devoted to Brank Asylum. Nell checked it out as a loan and drove out to collect Beth, who had apparently had a brilliant day at school and was more interested in having come second in the spelling test than in what she regarded as a sleepwalking experience.

They had supper, and Beth did her homework, which consisted of reading an allotted chapter of a Philip Pullman book and writing her own explanation of it.

Nell watched her for a few moments, seeing, with a pang, how much Beth's tumble of hair resembled Brad's. In the months after his death she had often believed she saw him standing by Beth, smiling down at her. She had known this was a projection of her own longing, but it had brought a faint comfort. Now, as she watched Beth, she realized the image was still there, but it had grown faint. It was as if Brad was only a light pencil sketch on the air. Am I losing you? she thought in panic. But I don't want to lose you, not ever.

She closed her eyes, to dispel the image and the memories, and reached for the book. The only thing to do when the lonely grief struck was focus very determinedly on something else.

She had expected to find the book rather dry, but it turned out to be interesting. It was well written, and the author had included a number of photographs. He also appeared to have carried out considerable research: there were copious footnotes, with sources quoted. Nell thought these might turn out to be useful and reached for a notebook to write down any likely ones.

Brank House had, it seemed, been built in the mid nineteenth century, and had been for the 'care and safe housing of the severely mentally afflicted'.

There were several photographs of the place – early sepia ones, and later black and white shots. It was a bleak, sprawling place, and whoever had taken the photographs had apparently done so at midnight or in the middle of a thunderstorm.

The asylum had been demolished at the end of 1966 to make way for a road-widening scheme patients had mostly been transferred to the county's psychiatric unit. Nell glanced at the date of the book's publication: 1968.

By some means or other, the author had gained access to some of Brank's records, and extracts were included, along with rather blurry images of the originals. The author particularly drew the reader's attention to two of these documents, whose text was reproduced in full. The first account was of the youngest known patient. She had been admitted to Brank Asylum in the year 1888, and she had been eight years old.

Eight years old, thought Nell. She looked up from the book, to where Beth, sane and safe and healthy, was frowning over her homework.

Brank House. Asylum for the Incurably Insane.
County of Shropshire
Patient's record.
Name: Elvira Lee.
Address: Mallow House, Marston Lacy, Shropshire.
Date of Birth: 10th November 1881.
Date of admission: 3rd April 1889.
Next of kin: No relatives believed living.
Religion: Church of England.
Diagnosis: Delusional and strongly hysterical.
Admitted under the Lunacy Act of 1840, certifying
    Elvira Lee (minor) as being of unsound mind and a
    proper person to be taken charge of and detained.
Signed by the under-named, who both hereby assert they
    are not related to the patient and have no financial
    interest in connection with her treatment and care
    under detention.
Signed: *Dr J Manville. Dr C Chaddock*

Elvira, thought Nell, staring at the page. That must be what Michael meant when he said he had found her. She thought back to the hasty phone call. He had said Elvira was born in 1880 and had died in Brank Asylum in 1938. That meant she had lived almost her entire life inside the place. Fifty years. The pity of it – the thought of a girl of Beth's age being locked away for her whole life – was so overwhelming that for several minutes the print on the page blurred. Nell frowned, put the book down, and got up to pour a glass of wine.

'Can I have some orange juice?' asked Beth hopefully, looking up from her homework.

Nell would have given Beth anything she wanted at that moment, purely for being here and for not being that poor child in 1889. She poured the orange juice, found the biscuits Beth liked, ruffled the soft chestnut hair, and went back to the book.

In April 1889, Charect House had still been known by its original name of Mallow. Nell scribbled the date down in case it might help in pinpointing the precise year the name changed, then returned to the book.

The author had included extracts from some case notes from

Brank Asylum. Nell wondered by what means he had got hold of them, but from the look of the dates they were all sufficiently far back for patient confidentiality not to matter.

The first was headed 'Chaplain's Report' and was dated 1905. She hardly dared hope Elvira's name would be there.

But it was.

SEVENTEEN

CHAPLAIN'S REPORT: BRANK HOUSE ASYLUM
November 1905

The condition of the patient, Elvira Lee, is increasingly difficult since the visit of two distant members of her family earlier this year – a Mr Frederick Anstey and his daughter, Harriet.

Miss Lee's intelligence has not deteriorated, but the terrors which have driven her for so many years have increased tenfold. She spends much of her time crouching in a corner of her room, her hands stretched tremblingly before her, as if to push away an encroaching enemy. At those times it is very difficult to reach her – even to make oneself heard.

However, a week ago some rags of her sanity appeared to have returned for a brief time, and I was able to talk with her for almost twenty minutes.

The outcome is that she is to allow me to perform a religious ceremony of healing. I am hopeful it may be a way of persuading this poor haunted soul that God's love and God's strength have banished the demons she undoubtedly believes lie in wait for her.

This morning I received permission from the Bishop to hold the ceremony and the doctors have given their consent, although stress it cannot effect a cure. At their request, I am making an official record of the event. The notes are to be appended to the patient's medical history.

Nell paused to refill her wine glass. So Elvira Lee had been thought of as haunted. How much of that had been due to her being incarcerated in an asylum since the age of eight? She remembered again how Beth, and also Ellie Harper, had insisted it was 'Elvira' the man in their nightmares was trying to find. Ellie in particular had been terrified for Elvira. 'He mustn't get her,' she had said. 'Promise you won't let him get her. She's so frightened of him.'

Nell pushed this troubling memory away and looked across at Beth, who was still absorbed in her homework. Then she returned to the chaplain's account of the ceremony performed on Elvira Lee more than a hundred years ago.

The ceremony began at three o'clock today, Sunday 16th November. It was not that of exorcism, for that takes much preparation and is rarely performed in these enlightened times.

Dr Manville and Dr Chaddock were both in attendance – partly in case Miss Lee should require their intervention, but more, I believe, from curiosity.

The attendants brought Elvira Lee to the chapel. She was calm, and there was not the sense of 'otherness' that is so marked when the madness seizes her. I took her hands and assured her she was in God's house, and that no harm could come to her in this place of refuge and sanctuary.

I began a simple prayer asking for peace and serenity to surround this troubled soul. At first Miss Lee murmured suitable responses – she has regularly attended all church services, as have most of the patients, and despite her affliction is well acquainted with both the New and Old Testament.

I had begun to entertain hopes that the peace I sought for her was beginning to soak into her mind, when she suddenly snatched her hands from mine and began to speak. Her voice was slurred and harsh. It is foolish to say this – and this is intended as a factual account – but the words rasped through the small, hallowed chapel like raw nails scratching across silk.

'You waste your time,' she said. 'You can never drive out the creature that seeks me.'

I reached for her hands again – they were hot and dry and the very bones seemed to push through the flesh and clutch me. She pulled away and backed clumsily into a corner of the chapel, crouching against the pew in a huddle, her hands over her head – I know that to be the classic gesture of someone seeking to defend him or herself from attack.

'He comes to me most nights now,' she said. 'I hear him making his blind fumbling way along the dark passages. He knocks at every door until he finds me. Just as he did the night my mother died.' She paused and half-raised her head in a listening attitude. 'Hear him now,' she said, and so forceful

were her words that I swear before God I heard three sharp
raps on the chapel door. The two doctors heard it as well, for
they both started and looked sharply round.

I said, in a low mutter, 'There's no one there, of course,'
and turned back to Miss Lee.

She had begun to sing the macabre verse she so often sang
when the madness visited her, and even though I had heard it
so many times, it still chilled me.

'*Open lock to the dead man's knock . . .*
Fly bolt, and bar, and band . . .
Nor move, nor swerve, joint, muscle or nerve,
At the spell of the dead man's hand.'

As she began the second part of the song, a curious little
echo picked up her voice, and the chant seemed to trickle in
and out of the corners, a half-second behind her, almost as if
a second voice was trying to join in. I saw Dr Manville, the
younger of the two, shiver and glance nervously round the
chapel.

I said, 'Miss Lee – Elvira – who is it you think comes to
find you?'

A great shudder shook her body, and she said, 'The man
who murdered my mother. I saw him do it, and that's why he
has to find me.'

This time it was Dr Chaddock who spoke. 'Elvira,' he said,
'the man who killed your mother is dead.'

'Is he?' she said, in a dreadful, harsh whisper. 'Can you be
sure? Because I hear him singing to himself – I hear him
chanting the rhyme I heard the night my mother died. If he
is dead, how do you explain that? And,' she said, 'if he is
dead, then who is it who creeps through the dark, searching
for me?'

Nell was unable to go on reading. She put the book aside, saw
it was almost half-past seven, and chased Beth up to bed,
grateful for an interlude of normality. Back downstairs, she
sat by the fire with a glass of wine, trying to persuade herself
to read the rest of the chapter. When the phone rang at twenty-
past eight, she was not prepared for the leap of delight at the
sound of Michael's voice.

He said he had not heard from Jack Harper yet, but had left
messages on both phones.

'I found out a bit about Brank Asylum,' said Nell, pleased to have something definite to report.

'Did you?' His voice seemed to fill with light when his interest was caught. 'What is it? Did you find Elvira?'

'Yes, I did. How did you know I would?'

'I didn't know, but I hoped,' he said.

'You found her as well,' said Nell, making it a statement.

'Yes. When I was in Charect House – oh hell, I was going to confess to you sooner or later. The builders were demolishing part of the attic wall. I found a second set of papers.'

'Really? To find one set of papers is surprising; to find two looks like a fake,' said Nell, deadpan, and he laughed softly.

'I don't think they're fake, Nell. I haven't read them all yet though; in fact, the last few pages are very nearly illegible – I might have to get someone here to help me decipher them.' He paused, and Nell waited. 'I don't know why I didn't tell you about them yesterday,' he said.

'If I'd found something like that I think I'd want to savour it on my own,' said Nell. 'After everything that's been happening here, I mean.'

'I did want to savour it,' said Michael, sounding grateful. 'But I'd like to tell you about it now – at least, as far as I've read. I've made a bit of a precis as I've gone along. Or are you in the middle of something?'

'I'm not in the middle of anything, and I've got all the time in the world,' said Nell. 'Beth's in bed, and I'm curled up by the fire with a glass of wine.'

'That sounds nice. I'm having a glass of wine here, as well. I've got a stack of second-year essays I should be reading and marking, but I'll do them later. Oh, and Wilberforce is here too – he's asleep in front of the fire.'

When he said this, Nell had a sudden image of him in a deep armchair, surrounded by books, the firelight bringing out lights in his hair, the cat contentedly asleep at his feet.

'Can I hear what you found first?' said Michael.

'I haven't read the whole chapter yet,' said Nell, reaching for the book. 'But it doesn't look as if there's much more – and what there is doesn't look particularly relevant to our search. What I have read, though, is an extract from some case notes – a kind of healing ceremony they attempted for Elvira. Could you listen now if I read it out? It's not very long.'

'Yes, of course. Hold on while I get a pen and paper. All right, the floor's yours.'

She read the chaplain's account to him, strongly conscious that he was listening very intently. Several times she heard the faint rustle of paper as he made a note, but he did not interrupt.

'His report ends there,' she said. 'With Elvira asking that question about who was creeping through the dark. Either the chaplain didn't want to write any more, or there was nothing more to say. Or, if there was more, the editor of the book decided not to include it.'

'It's remarkable,' he said. 'You have a very good reading voice, by the way.' Before she could think how to respond to this, he said, 'Whoever that chaplain was, he had a vivid way with words, didn't he? I wonder how much we can take as actual fact.'

'I've thought about that,' said Nell eagerly. 'And although some of what he says is a bit off-the-wall, there is one thing that can be checked.'

'Whether Elvira Lee's mother really was murdered,' he said promptly.

'Yes. There'd be police records – most likely newspaper reports. And if the chaplain's report is genuine – and if Elvira herself can be believed – she saw the murder take place. That could be true.'

'Yes, certainly it could.'

'Which means,' said Nell, encouraged, 'that Elvira would have known the killer's identity.'

'But would she?' said Michael, a shade doubtfully. 'She was only seven at the time.'

'She would have recognized somebody she already knew.'

'That's true,' he said. 'But that doctor – what was his name?'

'Chaddock.'

'Chaddock says the killer was dead. Hanged for the murder, would you think?'

'It's possible, isn't it? Not definite, though. Because Elvira believed he was still searching for her – even after she was in Brank Asylum, even after all those years. It sounded as if she thought he wanted to silence her.'

'Maybe he did. Maybe they hanged the wrong man. But that account was written twelve years after it happened. That's a long time for someone to go on searching. Elvira had been in the asylum all that time, remember. Easy enough for him to find her, one would think.'

'Yes. And it's a long time to go on being terrified, as well. I'm not sure we can trust Elvira's story. Twelve years in a mental institution would dent anyone's sanity. And if she really had seen her mother murdered when she was seven, her mind might already have been damaged beyond help. Oh, Michael, that poor little girl . . .'

'It happened a long time ago, whatever the truth of it,' said Michael.

'I keep trying to remember that. But how about the incidents that came later? Beth's abduction. Ellie's nightmares. Those don't come from Elvira. And—'

She broke off, and Michael said, 'There's something else?'

'I'm not sure. But that day when we were in the old graveyard – you went back for an umbrella, you remember?'

'Yes.'

'I thought I heard someone while you were away,' said Nell. 'A sort of soft singing.'

'*Ingoldsby Legends* among the graves? That macabre verse again?'

'That's what I thought at the time. But now I'm not so sure. My judgement probably wasn't very reliable that day.'

'Understandable,' said Michael. 'But let's remember two more girls were taken like Beth was taken. That one in the nineteen sixties – the one who was found in St Paul's Churchyard – and the earlier one in the nineteen thirties.'

'Could it be some kind of copycat crime?' said Nell, rather doubtfully. 'I know it's an awfully long time-span in-between, but—'

'Elizabeth Lee's murder would have been remembered in the nineteen thirties,' said Michael. 'Marston Lacy's a very small place, and it sounds as if the Lee family were quite prominent people. If there was a murder in their house, I'll bet it was talked about for years.'

'Could the nineteen thirties' case even have been Elizabeth's killer?' said Nell. 'No, it's a fifty-year gap. And what would be the motive?'

'Some local weirdo might have become obsessed by the original case. Or fixated on the Hand of Glory superstition.

He might have believed he was the reincarnation of the killer, or thought he had to complete the killer's task.'

'You shouldn't be teaching fiction, you should be writing it,' said Nell, smiling. 'I can just about accept the obsession theory once – for the child taken in the nineteen thirties. But I can't accept there was a second weirdo in the nineteen sixties with the same obsession, and then a third one again this week. And it can't be the same person – the gaps are too long.'

'It's not as far-fetched as believing in ghosts,' said Michael, sounding defensive.

'True.' Nell did not know if she would rather think Beth had been taken by a madman obsessed with a Victorian murder and hell-bent on child mutilation, or by a ghost. She said, 'Tell me about the papers you found. Wait a bit; I'll top up my wine first. I don't normally slosh vino at this rate—'

'But it's a three-glass problem, isn't it? I'll join you.' There was a faint chink of bottle against glass. 'Here goes with my findings,' he said. 'I'm condensing it a fair bit, and you can read the complete text when I've got it deciphered if you want – well, the photocopies. But this is the gist.'

He had a clear, concise way with words which Nell would have expected. She listened intently and with deep interest to Harriet Anstey's story – he had, as he said, written a precis, but he read sections of the actual journal to her. Nell found herself strongly drawn to Harriet.

'I wonder if we could find out what happened to her,' she said, when Michael finished.

'Well, Anstey isn't a very common name, and we know she lived in Cheshire. But it was only a few weeks before the outbreak of WWII, remember, and a lot of records were lost in the bombing.'

'I'd like to think of her meeting someone to take Harry's place,' said Nell, thoughtfully. 'And helping with the war that was coming – maybe running a canteen in the middle of Coventry while it burned or helping bombed out people in the East End. But I know that's being ridiculously romantic.'

'Actually, I thought the same,' said Michael. 'So I'm as bad as you.'

'It's a bit of a coincidence that she and Alice Wilson were about the same age, isn't it?' said Nell. 'And they both lost someone to a war.'

'Yes. Nell, I've just seen that we've been on the phone for an hour and a half – I've taken up your whole evening.'

'That's fine.' Nell did not want to say she had not had anything else to do with her evening. She said, 'Will you let me know about hearing from Jack?'

'Yes, certainly. If I can't catch up with them, they'll be arriving here, though. I've booked them into the Black Boar – at least that might keep them clear of Charect House. I've booked a room there for myself as well.'

'You'll be here over Christmas?' Nell had not expected this.

'It seems like it. Most of the Oxford people go to families, so college is pretty dismal. My father's lived in Manilla for the last five years – he works for the World Health Organization. It's a nice place for him to live, but it's a hell of a journey for me, specially at Christmas. Marston Lacy's a walk to the end of the garden in comparison. So maybe we can meet for a drink or a meal over the holiday? We'll hunt ghosts between eating plum pudding and scoffing turkey.'

'I'd like that,' said Nell. 'I'm hoping to have a sort of Open Day at the shop on Christmas Eve – mulled wine and mince pies and music.' It was part of a Chamber of Commerce project – most of the local businesses were participating, and she was going to have Victorian Christmas decorations in the shop. 'If you're around, you could look in,' she said, hoping this sounded casual. 'And the Harpers as well, if they're here.'

'That sounds nice,' he said. 'I will. Thank you. Goodnight, Nell.'

'Goodnight.'

After he rang off, the flat felt annoyingly silent and lonely. Nell stirred the fire, which had become desultory, washed up the wine glass, and sat down again. It was ten o'clock. She switched on the television news, found everything too gloomy for words, and switched it off again. The book about Marston Lacy lay where she had left it, and she supposed she might as well finish reading the chapter. It had not looked as if there was much more of any interest about Brank Asylum, but she would make sure.

The semi-religious ceremony focusing on Elvira Lee was followed by a short paragraph introducing the next set of case notes. The author explained it was a mixture of material taken from the records of someone who had been Brank's final patient and a written account provided by that patient. 'She was the last patient to walk out through those doors,' he said, sounding pleased at having hit on this phrase. 'Everything in this account is reproduced with her full permission.'

Nell rearranged the cushions in her chair, and began to read.

'They said, two years ago, that I was mad. I can no longer judge if that's true. But if mad means seeing things that aren't visible to other people, and hearing things not audible to anyone – such as a fleshless voice, chanting a grisly old rhyme . . . Yes, if those things made for madness, then I certainly was mad for a time – possibly for all of the time I was in Charect House.'

At these last words, Nell felt as if every nerve-ending in her body sprang to attention. Brank Asylum had closed at the end of 1966, and Alice Wilson had been at Charect House in the early 1960s. Was she making too many assumptions? But Alice had stashed her diary in the old clock, making some light remark about returning to reclaim it. But she didn't, thought Nell. Did she encounter something that night that brought about some kind of nervous breakdown? Is this Alice's account I'm reading?

She glanced towards the phone, wondering if she dare ring Michael, but thought it was a bit late. And this extract might not be anything of any value. She would read it now, and if necessary she could email him.

As she began to read again, the light from the table lamp mingled with the flickering of the fire, sending shadows dancing across the chimney breast, and she had the familiar sensation of unseen hands tugging her down into the past once more.

EIGHTEEN

'Occasionally, I worry that I might still be slightly mad – like a cracked piece of pottery – but the medics are being very breezy and cheerful, and saying I'm entirely recovered. Perfectly capable of going out into the world again, they say. It's a cold and very large world beyond the walls of Brank Asylum, but I dare say I can put up a good enough show of sanity in front of most people.

The doctors here never did put a label on what was wrong with me – I shouldn't think there was a suitable label for it really. Instead, they talked about a breakdown from overwork and stress. Stress! Ha! I've never suffered from stress in my life, and as for overwork – I'll bet I could overwork the doctors here into the ground any day.

When I asked if they had any objection to my drafting out a few notes for this book that's going to include Brank, they said not at all and added that writing was therapeutic, pronouncing this solemnly as if it might not have occurred to me.

I've told the historian I'm as sane as he is (ha!), but that I unravelled a bit at the hem a couple of years ago. Like that sweater you're wearing is unravelling at the hem, I said. (It was what we use to call Fair Isle, although I don't know what they call it today. I dare say if he uses any of this stuff in his book he'll leave that bit out.)

If he does decide to put that in, I'd like it understood that I consider I was entitled to unravel a bit at the hem two years ago. I think anyone would have unravelled if they'd seen what I saw in that hellish house.

The historian-cum-author can print this verbatim in his book if he thinks it will be of any interest, or it can be clipped to my medical records or flushed down the nearest lavatory for all I care. But perhaps if I write it down, it'll drive the memories from my mind once and for all. Then I can draw a line under it and write QED. That which was to be proved. And *now* I'm reducing Charect's darkness to a mathematical equation.

Charect. It's a very old form of word. In essence, it means an inscription, as in 'character'. But before the word became virtually lost, it signified something rather dark and often forbidden. I was allowed books while I was in Brank – and I found a number of interesting applications of the term. One fifteenth-century document recommends a specific charect to promote easy childbirth, while another was created as a defence against violent death, although there's a counter-warning against that one, which says, "What wicked blindenes is this than to thinke that wearing Prayers written in rolles, thei shall die no sodain death, nor be hanged, or, yf hanged, shall not die." That warning seems to have been issued after a charect was found on a murderer in Chichester Gaol in 1749. Curiously, it appears the man who possessed the charect actually did cheat the gallows, although there's an ironic twist to the story. It seems the condemned man was struck with such horror on being measured for the irons in which his hanged body would later be displayed (they say the twentieth century is violent!) that he expired on the spot from sheer terror. Which goes to prove the old saying that the devil never keeps his side of a bargain.

What's interesting on a purely local level is that a seventeenth century source states a charect can be used as a defence against: "Witchcraft, evil Tongues, and all efforts of the Devil or his Agents who walk the world seeking prey." Is that why Charect House was so named? It wasn't always called Charect – I discovered that early on. Its original name was Mallow House. That's a lovely name for a house – it's a deep purple name, redolent of scented summer nights with pale lilac flares in the dusk . . . There was a mallow at the house – I remember seeing it. But the house's name was changed in 1890 – one of the older attendants in Brank says her father told her how the name was changed to give the house protection from what walked there.

"Did it work?"

"They say not. They say whatever haunted that house, still does."

It does, of course. I was haunted, that night. And I think that whatever haunted me is still there.'

A log broke apart in the fire, making Nell jump. She watched the cascade of sparks die away before returning to the printed page. Could it really be Alice who had written all this? The style was very similar to that of the journal Nell had found.

But I won't cheat and turn to the end though, she thought. I'll read properly and objectively, all the way through.

'I always believed the real haunting started when I set the old clock going. I do know that sounds peculiar, but it's how it seemed at the time, and the years have done nothing to alter my opinion.

It was shortly before two a.m. when I saw the figure at the top of the stairs in Charect House. At first I tried to pretend it was simply the huge damp stain on the wall, but deep down I knew it was not. I can still remember how I ran back into the library and slammed the door, my heart pounding so hard that I'm surprised I didn't drop down dead of a heart attack there and then.

I sat in the library for a long time, huddled into a corner of the window seat, trying to summon up the courage to go back out to the hall. All around me the house was silent, but every so often a tiny creak sounded in the hall, and I knew he was out there. Do ghosts walk? I don't mean in the haunting sense, I mean really physically walk across a floor, causing worn floorboards to creak? I didn't know then, and I don't know now, but I know that on that night *something* walked across the old floors of Charect House, and it didn't do so silently.

The grisly old clock chimed two a.m. as I crouched there irresolute. (Me, irresolute! Never before, and I hope never again.) I hated the sound of that clock: it was distorted and uneven, as if it was struggling to make itself heard from beneath a murky lake. When I remember that night, the sound of that clock ticks and chimes slyly through the memories. I waited for the faint reverberations to die away, and that was when I heard the other sound. Not soft, stealthy footsteps this time, but something quite different. Somewhere in the house, something was tapping on a wall.

It's extraordinary how chilling it was. For a moment I thought it was part of the knocking I had heard earlier – the knocking *he* had made on the window and the door, asking to be let in – but I knew almost in the same instant that it was not. This was a light, panic-filled tapping – a trapped-bird sound. Except that whatever was making it was certainly not a bird.

That was the point at which I knew I should have to go out into the hall. I would have to see if I could capture that figure on film and those tapping sounds on the tape recorder. I buoyed myself up by thinking about the paper I would write afterwards for the Society for Psychic Research, and how people would say, "Goodness, imagine that sensible Alice Wilson – lifelong disbeliever and cynic! – writing such an account." Perhaps some of them might even say that it must have been a remarkably convincing encounter to affect me so strongly, and speculate as to the truth of it.

I set off up the stairs, the camera around my neck, the heavy-based torch grasped firmly in my right hand. For a relieved moment I thought he had gone, then I saw he was still there, turning his head this way and that, as if searching for something.

I was shaking so badly that I couldn't operate the camera shutter, but as I tried to force my hands to behave calmly, he began to sing, very softly:

"Sever quickly the dead man's fist—
Climb who dare where he swings in the air,
And pluck five locks of the dead man's hair.
Then twist into wicks,
With the grease and the fat,
One on the thumb and each finger to fix."

All ideas of using the camera fled, and I began to back away. As if the movement was a cue for which he had been waiting, he began to descend the stairs. He came slowly and warily, lifting one hand aloft, in the way people used to lift an oil lamp aloft. But it was not a lamp he carried.

Dear God, I can't believe I'm writing this, and I certainly don't expect many people to believe it, but—

In his hand he clutched a second hand – a dreadful, misshapen dead hand, with glimmers of light oozing greasily from each fingertip.

The hand taken at the midnight hour from the gallows tree.

For the second time that night I ran away. This time I didn't run into the library though – I wasn't going to risk being trapped in there – I ran along the passage leading to the kitchens. My feet rang out eerily on the stone-flagged floor, but I reached the main scullery safely and tumbled inside, dragging the door shut. It was dark, but it was not absolutely pitch black: moonlight trickled in from the small, grimed windows.

Where now? Opening off this room was a smaller one, with a deep, old sink and an ancient copper boiler. A door opened off that room to the side gardens of the house. I had locked that door earlier, and the key was in my bag in the library. But had *he* got in by this door? He had caused a door somewhere to open – *fly bolt, and bar, and band* – but which door had opened to his words? And would it have stayed unlocked?

The singing was suddenly nearer, and I dived across the floor and into the old scullery, which was at a lower level than the rest of the house and had three worn stone steps leading down into it. The stench of clogged drains and damp reared up to meet me like a solid wall, and black beetles and spiders scuttled away from my footsteps, but if the room provided an escape route I would not have cared if it smelt of a charnel house or if the Pied Piper's battalion of rats inhabited it.

The garden door was directly ahead – a solid, old door with a tiny, glazed panel at the top. I don't remember crossing the scullery, but I do remember how I felt when my hand closed round the handle. Because I knew at once the stubborn old lock was still in place, exactly as I had left it.

I tried to dislodge it, of course. I threw my entire weight into forcing that door open, but nothing short of a battering ram and four men would have opened it. Or, of course, the key. But the key was in my bag in the library on the ring with the others.

Behind me the door to the main kitchen opened, and the greasy light I had seen earlier cut through the darkness.

I shrank back, then darted behind the old copper. It was thick with cobwebs and verdigris had eaten into it in places. The smell of mould and dirt was almost overwhelming.

He stood in the doorway, still singing softly, and it seemed that the words and the cadences of the song floated across the air in filaments of light, turning the cobwebs into spun gold and scattering tiny specks of soft light everywhere.

"Sleep all who sleep . . . Be as the dead for the dead man's sake."

And here's the most frightening thing yet. I felt my eyelids becoming so heavy that the compulsion to let them close – to slide down into sleep – was impossible to ignore. His voice and the light he carried with him are the last things I remember . . .

When I woke it was to find myself on the attic floor, half lying against a wall. Of the macabre figure, there was no sign, and the house was silent, save for the maddening ticking of the clock downstairs.

I lay where I was, memory unrolling in front of me like a ribbon of road at night. Had he brought me up here, that figure? Why?

It was at that point I realized it was not the ticking of the clock I was hearing. It was the tapping I had heard earlier on. It was up here. Someone was behind the wall.

That's where they say they found me. Huddled on the attic floor, exhausted and severely dehydrated, my fingernails torn and bleeding.

I think I tried to tear down the wall – when they found me I was sobbing and insisting someone was trapped there. But after the ambulance people had given me some fluids intravenously and got me a bit warmer before trundling me off to a hospital, I understood that it was impossible for anyone to be behind the wall. It was part of the house – the plaster was cracked, old and discoloured. What I thought I had heard would have been a bird or a rat in the roof void, they said. And it's the logical explanation, of course.

My memory of that night isn't absolutely clear, even now. It's blurred, like trying to see through one of those Victorian fogs where insubstantial shapes, fuzzy at the edges, come and go. The memories come and go, and sometimes they're startlingly – frighteningly – clear, but at others I can't make out what they are at all.

But one thing remains stubbornly clear. I'm convinced that the figure I saw inside Charect House – the man who tapped at the window and who walked through the dark rooms with that grisly lump of flesh casting its horrid light – is still there.

**Brank House. Asylum for the Incurably Insane.
County of Shropshire
Patient's record.**
Name: Alice Wilson.
Address: Goldsmith Mansions, Peckham, London.

Date of Birth: 8th June 1925.

Date of admission: April 1963.

Next of kin: No relatives believed living.

Religion: Church of England.

Diagnosis: Delusional.

Admission: Patient was admitted to Brank Asylum under
the Mental Health Act 1959 as emergency case. Later,
she became a voluntary patient.

Released into care of: Family connections in New
Jersey, USA. Notes forwarded to State of New Jersey
Division of Mental Health Services.

The part that leapt from the page and burned into Nell's
consciousness was not Alice Wilson's macabre experience. It
was not even the fact that it really had been Alice who wrote
the account for the local history publication.

It was that Alice had apparently gone to live with family
connections in New Jersey.

New Jersey was where Liz Harper's cousins lived.

NINETEEN

Michael's study felt rather dismal when he finished the call to Nell.

It was just after ten o'clock. He considered seeing who might be in the Senior Common Room, but his room was warm and snug and he thought he would make a stab at deciphering some of the remaining pages of Harriet Anstey's journal. He had already decided to enlist the help of someone in the history department. They had astonishing methods for enhancing old documents – Michael had only the vaguest idea of how it was done, but he knew surprising results could be achieved.

But it would not hurt to spend an hour or so seeing what he could make of the faint, faded scribble. Two or three of the pages looked as if they were still reasonably legible.

23rd April 1939

The builder's report was delivered to the Black Boar's reception desk shortly after breakfast. It's so pleasant when people do what they promised, and the report is a properly itemized list of all the work needed, along with estimates of the cost of each individual task. When I read the total I blinked though, because it's a shockingly large sum. But I think I could manage it – Father did not leave a great deal of money when he died, but he left a little, and Mother did too. And there's the undoubted fact that Charect House, put into reasonable order, should sell for a very comfortable price.

The builder has added a handwritten note to the effect that I should not be too dismayed. Everything about the house is shockingly old-fashioned, but the fabric is sound. He also says even if I decide not to have the main works done, he strongly advises that the worm-eaten beams in the attic are shored up. They are causing the rafters to sag, and a section of an inner attic wall has already partly collapsed. It was a load-bearing wall, he says, and there's a very real danger of that section of the roof collapsing.

He finishes by saying if the quote is acceptable, they could start work soon.

I don't suppose many people are having building work done at the moment, since, despite Mr Chamberlain's reassurances, we're clearly on the brink of war.

24th April

I have accepted the builder's estimate and have asked him to start the work as soon as possible. (The part about the roof collapsing terrifies me.)

The men will begin with the basic building work and the roof repairs, and will also renew the electrical wiring, since that will mean ripping out wires and gouging into the walls anyway. New beams will be put in, and the old ones torn out. Afterwards, they will build up the collapsed attic wall to provide extra support to the roof. Then they will replaster everywhere.

I think this is going to plunge the house into massive upheaval.

2nd May

I was right about the upheaval. Charect House has become the temporary home of five or six builders, along with an astonishing miscellany of their accoutrements – hods filled with bricks, and lengths of plasterboard which are never the correct size and have to be sawed into pieces, and huge tubs of plaster and cement and paint. There are miles of electrical wiring everywhere – I have no idea which is the old wiring and which the new, and am keeping well clear of both on principle.

The newspapers are saying Herr Hitler has issued a directive to the German High Command to prepare for an attack on Poland. The Prime Minister has announced that Britain will stand by Poland.

I find all this so worrying – it takes me back to the Great War. Harry once said he believed that although we should eventually win that war, it could linger as unfinished business for a very long time. What would he say if he could see what's happening in the world now, I wonder? Would he want to be back with his regiment? Sometimes, as I work in the house, sorting out the boxes and trunks, with the sounds of hammering and sawing all around me, I have the strangest feeling that Harry is close to me.

4th May

The main annoyance from the renovation work is the frequency with which the men keep turning off the electricity. It's apparently necessary to do this, although I don't understand why. Sometimes they give a cheerful shout of warning, and sometimes they don't – or, if they do, I don't hear it because they're at one end of the house and I'm at the other. It doesn't matter so much if I'm at the front of the house because the sun streams into most of the rooms, but it's disconcerting if I'm in the kitchen, which is rather dark. This morning when it happened I tripped over an uneven section of floor, trying to get to the matches to light the oil lamp, and laddered my last pair of stockings.

6th May

I've taken to wearing a skirt with deep pockets in which I can store a box of safety matches. If the lights go off without warning, I can at least strike one and find my way to the nearest oil lamp. There are six lamps placed at strategic intervals around the house – three that were already here, and three more which my friend the taxi driver helped ferry out here yesterday.

I've had a good morning's work – I've been putting out the boxes of what seem to be genuine rubbish. The builders have promised to take them away in one of the skips after the weekend. They're finishing early today on account of it being Friday afternoon. That seems fair enough: they start quite early in the morning; in fact, when I arrive here around ten, they've usually put in a couple of hours' work already and are settling down to a fry-up over the primus stove. I'm usually offered a bacon and egg sandwich. It's all very democratic, and the bacon and egg sandwiches are delicious.

I brought a newspaper with me to read with my lunch. Today the Black Boar have given me sausage patties, which make a nice change from sandwiches. There's also a slice of Victoria sponge, and an apple to round it off. I ate it all while reading newspaper headlines about how two warships are escorting the King and Queen to Canada, and how each ship carries several million pounds in gold for safe-keeping in that country. I don't think there's much doubt about the war. I think Harry would say we shouldn't trust Adolf Hitler *or* Mussolini.

It was on the following page that Harriet's writing became uncertain, and Michael put the diaries down for a moment, considering whether he should hand the rest of the pages to his colleague in the history department. But when he took the journal to the desk and switched on the table lamp, the next two pages were legible, although the writing itself was straggly and erratic. He would read as much as he could.

Harriet Anstey's journal: concluding entries

I'm writing this by the dimmest light imaginable. I'm trapped in Charect House, and I can't see any way that I can get out—

That's absurd. Pure hysteria. Of course I'll get out, either by my own efforts or because somebody will miss me and come to look.

But in case they don't, I'm going to set down an account of what happened. I don't know who might one day read this, so I'm making it as legible as I can. But it's very difficult. There's hardly any room to write. There's hardly any light to write by.

It was half past four, and I was in the library.

I'd finally finished sorting through the boxes, and I was folding some curtains to take back to Cheshire. Beautiful material, excellent quality, and whoever had chosen it had very good taste. They would cut down very nicely for the spare room at home.

Normally, on a May evening it would still be bright sunlight, but a storm seemed to be brewing: there was that swollen, bruised look to the sky and the feeling of something pressing down from overhead. I thought – if this continues I shall end with a headache. The ticking of the clock in its corner seemed to be in exact rhythm with the slight throbbing against my temples, and I wondered whether to get up and stop the mechanism, but the builders seemed to be winding it up regularly, probably so they would know when it was time for their various breaks.

The builders had already left, driving off half an hour earlier in their rattletrap vehicles. The plasterer, they said, might come in early on Saturday morning to do the plastering in the attic. Only a couple of hours' work, it was, then it could dry out over the weekend. I thought I knew which the plasterer was: he wandered around with large tubs of cement and whitewash, dabbing at walls with brushes, apparently at random.

I listened to the lorries go down the drive, then returned to the boxes. I was intending to work until about five o'clock: I had dispensed with the taxi driver since the work on the house commenced – shockingly expensive to have two taxis every day! – and had discovered that if I walked part-way along the lane, a little country bus came along every two hours and went all the way into Marston Lacy. Today I would catch the six thirty bus and be at the Black Boar in time for seven thirty dinner.

When footsteps walked across the room directly above me, I was startled, but not overly alarmed. I thought all the men had left, but it was possible one was still here – the electrician certainly came and went according to his own timetable, and both he and the plumber drove their own vans.

I got up, dusted down my skirt (old papers gather a remarkable quantity of dust), put my diary and pen in the pocket where I keep the matches, and went up the stairs.

At first I thought he was standing at the top of the stairs, looking down, then I saw it was only the mottled wall where a huge, damp stain had spread. In the dimness of the hall it looked like the outline of a man – I had noticed it before. But as I started up the stairs, I saw that after all it wasn't the damp stain – it really was one of the workmen.

'Hello,' I said. My voice echoed in the enclosed space, and I saw him give a start of surprise as if he hadn't realized I was there. 'I didn't know anyone was still here,' I said. 'I'll be leaving and locking up in about ten minutes – have you finished?'

He did not answer. He began to come very slowly down the stairs – fumblingly, that's the only word I can think of to describe it – and as he came, he was humming very softly to himself.

The throbbing headache that had started earlier increased, making me feel slightly dizzy, but – and this is the really curious thing – the soft humming was trickling in and out of my brain. Prowling music – beckoning music. Music that said: *follow me* . . .

I reached out to the banister to steady myself and began to say something else about intending to leave. Only, I don't think it got said. The headache swelled to enormous monstrous proportions, and the music swooped and whirled around me, and the man seemed to come towards me through a kind of amber glaze. Like those insects you see trapped in resin – only, I was the trapped insect, looking out.

I have no recollection of moving up the stairs – I can only remember the soft cadences of the music and the overwhelming need to get closer to it. I think there was the feel of the new floorboards under my shoes, where the builders had nailed new sections of oak strips into place that day, but I can't be sure.

And then, little by little, the humming faded, and I sank fathoms deep into sleep – only, I don't think it could have been sleep in the normal sense of the word. I think it was much too deep and dense for that. I think I might have fainted.

When I opened my eyes, the amber glaze had gone and I was lying in a small, cramped space, half covered by pieces of old sacking. There's the smell of new plaster, and it's stiflingly hot and ominously quiet. Or is it? Isn't that soft singing still going on somewhere, a long way away? No, there's nothing to be heard.

I've pushed the sacking aside and managed to stand up, although I'm stiff and uncomfortable, as if I had been lying up here for a long time, and I've got pins and needles in my legs. But I've rubbed them to get the blood flowing again, and I've tried to see where I am. The matches I've been keeping in my skirt pocket are still there, with the diary and pen, and a few minutes ago I struck a match. Oh God, that was the worst moment of my life. The tiny flame flared up in the airless space, showing that I was in a small, narrow space, completely enclosed by four walls. And the walls are unbroken . . . I sat there on the floor, staring about me, until the flame burned all the way down and scorched my fingers.

The knowledge of what I saw in that too-brief flare of light is drumming into my brain. I'm in the attics of Charect House, on the other side of the damaged wall the men rebuilt. I have no idea how I got here, except that I know I tried to follow that sly, beckoning humming . . . Did it bring me up here? It must have done. And then I sank into that deep, dark sleep.

Heaven knows how long I was unconscious, but while I lay there, the plasterer must have come in to finish the work to the newly-built wall. A couple of hours' work, early on Saturday morning, so the plaster can dry out over the weekend, that's what the builder told me. Or perhaps the man even came back on Friday evening, to get the job done and out of the way. Whenever it was, he wouldn't have seen me, because I was lying in the far corner, in a little recess created by a section of jutting wall, most likely part of the chimney breast. And I was half covered by sacking, so he would just have seen a pile of household debris. Some old sacks, a couple of discarded dust-sheets. No need to bother carrying them down the stairs.

I've struck a second match, and it might not be quite as bad as I feared. There might be a faint chance of escape. There's a tiny window, set high up, and surely I can break the glass and climb out.

I can't. The window is too small – it's a tiny, round window, barely a foot across, hardly more than a ventilator. It lets in a few threads of light at the moment, for which I'm deeply grateful – I can just about see to write these lines. But I think when night falls, it will be pitch dark in here.

I don't know if this is still Friday or if it's Saturday. What I do know is that the builders won't be returning until Monday morning, and that means I'll be here for two, if not three, days. Trapped up here in the silence and the dark. The prospect terrifies me . . .

Michael was unable to make out the writing on the rest of this page – it trailed off as if the writer could no longer hold the pen. There were sections of blank paper, then it resumed near the foot of the page. Oh, Harriet, he thought, please be rescued.

I've used up a third, precious, match examining this place very carefully, and now I'm sitting under the little round window, writing this. It's a surprisingly calming thing to do – although I won't answer for the clarity of what I'm actually writing. But it gives me hope to be writing it – it makes me believe I'm sending a letter to someone and the unknown someone will respond. I might still get the letter to the outside in some way, although at the moment I can't see how. The window is hopeless – too small and too high. I can just manage to see out of it, and I can just touch the glass with my fingers, but even if I could break the glass I couldn't climb out.

The walls are solid. I've tapped them all the way round, and three of them are obviously the brick outer wall of the house itself. The fourth seems to be the new one – there's a different feel to the surface, and there are one or two slightly damp patches, as if the cement or something isn't quite dry. But although I've banged this wall, and tried to gouge out the damp-feeling plaster with the heel of my shoe, it's set hard and I've made no impression on it.

A little while ago I managed to stand on tiptoe and look through the tiny window. Far below are the familiar tanglewood gardens. The window looks down on to the side patch – what would have been the kitchen garden. Vegetables and herbs. It's a ruin now, but it's still recognizable for what it once was.

In terms of actual distance, that patch of garden is only forty or fifty feet below me. In reality, it might as well be forty or fifty miles, because I can't get through the window; I can't even get high enough to break the glass. And if I could, what good would that do? Could I throw something out? What? What would attract attention? Shoes? A note? But a note would blow away at once, and shoes would simply become part of the miscellaneous debris that's already scattered around the house.

But it will be all right. The builders will be back on Monday (how far away is Monday?), and I'll hear them and I'll be able to make them hear me. I've only got to sit it out and wait. I'm dreadfully hungry. Worse, I'm dreadfully thirsty.

At this point the writing deteriorated so badly and was so damaged by damp or age that, although Michael spent almost an hour poring over the faint marks on the pages, he finally had to admit defeat. Harriet had certainly written more – there were two and a half pages left – but it was plain that by that time she had been writing in what must have been virtual darkness, perhaps striking a match every so often. What demons had gibbered at her while she huddled up there?

But she got out, he thought determinedly. Of course she did. They'd have found her body when they broke that wall down if she hadn't. I was there when they did that – I'd have seen her body. Her own builders would have returned and heard her calling for help. Or she would have managed to finally break the glass of the tiny window and attract someone's attention.

The window.

He turned back to Harriet's description of the small space in which she had been imprisoned. He would deal, afterwards, with the question of why and how she had been imprisoned. For the moment he would focus on the practicalities. On the window. A tiny, round window, she had written. Barely a foot across, hardly more than a ventilator.

A round window. *Round.* His mind presented him with the memory of the small window that had been uncovered when the builders broke through the attic wall. It had been small, but it had been a traditional oblong, perhaps eight by ten. He had looked through it on to the shrubbery directly below. He had not seen the kitchen garden, as Harriet had. Because the window she had looked from was on a different part of the house?

He switched on the computer and, after a few false attempts, found the photographs he had mailed to Jack and Liz. Which one was it Jack had joked about? 'You should have told your girlfriend not to stand at the window while you photographed it,' he had said.

Michael opened the first three, and then, suddenly and heart-stoppingly, the one he wanted was there. The slightly shadowy figure of a dark-haired female, one hand raised as if waving to someone on the ground. Or was she trying to bang on the glass to attract attention? It was exactly as he remembered it. What he had not remembered, though, was that the window itself was round. And he was as sure as he could be that he had not seen a round window anywhere inside Charect House.

He sat back, his eyes still on the screen, remembering how he had been vaguely surprised when the demolished wall had disclosed such a small space, and how he had expected it to be larger. Jack, working from a ground plan the builders had supplied, had seemed to expect it to be larger as well.

Was it possible there was another attic? An attic that had a small, round window?

'Well, Michael, you've handed me an odd one with this,' said the head of the History Faculty. 'Where on earth did you dig this up? Oh God, you didn't actually dig it up, did you? Because it smacks of mist-shrouded graveyards and heroines walled up in crumbling dungeons, and—'

'Did you manage to decipher any of it?' said Michael, who had spent a virtually sleepless night before delivering the remaining pages of the diaries to the History Faculty Head at half-past eight, and had paced the college impatiently until lunchtime, waiting for the results.

'Only about three-quarters, but enough to get the gist of it.' He reached for a large envelope on the edge of his desk. 'I've put a rough transcript in here for you, but some of it's guess-work. Michael, tell me you haven't been cavorting around sepulchres in your spare time? Or was it a macabre treasure hunt you went on for Halloween?'

'It's something that turned up in an old house a friend's renovating.' Michael had to restrain himself from snatching the envelope out of the man's hands.

'Oh, I see. Simple as that. Interesting though. It's a genuine document, then?'

'You tell me.'

'I haven't done any dating tests – you didn't give me time – but I can do some if you really want. It seemed authentic, though.'

'That's what I was afraid of,' said Michael and managed to get out of the office before he was asked any more awkward questions.

He had hoped there would be a message from Jack when he got back to his rooms, but there was not. Still, it was only twenty-four hours since they had set off for New Jersey. Plenty of time for Jack to check phone messages and call back.

He got through the afternoon's session with a group of first years on the structure and origins of iambic verse, and by six o'clock was seated at his desk, taking Owen's semi-guesswork transcript from the envelope.

*   *   *

The light is fading, and I only have twelve matches left. I've counted them several times – it's something to do.

I've shouted and banged on the window at intervals, but it's no use. My voice is so cracked and dry that I don't think anyone would hear me.

I think it might now be Saturday evening, which would account for no one being here. Whatever day it is, no one has heard.

But I'm not alone in the house. Every so often I'm aware that someone's out there. Like the way your skin prickles before a thunderstorm. Each time that happens, I wait, listening, and presently I hear the attic stairs creak, and a slow tread comes across the floor. I've tried calling out in case it's a tramp or a gypsy looking for a night's shelter, but there's no response. But whoever is out there doesn't go away. Whoever is there, stands on the other side of the wall for a very long time.

Have to stop writing now – light almost gone. I'm so thirsty . . . My head throbs agonizingly, and I can hear the blood pulsing in my temples. Or is it the hammer-blows of the old clock ticking away . . . No, stupid, the clock's all the way down in the drawing room, I couldn't possibly hear it up here.

I have the feeling that Harry is quite close to me tonight.

Owen from the History Department had added a note of his own at this point:

Michael – sorry, impossible to make out the next few sentences. The words clock *and* singing *seem to be indicated, though. Best I can do. O.*

The transcript resumed on what seemed to be Sunday morning, with a faint light filtering through the tiny window into Harriet's prison.

Grey light coming in now. Good. Another day – a day when I'll be rescued. Head throbbing as if it's swollen to three times its normal size. Is that lack of air?

I drifted in and out of sleep – the utter darkness very frightening, though. Lips cracked and dry – keep thinking about tall glasses of cold water . . . But today I will be rescued. Or I will think of a way to get out. If only I could tear down this wall . . .

I can't tear it down, but could I burn it down? Matches – ten of them left. I could make a torch from the sacking. I might be able to break the window from the fire . . . Harry would say that's a good thing to do – practical. He was so practical, Harry.

Fire no use. Cement probably still too damp. Sacking burned up but then burned itself out too quickly.

I'm going to try pushing these pages into the new wall where I burned part of the plaster. They might reach the other side.

Whoever reads this – whoever you are – please help me. Please break down the attic wall and get to me . . .

Harry seems very close to me now. As if he's waiting for me somewhere quite near. If I put out my hand I have the feeling his hand will close around it. Warm and safe and very loving, just as it always was . . . I always knew he would come for me one day . . .

TWENTY

The diaries stopped abruptly. Michael sat back, a huge wave of emotion sweeping over him. Did she get out? he thought. Surely someone missed her and went looking for her.

The phone rang, startling him, and hoping it was Jack he snatched it up. Nell's voice said, 'Michael? Is this a good time to ring?'

'Any time is good if it's you,' said Michael, before he could stop himself. Before she could speak, he said, 'I mean, I'm glad it's you – I've got several things to tell you about Harriet.'

'Did you finish her journal?'

'Yes. It's a bit emotional, though. I'm not sure if I can actually read it out. I thought I'd get photocopies made – I could post them to you.'

'I'd like to read them,' said Nell. 'Yes, please post them.'

'You sound as if you've found something else.'

'I have,' said Nell. 'I read to the end of that local history book last night – the one that had the information about Elvira. The author included another case history. He said it was the last person to be a patient in there – the last one to walk out through the doors, is how he put it. It sounded as if Elvira was the youngest patient he could find, so he put the asylum's last one in as balance. Michael, it was Alice.'

Michael's mind had been so filled with Harriet that he had to think who Alice was. Then he said, 'Alice Wilson? Alice was in Brank Asylum? Are you sure?'

'Yes. She was taken there after being at Charect House. The admission notes are included, and there's an article she wrote for the author when he was compiling the book. I'll see if I can get it photocopied, and if so I'll send it to you. The writing sounds exactly like the journals I found in the old clock. Sorry, that sounded a bit Lewis Carroll, didn't it? Like the dormouse going to sleep in the teapot.'

'I didn't think anyone read Lewis Carroll any more,' said Michael. 'To children, I mean.'

'Beth loves *Alice in Wonderland*. She likes the story about the girls who live in the treacle well.'

'Of course she does,' said Michael, secretly entertained.

'But,' said Nell, 'I think Alice – I mean our Alice, not Lewis Carroll's – saw that figure while she was in the house. The one Elvira saw, and the one who took Beth. I think it sent Alice mentally off-balance for a time.'

'I'm not surprised.'

'No, nor am I. And she heard sounds from the attic, as you did. That's where they found her after she collapsed. On the attic floor in a kind of semi-coma.'

'The attic,' said Michael, half to himself.

'Yes, but there's more. She was inside Brank for a good two years – initially as an emergency admission, maybe she was even sectioned, although I think she was a voluntary patient afterwards.'

'Two years is a long time.'

'I know. It's my guess she clung to the safety of being inside the place as long as she could. But, listen, when they released her from Brank, they did so into the care of family connections in New Jersey.'

Again it took a moment for this to sink in, then Michael said, 'But that's where—'

'—Liz Harper's cousins live,' said Nell.

'It's coincidence,' said Michael. 'New Jersey is a huge place.' But his voice did not sound very convincing, even to him.

'Yes, but Liz inherited the house from someone,' said Nell. 'There's a family link between Liz and Charect, we know that. Supposing the link is through those cousins. Supposing it's even through Alice?'

'Alice's journal doesn't make any mention of having a connection to the family,' began Michael. 'Or does it? Wasn't there something about her pulling strings to get that particular ghost-hunting assignment?'

'Yes, there was. I checked her journal. You have an incredible memory.'

'Only for things that interest me.'

'She talks about Charect being special in some way, too,' said Nell. 'I read it again – well, parts of it – and some of the things she writes could indicate she knew a lot more about the house than she was letting on. I'm trying not to leap to conclusions, but I do wonder if she was related to the Lees. Have you heard from Jack or Liz Harper yet?'

'No, but I haven't checked my emails since lunchtime. Hold on, I'll do it now.'

The laptop had gone into its sleep mode; Michael activated it, and opened the email programme.

'There is an email from Jack,' he said. 'That's something at any rate, except—'

'What? Michael, what is it?'

Michael said, 'I'll forward the email to you in a minute, but listen.'

Michael—

I got your email and voicemail message, and I know you said the house is pretty much derelict, but we think we'll still come over. Liz is really keen to see the place as soon as possible, particularly since— Well, since the most astonishing thing!

We got to New Jersey two days ago, at least I think it was two days ago, because time has got a bit skewed for us with everything that's been happening. But we were greeted with some very sad news indeed. Liz's doughty old godmother died two days earlier. She was in her late eighties, the grand old girl, and she's been living with the cousins for about four years. Apparently, she just sat down after supper, said, 'I feel a bit peculiar,' closed her eyes and died. Way to go, as they say, but think of the shock to everyone. Liz cried, because she was really fond of her, and so was I, despite all the things I used to say about her. (I didn't cry, of course.)

Godmamma was English – can't remember if you knew that – and one of that wonderful tough breed that went through World War II and came out the other side. She never married, but she was engaged to one of Liz's cousins – the previous generation of cousins, or maybe even the one before that. He was in the army, and he went out to Hiroshima and was there when they dropped the atom bomb in '45. Alice always kept in touch with his family.

Michael broke off as Nell gasped.

'Alice,' she said. 'It's our Alice, isn't it? That's the link. She contrived to get the Charect House investigation because it had been in her fiancé's family.'

'That's what it sounds like.'
'Sorry, I didn't mean to interrupt. Go on.'
Michael resumed reading.

We got there in time for the funeral – Ellie stayed behind at
the house for that, and one of the cousins' teenage daughter
stayed with her – but Liz and I went. Afterwards, we were
able to help with sorting out the dear old love's things. Liz
gets a few of the pieces – some glassware and really beautiful
porcelain. God knows how we'll get it to England without it
smashing, but we're going to try. Ellie gets a little legacy that's
to be put into a savings fund to mature when she's eighteen.
"So she can opt to study or go round the world or squander
it on lush living, whatever she wants," Alice had specified.
My guess is it'll be round the world, and I think Alice would
have approved of that.

Locked away in a kind of travelling desk that she must have
had for fifty years, were all her papers – birth certificate, life
insurance, passport. Photographs of the guy who was burned
to a crisp in Japan. Michael, I didn't weep at the funeral, but
I did then, seeing those photos, although I pretended to Liz I
had something in my eye.

(She said, "Oh yes? And is that Rachmaninov's Second
Piano Concerto I can hear drifting down the rail track?" She's
such a cynic, that Liz.)

So there were these photos – good-looking guy he was, warm
smile, absolute tragedy he died like that. And books. A lot of
books. I should think they're worth a bit – we might send Nell
West an inventory to see if she'd know of a market for them.
Terrific old tales of legends and ancient British folklore, and
even some on magic. Plus a really battered book called *The
Ingoldsby Legends*. (What, or where, is an Ingoldsby?) I did
glance at a couple of pages of that one, and trust me, it's a
chiller in places, although I think a fair amount might be what
you lot call black humor. The humor we aren't supposed to
get.

We all sat on the porch after the funeral, remembering her,
telling anecdotes about her, as you do when somebody's died.
I haven't pieced her life together completely, because everyone
had a different memory, so it's like putting a jigsaw together.
I dare say there are a lot of pieces still missing.

But as far as I can make out, she worked with various societies for psychic research in England – I know it sounds off-the-wall, but she was that kind of lady. She'd have taken huge delight in debunking fraudsters and scams, but secretly she'd have loved it if she came across anything that smacked of the real thing. Not that I think there is a real thing. No ghosts, no pack drill.

Here's the amazing thing. She went to Charect House. She actually went there, sometime in the sixties. I don't know why or how, or if it was a psychic investigation, or what it was. Because around that time she got ill – no one here knows the details, but some kind of nervous exhaustion from over-work is the popular view. That's when she came to live in New Jersey, to be near Joel's people. She looked on them as family, and they looked on her as the daughter-in-law or sister-in-law she should have been. She was an adopted aunt to half a dozen of the kids, as well as godmother to Liz and one or two more.

But this is the explanation for Ellie's nightmares. Ellie used to stay with these cousins for weekends, and she was there this summer for almost a month. Alice was there as well, and Ellie took to her. You know how it is with kids and old people – they often have a remarkable affinity.

We've talked to Ellie as much as we dare – not wanting to revive the nightmares which, thank the lord, have been quies-cent for the last week – and she says, in that unconcerned way, that yes, Aunty Alice did used to tell really great tales. An old house in England, and a man who used to sing and knew spells for putting people to sleep. "Sleeping Beauty stuff," she said. "I don't believe all that, of course. It isn't cool to believe fairy stories."

We asked what kind of a man Aunty Alice talked about, and Ellie shrugged. 'I don't know. He had black eyes.'

I don't know about you, Michael, but it seems clear to me that Alice had talked to Ellie about some of the psychic investigations she did – not spookily or frighteningly, because beneath the crusty exterior she had a heart of gold and she loved kids. But she'd tell stories they might find fascinating – stories they wouldn't have come across before. And she was a world-class raconteur when she got going, I'll say that for her.

So there you have it. The explanation for Ellie's nightmares, we're absolutely certain of it. Happy ending. And we're setting off for JFK tonight – there's a stopover in Paris, and Liz says we should make it a three-day stay at the very least. I dare say I can be made bankrupt as easily on the Left Bank as I can anywhere else. Then it'll be London on or about the 22nd. OK for you?

Liz and Ellie send you their love. I send whatever's appropriate and manly!

Jack.

'Is it the explanation?' said Nell, after a long pause.

'It could be for Ellie. But it doesn't explain what I saw,' said Michael. 'Or what happened to Beth.'

'Or what I saw and heard in the old churchyard where we found Beth. Or,' said Nell, 'what Alice saw for herself forty years ago.'

'Harriet saw it as well, thirty-odd years before Alice,' said Michael.

'There are two things I could bear knowing more about,' said Nell, thoughtfully. 'The first's William Lee himself. There didn't seem to be a grave for him in the churchyard, if you remember? And Alice mentions a local legend—'

'That he was dead and underground these seventy years, but sometimes still seen in the house,' said Michael. 'Does that mean William is the man we both saw?'

'I don't know. But it sounds as if there's something peculiar about his death,' said Nell. 'You remember the clock I bought for Liz?'

'The one in the drawing room? The property of a lady.'

'Yes. Nineteenth-century long-case clock, mahogany and rosewood, and it was made—'

'By Brooke Crutchley.'

'Yes! How did you know that?'

'Because I've got a photocopy of the catalogue on my desk. Jack sent it. It says, "Brooke Crutchley was the last of the famous clockmaking family, and this piece was made for William Lee. In view of the manner of William Lee's death, this item is expected to realize a high figure".'

'I suspect,' said Nell, rather drily, 'that the auctioneers added that bit about William to push up the price. But the clock came from Charect all right. Alice and Harriet both mention it, if you remember.'

'I do. And I thought I heard it ticking that first day I was at the house,' said Michael. 'Only, I couldn't have, because there was no clock in the house at that stage. Sorry, did you say something?'

'I think I shivered,' said Nell.

'You said there were two things. What was the other one?'

'Oh, to try to pin down when and why the name of the house was changed. It was Mallow House until around 1890. If a ghost legend started up around then, that's probably the reason for the change.'

'You mean somebody local thought it might ward off the evil influences?' said Michael incredulously.

'I do know how flaky it sounds,' said Nell, a bit defensively. 'But this is a small market town, remember, and in 1890 it wouldn't have been much more than a village. They probably still had a resident witch and leapt through the bonfire at Halloween.'

'And they say the countryside is boring,' said Michael, smiling. 'Nell, I'm coming back next week. Term finishes here on Tuesday, and unless I can catch up with Jack and head them off, I'll have to be around to explain what's been happening. I thought I'd drive up on Wednesday.'

'I wonder if I'll have found William Lee by then.'

'I expect you and Beth will have family things to do for the holiday, but if not, would you both come out to lunch somewhere one of the days?'

He had no idea how she would respond, and he thought there was the tiniest pause. Then she said, 'I think we'd like that very much. We haven't got any family things to speak of. Thank you.'

'I'll ring you when I get to the Black Boar. Oh, and I'll post the photocopies of Harriet's journal tomorrow. Till next week, Nell.'

Nell had decided to start the search for William Lee with death records. This would mean the archives office again, where she had found the initial letters between Alice Wilson and the local council official who had called her in. She would drive over there after dropping Beth at school.

Beth was pleased to hear they were going to have lunch with Michael and excited about the Christmas preparations for the shop's open day. Nell had found some Victorian glass decorations, and they were going to spend the weekend putting them up. There would be gold and scarlet everywhere, and a huge tureen of warm punch, together with mince pies. Beth thought this was pretty good.

'Um, Dad would have liked us doing this, wouldn't he?' she said. 'I mean – he wouldn't mind that we enjoyed it without him.'

'He'd have said have a ball,' said Nell, fighting to keep her voice steady.

'And he wouldn't mind us going out to lunch with Michael?'

'Certainly not.'

'I think he'd have liked Michael, don't you?' said Beth, and then, in a rare show of emotion, leaned over in the car and put her arms round her mother's neck. She smelt sweet and young and fresh, and Nell thought: oh God, I can't bear the thought of Christmas without Brad. I can't bear that he won't see Beth laughing and enjoying a Christmas party, and opening presents . . .

But she hugged Beth back and said, yes, Dad would have liked Michael very much, and the shop's open day would be great and had Beth remembered her gym shoes?

When the longing for Brad overwhelmed her like this, the only thing to do was focus on the practicalities of life.

The archives office had births, deaths and marriages on microfiche. Nell typed in a request for William Lee and, asked to provide a date within five years, added 1887 to 1892.

The microfiche ticked and scrolled along, and Nell waited, her heart pounding. It was absurd to feel apprehensive; it could not matter very much whether William Lee had died of honourable old age or succumbed to some peculiar and unpronounceable disease in a far-flung outpost of the empire.

Here it was now. A smudgy facsimile of a death certificate. The date was January 1889. William Lee was described as a widower, and his wife's name was Elizabeth. This all fitted. He had been born in 1850 in the County of Shropshire, and under the column for profession was the word 'Gentleman'. This fitted as well.

The cause of his death was given as dislocation of the neck and severance of the spinal cord.

The place of his death was Shrewsbury Gaol.

William Lee had been hanged.

It should not have come as such a shock – the clues had all been there – and yet Nell was sat staring at the screen for several minutes. Then she entered a new search request for Elizabeth Lee. This time she knew the exact year of death. 1888.

And there it was. Elizabeth Alexandra Lee, born 1858. Wife of William Lee in the County of Shropshire. The cause of death was given as trauma to skull.

The facts were as clear as if they had been printed on the screen. William Lee had been hanged at Shrewsbury Gaol for murdering his wife. And three months later, his seven-year-old daughter, Elvira, had been confined to Brank Asylum, where she had lived for the rest of her life.

TWENTY-ONE

From the archives to the newspaper offices was a logical step mentally, and a relatively brief drive physically.

It was not a very pleasant drive though; the sky was iron grey, and a bitter sleet drove in spiteful flurries against the windscreen. Had it been a morning like this when William Lee was hanged? As he was led into the execution chamber, had he glimpsed a leaden sky through prison windows, or had his thoughts been only for his daughter left behind? Nell tried to imagine the small Elvira Lee on that morning and could only see Beth's bewildered little face when she had to tell her about Brad. Beth had not cried when she knew about her father's death; she had sunk into a small, frozen huddle of confused misery. Had Elvira done the same thing? But what about Elvira's blindness? She had talked to Harriet about that little tree-planting ceremony – she had described how she had worn a scarlet hat and scarf that morning, so she had had her sight then. When had she lost it? And how?

The newspaper offices were warm and welcoming after the bleak morning. Nell found the report of the case quite quickly; the *Marston Lacy and Bryn Marston Advertiser* had reported on it with diligence and commendable restraint. The article explained that on a night in October 1888, William Lee, for reasons best known to himself, had woken his wife from sleep and killed her by smashing in her skull. Then he had pushed her body down the stairs of their house, Mallow House in Marston Lacy, clearly hoping the fall would inflict other injuries and disguise the blow he had dealt:

'Police investigations, although thorough, did not immediately encompass the hapless widower, and his assertion that a common housebreaker had been in the house was accepted.

After his arrest, William Lee held by this account of a burglar throughout the trial, repeating his description of the man, while admitting he had only seen a fleeting glimpse of him. 'A thickset man,' he said. 'Pallid of complexion and with deep-set eyes.'

A search was made, but no one answering this description was ever found.'

Thickset, pale and with deep eyes, thought Nell, rereading the description. It was exactly how Michael had described the man he had seen that day in the house. It was Beth's description and Ellie Harper's as well. She repressed a shiver and read on:

'Until this tragedy, William Lee was a respected and well-liked gentleman in Marston Lacy, known to be scholarly by nature. After the death of his wife, he continued to go about his lawful occasions for several weeks, his behaviour exciting no suspicion. He was sometimes seen with his small daughter – they were forlorn figures, people said; he, tall and thin and clothed in black, the child solemn and pale, clinging to her papa's hand as if she was afraid of losing him.

Lee even took delivery of a long-case moon-phase clock from the workshop of the local clockmaker, Brooke Crutchley, such clock having been commissioned in the autumn of 1888 as a Christmas gift for the ill-starred Elizabeth. Mr Crutchley himself oversaw the delivery and installation of the clock, and a human note is added in that one local resident reports how, on leaving Mallow House afterwards, Mr Crutchley was seen to be visibly distressed.

But eventually, William Lee was arrested on the 30th of November, and found guilty of wilful murder by a jury of his peers on the 21st of December at Shrewsbury Crown Court. His execution took place in Shrewsbury Gaol on 11th January 1889.

William Lee was a scion of the well-known Shropshire family of landowners. He married Elizabeth Marston in 1879, on which occasion the entire village of Marston Lacy was treated to a celebration supper at the village hall to commemorate the event.'

Brooke Crutchley again, thought Nell. It was odd how he kept cropping up. Why had he been so particularly upset that day? Surely clockmakers and squires did not move in the same circles in that era? He could not have known the Lee family, other than as customers.

The paper did not refer to the small Elvira, but this was most likely because children were not regarded as suitable subjects for newspapers. Nell thought the laws restricting journalists had been more stringent in those days.

She was about to request a printout of the article, when a small block of text on the screen caught her eye. It was at the foot of the same page as the report of William Lee's death and was enclosed in a box, in the way of advertisements in those days:

'Messrs Grimley and Shrike, solicitors, request information leading to the finding of descendants and relatives of the Lee family of the County of Shropshire. Or of descendants and relatives of Elizabeth Lee, née Marston, formerly of Mallow House in Marston Lacy, in the County of Shropshire.

It is also hereby notified that the said Mallow House, at the final request of William Lee, henceforth be known as Charect House.

Messrs Grimley & Shrike, Solicitors and Commissioners for Oaths, High Street, Marston Lacy.'

So it had been William who had changed the name of his house. And had Grimley and Shrike wanted to trace family connections because Elvira Lee had been certified as insane, or because she was a minor? Nell made a note of the solicitors, in case the firm still existed, and went out. As she drove home, she thought again that she could bear knowing more about Brooke Crutchley.

Where would she find him, though?

When Nell got back to the shop, there was a letter from the insurance company saying the annual premium on the buildings was due in January, and asking if she would confirm the exact date of her purchase of the premises. Nell had been able to take over the existing buildings insurance from the previous owners, paying the remaining eight months of the premium. It had been an arrangement agreeable to everyone involved, but the policy expired immediately after Christmas and the new premium was almost due.

The insurers asked that, because of the Christmas post, she phone or email the information, and the letter was dated a week ago so it had better be dealt with today – it was already the 17th. Nell could remember the date she had moved in, but the actual completion of the purchase had taken place a couple of weeks earlier and she was not sure of the precise day. She would have to dig out the conveyance.

She put the printouts about William Lee in a drawer until she could show them to Michael and smiled, remembering how his voice seemed almost to light up when his interest was caught. She might phone him this evening – no, better not. It was the last couple of days of the Oxford term, and there would be various events he would have to attend. She would scan the article on to the computer and email it to him.

The conveyance was in the office safe with the title deeds. Nell had turned a small room at the back of the shop into an office. It overlooked the courtyard and the workshop. She was hoping she could afford to have the workshop painted and the courtyard resurfaced by next spring so that she could set up her antique weekends, but it depended on how business went. Still, Christmas was traditionally a good time, and she was going to have a display of Regency miniatures and some early Victorian jewellery for the shop's Open Day. The jewellery had come from a house sale in Powys, and there were some really beautiful pieces, so some of it might sell for Christmas gifts.

The office was strewn with trade magazines, and the shelves were stacked with reference books. She unlocked the safe and found the title deeds in their box file. Earlier documents were in a perspex folder to protect them, but the more recent ones were at the front. Land registration, various surveys, abstract of title . . . Here was the conveyance with the date of legal completion: 11th January. The date jabbed at a memory in her mind – what was it? It was the date when William Lee had been hanged. That was a macabre coincidence if ever there was one.

Nell wrote down the date, then started to fold the papers

carefully back in place, wanting to keep them in sequence. She had bought the premises from a couple who were retiring and who had run a small coffee house-cum-craft business. It had not needed very much work to adapt it for antiques, although some general modernization had been necessary. The old couple had been here for thirty years; they told her that before they came the place had belonged to a carpenter – one of the old types of cabinetmakers. Lovely pieces he had made and sold, they said, and how nice to think the place would again be used to house beautiful furniture.

Here was the conveyance from the cabinetmaker to the coffee house couple. He had been here for a long time, as well. Nell turned back to find the date he had bought it, briefly curious. He had not bought it; he had inherited it from his father in 1940. There was a transfer of title. It had been drawn up by Grimley & Shrike, the solicitors who had advertised for descendants of William or Elizabeth Lee.

She turned over another document. It was an earlier transfer of title, and the names—

Something seemed to swoop down and press hard on the top of her head.

In 1897 the ownership of these premises had been transferred to a man called Josiah Crutchley, as being: 'The only known relative or descendant of Brooke Crutchley, on whom a presumption of death had been declared, *juris et de jure*, at Shropshire County Court.'

Michael had sent several emails to Jack and had four times tried the mobile number. On the last attempt there had been a different message, saying the service was discontinued. Michael had no idea what this meant, unless it was something to do with them having left the US and reached Paris.

He was worried, but in a fairly low-key fashion. It was not absolutely vital that he stopped Jack and Liz bringing Ellie to Marston Lacy – it sounded as if the nightmares had stopped, and the theory that they stemmed from Alice's stories was credible. All the same, there was something peculiar about Charect House, and if there was any chance that Ellie's nightmares might start up again she must not come within a hundred miles of it. And how about Beth's eerie abduction? There was no explanation for that at all.

At intervals he thought about what might still lie behind the attic wall in Charect House, and Harriet Anstey's words ran in and out of his mind.

Whoever reads this – whoever you are – please help me, she had written. Please somehow break down the attic wall and get to me . . .

I'm sorry, Harriet, said Michael silently. I would have got you out if I could. Then he thought – hell's boots, now I'm apologizing to someone who died sixty years ago!

He attended the Dean's end of term lunch, at which there was the promised goose, served in lavish portions, then went to a drinks party the same evening, given by Owen from the History Department. It was midnight before he got back to his rooms, where the porter greeted him with the information that Wilberforce had got himself stuck in a section of panelling in the Bursar's office, the Bursar having taken the opportunity afforded by the Christmas break to commission some refurbishment of the wainscoting. Nobody knew how Wilberforce had got into the Bursar's rooms, but it appeared he had become wedged half in and half out of the section of wall. According to the porter he had screeched fit to disturb the whole of Oriel, and Corpus Christi and Merton as well, and had finally been rescued by two of Michael's second years, whom he had scratched.

'I'm dreadfully sorry,' said Michael, making a mental note to look out for the second years in question and treat them to a large drink each, and to double the porter's Christmas tip.

He swallowed two paracetamol, wished he had not drunk the Dean's hock and Owen's claret on the same day, and finally got to bed shortly before one a.m.

Next morning he got up early and went into several of the Oxford bookshops to find something for Nell and Beth for Christmas. It had better not be anything too elaborate or expensive in case it made Nell feel awkward, but he would like to find something.

The trouble with bookshops was that you always spent more time and usually more money in them than you intended. By lunchtime Michael was still only on the third shop and had already acquired six books. It was not until he had chased away the lingering memory of the Dean's hock and Owen's claret with a cup of strong coffee that he found a framed print

from a John Tenniel illustration, intended for the first publication of Alice's Adventures in Wonderland, but never actually
used in the book. It showed the Cheshire Cat, looking extremely
pleased with itself, lying under a tree and Alice standing over
it, waving a severe and admonitory finger. Michael loved it,
and he thought Beth in particular would love it as well. The
frame was slightly scuffed, but the shop offered to clean it up
a bit. An application of Danish oil, then a good buffing with
beeswax and turpentine. Would tomorrow morning be convenient for it to be collected?

'It would indeed,' said Michael, and he left a deposit and
his name.

When he got back there was an email from Nell, attaching
an article she had found about William Lee. 'You'll see,' she
had written, 'that his death conforms to all the traditions of
hauntings. And his description of the "burglar" is eerily like
the man you saw. I've found another piece of jigsaw as well
– it's interesting but probably not relevant, so I'll save it until
you're here. Beth and I have decorated the shop; Beth thinks
it looks pretty cool, and I hope it looks like something out of
Dickens. Our Open Day is on Monday, and there's a glass of
mulled wine and a mince pie with your name on it.'

Michael would certainly look in for the mulled wine and
the mince pie, and he would book the promised lunch for
the three of them for Tuesday or Wednesday. He remembered
to phone the Black Boar to confirm his reservation and the
reservations for Jack and Liz, tried to reach Jack yet again,
then gave up.

He drove to Marston Lacy two days later, the framed print,
wrapped by the shop, carefully stowed in the back of the car.

Nell's shop did indeed look like something out of Dickens.
Michael stood in the street for a moment, enjoying the scarlet
and gold decorations and the glinting candlelight reflecting on
the spun-glass stars and globes. The inside looked fairly full of
people, and it looked as if quite a number were buying as well.

When he went in, the warm scent of cloves and cinnamon
from the huge tureen of mulled wine greeted him. There was
a buzz of conversation from the people, and music was playing
quietly but pleasantly. After a moment Michael identified it
as Tchaikovsky's Nutcracker Suite.

Nell was absorbed in discussing something with two of the guests, but Beth saw him and came over. She was wearing a garnet-coloured dress, which gave her a Victorian look of her own.

'I'm allowed to speak to people and offer them a mince pie,' she confided. 'But I mustn't get in the way, 'cos it's a grown-up party. I didn't think you counted as a grown-up, however.'

'I don't think I do.'

'Was that rude?' asked Beth, anxiously.

'Not a bit.'

'Have a mince pie? How's Wilberforce?' said Beth hopefully.

'I'd love a mince pie, and Wilberforce has been very bad,' said Michael, and he saw her face light up with glee, suddenly turning her into a gamine. For the first time he was aware of a pang for the dead Brad West who would never see his daughter grow up. He said, 'I've typed out Wilberforce's new adventure for you.'

'Oh, brilliant. Could I have it tonight, d'you suppose? On account of I'm going to a party on my own tomorrow.'

'Yes, of course.'

'It's a party with a girl at school in my class,' explained Beth. 'And four of us are staying at her house all night. We might have a midnight feast, only I mustn't tell Mum about it.'

'I won't say a word,' promised Michael. 'But I'll want to know what you had to eat.'

'Um, OK. Shush, here's Mum now.'

Each time Michael saw Nell the sight pleased him all over again. Today she was more formally dressed than he had yet seen her: her outfit was the colour of horse chestnuts, and with it she wore a pendant of beaten copper and earrings to match. The colours brought out the red lights in her hair.

She smiled at him. 'I'm so glad you made it. Is Beth looking after you?'

'She is, and I've had two mince pies and I'm about to head for the mulled wine,' said Michael promptly. 'And Beth says she's going to a party tomorrow night, and your notice on the door says you're closing the shop on Tuesday, so will you both have lunch with me on Wednesday?'

Beth looked at her mother and Nell said, 'We'd like that.'

'How long does today's party go on?' asked Michael, glancing at the shop, which by now was quite full.

'Until six.'

'It's a lot of hard work for you.'

'I've got a couple of local girls in, helping,' said Nell. 'They're being very good.' She paused, then said, 'You got the email?'

'Yes, and I'm looking forward to hearing what else you found.'

'Well, if you feel like coming back for a drink after we close . . . ?'

'Seven o'clock? Can I bring some food? The Black Boar seems a bit harassed with cooking about half a dozen turkeys, and I shouldn't think you'll want to cook after today, will you?'

'I hadn't thought about it—'

'We could order pizza,' said Beth hopefully, and Michael laughed.

'You sound like one of my students. Pizza it is. I'll order for half-past seven.'

The pizzas had been consumed with enthusiasm, and Michael had solemnly viewed some drawings Beth had done of Wilberforce and said they were extraordinary like him. He would take one back for his study at Oxford, he said.

Beth went contentedly to bed, taking with her the story of Wilberforce stuck in the panelling, which Michael had related over the pizzas. Nell had scooped up the pizza boxes and taken them out to the kitchen bin, and Michael had refilled the wine glasses.

'Nice,' he said as she came back to the sitting room and curled into a low seat by the fire. 'Firelight's traditional for ghost stories, isn't it? I read the article about William Lee. I've been trying to decide if he really did kill Elizabeth.'

'Twelve good men and true thought he did.'

'Elvira didn't seem to believe it, though. That part about how she clung to William's hand . . .'

'It's evocative, isn't it? But you know,' said Nell, 'I don't think a child would believe a thing like that about her own father. She was almost eight when he was hanged – she'd have known him very well, and she'd remember him quite clearly.' Her eyes darkened briefly, then she said, 'Also, most of this information is second-hand, if not third. Harriet's journal is a memory of something told to her when she was a child.'

'And the chaplain might have been painting purple patches,' said Michael, thoughtfully. 'Elvira said the murderer was still trying to find her. She said his mind had – what did she call it? – touched the black marrow of the world's history . . . Sorry, I didn't mean to spook you.'

'She said she heard him singing as he searched for her,' said Nell, who had shivered slightly at his words. 'He sang that song I heard in the churchyard.'

'Harriet heard that as well. Or,' said Michael, 'was Harriet simply dredging up the memory of what Elvira told her? Like Jack thinks Ellie did with Alice. Because that meeting with Elvira clearly made a deep impression on Harriet.'

'I heard the singing as well,' pointed out Nell. 'Oh, but that was after I read Alice's journal, so maybe I was doing the same thing.' She paused to drink some more of the wine.

Michael said, 'Have the police found any trace of the man who took Beth?'

'No. The policewoman who stayed with me while she was missing – Lisa – phoned yesterday to check she was all right. She said they hadn't got any leads at all. They're putting it down to a tramp, I think. Someone who took Beth, then panicked and beat it out of the area. She was left inside the church, by the way. They found traces of hair and shreds of wool from her scarf. There were a few hairs on a kneeler – they think that had been put under her head for a pillow, and a woollen cassock thrown over her. They said she'd have been perfectly snug and warm.'

'Who put her on that grave, though?'

'I don't know. Neither does Inspector Brent. Someone who wanted her to be found, maybe? I suppose,' said Nell, 'the tramp theory might even be the truth.'

'You don't think so?'

'What I think is so fantastic I don't really believe it myself,' said Nell. 'A tramp would be horrible, but it's easier to accept.' She frowned as if to push away the memories. 'Tell me what you thought about the article.'

'One thing that struck me,' said Michael, 'was that William's description of his burglar matched the description of the man I saw in Charect House that day. It matches Harriet's description of the man who stood over her that day, as well.'

'Then it wasn't William either of you saw?'

'It doesn't seem like it. But if William was hanged for a crime he didn't commit, it certainly gives him one of the classic reasons for haunting. D'you know, I don't believe I ever imagined myself discussing ghosts quite so rationally,' he said wryly. 'You have a remarkable effect on me, Nell.'

'It's more likely the wine,' she said, after a moment.

'I expect so. What was the other jigsaw piece you found?'

'Oh, that. Hold on, I'll show you.' She opened the drawer of the desk which housed the laptop and handed him a large envelope.

'Property deeds?'

'Yes. I've put the relevant one on top. It's fairly old, so you have to be a bit careful – sorry, you're probably used to dealing with old books and papers on a day-to-day basis.'

'Well, not quite,' said Michael, and he read the transfer of title on top of the deeds. Brooke Crutchley's name leapt out at him at once, but he looked through the whole list before setting it down on the table. 'So we're in his house,' he said thoughtfully. 'Brooke Crutchley – the man who made that sinister clock.'

'Yes. And I can't help thinking – feeling – that he's at the heart of all this,' said Nell. She was sitting on a low stool by the fire; the fire painted copper and bronze shadows into her hair, and Michael suddenly found he wanted to reach out and run his hands through her hair and cup her face between his hands.

'Elvira said the man looking for her was an ordinary man – what was called Everyman.'

'I remember that as well,' said Nell, eagerly. 'She said he enjoyed the company of his fellows and drinking beer with them at the end of his day's work.'

'Yes. What kind of man does that sound like to you?'

'A workman of some kind,' said Nell. 'Not a labourer, exactly. Not someone who dug ditches or worked in the fields. Someone who worked with his hands.'

'An artisan? A skilled craftsman?'

'Yes.' She turned from her contemplation of the fire to stare at him. 'A cabinet maker,' she said slowly. 'Or a tailor or jeweller or stonemason. Or—' She broke off, her eyes widening.

'Or a clockmaker,' said Michael.

TWENTY-TWO

'**B**ut,' said Nell, for the tenth time, 'how does that get us any further?'

'Do we really need to get any further?'

'I think we do if we can. There's still Ellie to think of. And there's what happened to Beth.'

'If we could find out what happened to Brooke Crutchley, that might give us a start,' said Michael. 'All we know is that he lived here – presumably he worked in the outbuildings behind the shop – and that he vanished and was presumed dead after— Wait a minute, how long was it?'

'Seven years,' said Nell. 'I think that's fairly standard in law for presumption of death.' She had made a pot of coffee half an hour earlier, and they were still drinking it.

'There'd have been a search for him, I should think,' said Michael. 'He sounds as if he was a well-known figure – modestly prosperous too, I should think. This house isn't exactly a hovel, is it?'

'No, and that auction catalogue refers to him as one of a famous clockmaking family. It was quite a reputable trade,' said Nell. 'Very skilled, and he'd have to have a knowledge of the mechanical side of things. Almost a jeweller on that score.'

'They'd have searched this house for him,' said Michael, leaning back in his chair and looking round the room. 'So I shouldn't think there'd be any clues after all this time. Even so . . .' He frowned. 'Nell, you might hate this, but I'd like to have a really thorough look at this place.'

'You can scour it from top to bottom if it will solve the ghost,' said Nell. 'I was going to close the shop at lunchtime, and Beth's going to her party at four. It might be better to do it while she's not here.' She smiled. 'They're planning a midnight feast at her party. She thinks I don't know, so I'm not letting on that I do because that's part of the fun for her.'

'I ought to go out to Charect House tomorrow,' said Michael. 'Jack's builders won't be there over the holiday, so I'd better make sure everything's left secure. Frozen pipes,' he said, remembering that this could be a problem for house-owners in the depths of winter. 'Would it be all right if I turned up around half-past four, after Beth's gone? It needn't take more than an hour or so, but if I'm still here by six we might go down to the Black Boar afterwards for something to eat.'

She hesitated, then said, 'Would it be easier to have a meal here? Nothing elaborate – I could just put a casserole in the oven and leave it to simmer until we're ready to eat.'

'That would be nice.' He got up to go. 'I'll see you tomorrow, Nell,' he said.

Nell spent most of the night wondering what on earth had possessed her to invite Michael to dinner. It was the classic move if you fancied someone. Well, all right, she did fancy Michael. But she was not going to do anything about it. And she was making too much of this. It was only a friendly, convenient meal, meant to round off the search for clues about Brooke Crutchley, during which they could discuss their ghost. It was not as if she was going to put candles on the table or wear a low-cut gown and slink around offering wine in a purry voice. Nell determinedly reminded herself it was just the ghost that was drawing them together, but she was starting to think it was more than that. She looked across at Brad's photo on the bedside table for reassurance. 'It's all right, isn't it?' she said to the photo. 'I'm not going to do anything. He's just a friend, and this is a bizarre situation we're both in, and it's about protecting Beth – and Ellie Harper, too.'

The photograph stared blandly back. There was no animation behind it, no spark, no life. I don't want you to become just a piece of paper in a frame, thought Nell, in panic. But I think you're moving away from me – you're becoming distant. Or am I going further away from you? You never saw Marston Lacy or this shop – you never even heard of the place. You don't know the people I'm meeting now, and you don't know Michael or anything about the Wilberforce stories he's making up for Beth. And it's starting to become really difficult to reach you in my mind, Brad, she thought, and I hadn't bargained for that and I don't know if I can bear it.

But when she finally did slide down into sleep, it was not

Brad she was thinking about, it was Brooke Crutchley. It was disturbing to know she was in his house.

It felt odd to be putting together a casserole next day, knowing she would be serving it in what Beth would call a grown-up way. Wintry sunlight filtered into the kitchen and some of last night's shadows dissolved. Nell enjoyed cubing meat and dicing bacon and mushrooms. She tipped all the ingredients into an iron casserole pot, poured in red wine, and added a sprinkling of herbs. The whole lot could go in the oven around three o'clock, where it would happily simmer on a very low heat for four hours, if not five. She would collect freshly-baked bread and cheese and fruit on the way to taking Beth to her party.

She had been determined not to watch the clock like a teen-ager on a first date, but after she dropped Beth off and got back home, she was very aware of half-past four arriving, and then quarter to five.

Michael arrived just before five, carrying a bottle of wine and apologizing for being a bit late. He had been out to Charect as planned and had got involved in a problem concerning a water tank, he said.

'The builders wanted to fire up the central heating so they could leave a bit of heating on over the holiday,' he said. 'But there was something wrong with the pump and they can't get a replacement until the second of January. So they're draining all the water tanks and pipes to stop them freezing. At least, I think that's what it is – does it sound about right to you?'

'Yes,' said Nell. 'Would you like a cup of tea before making a start on the clues for the ghost?'

'I'll start right away, I think,' said Michael. 'It's a pity it's the depths of winter, isn't it – it would be easier to do this in daylight. Because I was thinking the likeliest place to find anything is in the workshops, and I should think it's a bit cold and dark out there in this weather.'

'It's not too bad, actually,' said Nell, reaching for a jacket and woollen scarf. 'There's electricity out there, so we'll be able to see what we're doing.'

'I've brought a torch,' said Michael, sounding pleased at having thought of something so practical.

'Well, that'll be useful. And it isn't as cold in there as you might think. There's a horrible old iron stove, but I've never fired it. I had a couple of convector heaters put in.'

Nell was pleased to see that Michael liked the workshop. He prowled around, commenting on the scent of beeswax and oil, asking questions, and admiring a small Indian rosewood desk she had found under a heap of rubble in the Powys house sale and was stripping off several layers of Victorian varnish.

'Where did you study all this?'

'I'd like to say I did a Fine Arts degree, but I didn't,' said Nell. 'I got on to a training scheme with one of the big auction houses. Not Christie's or Sotheby's, but not far off. A great piece of luck for me. It was quite intensive – a three-year apprenticeship, half working in the showrooms, half in a kind of training school. I do love working with all these old things.'

'I can tell,' he said, smiling.

'I'm trying to think Brooke Crutchley did, as well,' said Nell. 'I find it a bit spooky knowing he worked here, and I'm not sure if I like the sound of him very much. But it's easier if I can think of him enjoying what he did.'

'I can't see anything in here to give us any leads to him, can you?' said Michael, shining the torch over the walls and up into the roof space and the rafters.

'No.'

'Is that the old stove? I don't blame you for not trying to fire it.'

'I hate it,' said Nell. 'It's like a monstrous black toad crouching in the corner.'

'I should think it dates back to Brooke's time,' said Michael, inspecting the stove, which was cast iron, with small doors at the front and a flue stretching up into the roof.

'It's Victorian design at its most florid,' said Nell. 'I'm going to have it ripped out when there's enough money and the vent capped outside.'

'There's a door on one side. Here, where the wall is set back a bit. It doesn't look as if it leads anywhere, but it's too large to be a cupboard.'

'It's not a cupboard. It's just a kind of alcove for cleaning the flue and raking out cinders and clinkers and things. In the days when they had cinders and clinkers.'

'Can I take a look?'

'Yes, of course.' Nell came to stand next to him as he opened the door, which was set into the wall about eight inches higher than the floor level. It stuck for a moment, then opened with a dry, scraping sound. A shower of black dust cascaded out, and the stench of ancient soot and dirt came out at them like a clutching hand. They both coughed and backed away.

'It's a disgusting smell, isn't it?' said Nell. 'It'll clear in a minute, though. Hold on, I'll prop the door open.'

'Have you ever looked in here?'

'Well, I did when I bought the place. I only glanced inside to see what it was, though. When the survey was done, the guy said everything seemed sound, but he didn't think I should fire the stove.'

'I shouldn't think you'd ever want to,' said Michael, glancing back at the stove, which jutted malevolently out into the room. He leaned forward into the recess, shining his torch over the walls. It was a small space, barely four feet square, and even with the door propped back against the wall it was still thick with the smell of dry soot and dirt.

'It's a horrible place,' said Nell as Michael leaned deeper in and moved the torch's beam over the walls, which were lined with sheets of cast iron. The wall backing on to the stove was pitted with centuries of heat. 'It's like a coffin standing upright.'

'That's an odd analogy to make,' he said, moving the torch over the walls and floor. 'There's nothing in here, though, in fact— Oh!'

'What?' Nell peered over his shoulder. 'Michael, what have you found?'

'Down there.' Michael moved back to allow her to see.

'It's a trapdoor,' said Nell, puzzled. 'I didn't know there was a trapdoor.'

'If you only glanced in that once, I don't suppose you would. And the floor's thick with soot and dirt.'

'There must be an old cellar down there,' said Nell, staring at the oblong outline of the trapdoor. It was wooden and very solid-looking, with an iron ring handle, flush with its surface.

'Might it just be some kind of underground storage vault – something to do with the stove again? Only, I can't think what,' said Michael.

'It's a very large trapdoor for a storage area.'

'It is, isn't it? Do you want to see if we can open it?'

'No,' said Nell. 'But if we don't, I'll have nightmares wondering what might be down there.'

Michael climbed over the low section of wall and knelt down on the edge of the trapdoor. 'There isn't much room to manoeuvre,' he said.

'Give me the torch.'

'Thanks. Shine it directly down, will you? That's better.' He reached for the ring handle. 'It feels as if it's rusted in place.'

'Try it anyway.' Nell was kneeling just outside the recess, directing the torch on to the oblong of solid oak. Cobwebs brushed against her face like ribbons of dead skin, and she shuddered.

'It won't budge,' said Michael, after a moment. He sat back on his heels. 'It feels as if it's brass or iron, and it's stuck fast.'

'Try turning it. Both ways. It might be a twist mechanism.'

'No good,' he said, after a moment. 'I don't think it's locked, though. I think it's just bedded in with rust and age. The same goes for the hinges.' He tugged the handle again, using both hands, turning first left and then right. 'It's absolutely solid,' he said, sitting back on his heels and wiping sweat from his forehead with the back of one hand. 'Damn. Nell, it'll take dynamite to get this open. Or an axe.'

He looked so crestfallen that Nell smiled. 'You really are the scholar in the ivory tower, aren't you?' she said. 'There are more ways than one of skinning a cat or opening a cellar. Stay here – I'll see what I can find.' She put the torch down and went across to the back section of the workshop, to the tool box.

'Try this,' she said, setting down two large chisels and a can of oil. 'We drench the handle and the hinges in oil and let it soak in for a few moments. It might free the handle enough for it to turn. If it does we'll tie my scarf round it – that'll make it easier to pull the door up. If we can raise it even a little way, we can put this larger chisel in as a wedge so it won't bang down again.'

'Do you know,' said Michael, 'you constantly delight me.'

'Do I?' said Nell, absently. 'That's nice. Here's the oil. Just slosh it straight on. You're nearer to the handle than I am.'

'Are you coming in here with me?' asked Michael, taking the oil and sprinkling it liberally over the handle and the hinges.

'Yes, I'm going to scrape out some of the accreted dirt around the edges of the trap,' said Nell, climbing over the low wall. The recess was as unpleasant as she had expected: hot and slightly claustrophobic, and when she knelt down she felt the crunch of the old, dried cinders from the stove under her knees.

'Are you sure you're all right about all this?' said Michael, reaching for the other chisel to help.

'Not really. But let's do it. There's probably nothing down there except years of dirt.'

'Fair enough.' He scraped diligently for several moments, then said, 'I think that's got most of the dirt out. Let's see if the handle will move now.' He grasped it firmly, and this time it lifted slightly. Michael looked up, his eyes shining. 'You clever girl,' he said. 'The oil's worked. Where's your scarf – thanks.' He knotted the long woollen scarf tightly round the handle and stood up, moving to the edge of the trapdoor, his back almost flat against the stove wall.

'Be careful the handle doesn't snap off or it really will be an axe job,' said Nell, moving back to give him room.

'You couldn't swing a cat in here, never mind an axe.'

At first they both thought that, after all, the door was too tightly wedged to move at all. 'And the wood has probably warped over the years as well,' said Nell, frowning. 'That won't make it any easier.'

'It's moving,' said Michael suddenly, and with a dry, scraping sound the trapdoor began to lift. It did so slowly and with a screech of splintering wood and protesting hinges that tore through the quiet workshop like a soul in torment. A thin black line showed around the edges of the door.

'Is it heavy?' said Nell anxiously. 'Let me help.'

'It's all right – it's nearly there. Put the chisel in place in case the scarf slips.'

But the scarf stayed in place, and the door, once freed, came up relatively easily. Dry, foetid air gusted out from the black gaping hole, and Nell gasped and backed away.

'The smell's even more disgusting than this recess,' Michael said.

'At least it doesn't smell of damp.'

'That's about all it doesn't smell of.'

They pushed the trapdoor back against the stove wall. It clanged against the pitted iron sheet, and Nell saw there was a deep indentation where the door must have rested many times before.

'There's a corresponding handle on the underside,' said Michael.

'That's unusual in a cellar. Or is it? Maybe somebody was frightened of being trapped at some time,' said Nell, shining the torch down into the cellar itself. The light sliced through the thick blackness, showing brick-lined walls with a floor at the foot that looked as if it was black brick or stone. 'How safe do you think the steps are?'

'They look like solid stone, but they might have crumbled in places.'

'I should think this was part of the foundation of an earlier building,' said Nell. 'Or these workshops could have been an old scullery wing or something like that.' She looked at him. 'What do you think? Do we go down there?'

'As you said, if we don't, we're going to wonder,' said Michael. 'Shall I do it while you stay here?'

'No fear,' said Nell, getting up and stepping out of the recess. 'Let me get another torch, and I'm coming down there with you.' She darted back to the toolbox and found the spare torch kept for power cuts. When she came back Michael was wedging the trapdoor more firmly against the stove wall.

'I'm making sure the hinges aren't about to disintegrate and bring the door crashing down on our heads,' he said. 'I wouldn't trust this handle to open from beneath, would you?'

'No, but let's not even think about being trapped down there.'

'Let me go first – no, I'm not being masculine and protective. Well, yes, all right, I am. But if I go head over heels down a section of crumbled stone, you'd still be up here to go for help.'

He started warily down, shining the torch as he went. Nell, peering anxiously over the edge saw the light sweep over ancient walls, crusted with soot and grime.

'I'm at the bottom,' he said. His voice echoed slightly and eerily. 'There are ten steps, and they all seemed sound, but they're very worn so make sure you don't slip.'

'Here I come,' said Nell. 'The smell's clearing a bit now, I think. That's something to be grateful for.'

But descending the stone steps was a grim experience. Once, thought Nell, someone lived here or worked down here – maybe was even held prisoner here – and whoever it was suffered such agonies of black and bitter despair, the feeling's soaked into the walls. She remembered how Harriet Anstey had said Brank Asylum made her think of people drowning in the dark. That's what it feels like down here, thought Nell, and for a moment she had to resist a compulsion to bolt back up the steps. But she reached the bottom of the steps and was grateful when Michael put an arm round her.

'For warmth,' he said.

'Was I shivering?'

'No, I was,' said Michael.

The cellar was bigger than they had expected – a narrow but fairly long room that must stretch under the whole work-shop and even extend under part of the courtyard. Nell had been expecting to see a traditional underground room, perhaps with a stone floor and walls, bare of anything saved the accu-mulated dirt of decades. But the room, although it was certainly stone, was not bare. It had been lived in. Standing against the walls were the remains of bookshelves – rotting and splintering with age, but recognizable.

'There are still books on them,' said Michael softly. 'Dear God, look at them.' He moved the torch, showing up rows of old yellowing books, many of them crumbled beyond retrieval, but some still with the leather or calf spines intact. Here and there a vagrant glint of lettering, perhaps once gold leaf, caught the light.

'An underground study,' said Nell in a whisper.

'A secret library,' said Michael. 'Forbidden works, I should think.'

The torchlight moved again, and Nell felt as if something had slammed a clenched fist into her throat. She gasped, and in the same moment felt Michael's hand tighten around hers.

At the far end of the cellar was a large writing desk, with a chair drawn up to it. Seated in the chair was the partly-mummified figure of what had once been a man. His head had fallen forward on to the desk, near an elaborate inkstand, and in the sweep of the torchlight it was possible to see the

fragments of dried skin that clung to the rounded skull. Hands
– not quite fleshless – reached across the desk, and Nell took
a step backwards, because it was dreadfully easy to imagine
the hands would suddenly move and reach out . . .

Michael said, very softly, 'I think this is Elvira Lee's nightmare man. Remember what she said to Harriet? That he had
learned spells from the black marrow of the world's history.'
He indicated the shelves. 'I think these are those spells,' he said.
'This is where he studied them. That's why he had to shut
himself away down here.'

'Brooke Crutchley,' said Nell, unable to look away from the
dreadful figure. 'It must be. It can't be anyone else.'

Michael took a cautious step towards the desk. Nell, who
could not have approached that figure for all the money in the
world, watched him.

'Look at this,' he said, in the same soft voice.

'What is it?'

'An oilskin packet. Sealed as well as anything could be
sealed down here.' He lifted it up gingerly. Showers of dust
came away, and Nell shuddered.

'Handwritten pages,' said Michael, cautiously unwrapping
the oilskin.

'A diary?'

'Some kind of record, at any rate. The top page is dated
January 1880. Let's take them upstairs and close this place up
again. We can report what we've found in the morning – although
I'm not sure who we actually report it to.'

'I'd better phone Inspector Brent. He'd know the procedure.'
Nell's eyes were on the oilskin package. She said, 'But before
we even attempt to look at those papers, let's go back upstairs
to the ordinary world and have a wash and a drink – oh, and
something to eat.'

They were both so covered with dust and dirt that Nell
suggested they took turns to shower.

'And let's eat your casserole before we even try reading
those pages,' said Michael. 'I don't know about you, but I'm
ravenous and it smells terrific. I didn't know it was such hungry
work exploring subterranean rooms.'

For a moment there was an echo of Brad's expression – I'm
extraordinarily hungry – but it was a soft and benign echo.

There was an intimacy in finding clean towels for Michael, then leaving him to open the wine while Nell showered after him. While she was doing so, he called through the bathroom door that he would check on the casserole if that was all right.

'Give it a stir if it needs it,' shouted Nell. 'There's a wooden spoon on the work surface somewhere.' She pulled on clean trousers and a loose shirt, and padded down to the kitchen. Michael had stirred the casserole and had poured her a glass of wine. His hair was slightly damp from the shower, and Nell wanted to reach out to touch it. Instead, she ladled out the casserole and passed him the bread.

'I think,' he said, between mouthfuls, 'that we might have found the – the core of the problem, don't you? Down there in the cellar, I mean.'

'The unhallowed spirit?' said Nell, smiling. 'The troubled soul that can't rest until it gets Christian burial – or burial according to whatever it believed in?'

'Don't mock me, you heartless wench, it's in all the best traditions of ghosts, in fact you said that yourself.'

'I'm not mocking you. I still don't believe it all – not logically and sanely. But then I remember what happened to Beth – and Alice's journal and Harriet's.'

'And Elvira talking about the man who tried to find her – the man she said must never find Harriet or she might lose her sanity,' said Michael.

'Yes.' Nell realized they were both looking across the room, to where the oilskin package lay on a low table. She said, 'Can you eat any more casserole? In that case, I'll dunk everything in the sink and bring the cheese and fruit over to the fire.'

Between them they carefully peeled away the oilskin covering and drew out the sheaf of papers. The writing was legible, although the ink was faded in places, and here and there the paper was spotted with brown mould.

With the fire burning brightly in the hearth and the curtains drawn against the night, they sat together on the sofa and began to read Brooke Crutchley's journal.

TWENTY-THREE

December 1880

I never expected to become entangled quite so violently with a lady. But anyone reading these pages may be familiar with that sudden lightning-sizzle of emotion that sears through the mind so that one is unable to think of anything else.

I must qualify that statement, because for some of the time I have certainly managed to think of other things, although that may be because I must. The poets talk about counting the world well lost for love, which I dare say is all very well for poets, who seem able to live on about half of nothing and appear to have no responsibilities, and who think nothing of starving in garrets where they usually end up with a galloping consumption. I see no benefit in any of that, and certainly not in wasting away for love's sake. I enjoy my food and think of myself as a robust figure of a man with a healthy appetite. (Only the unkindly-disposed would call me portly.)

Nor do I have any family responsibilities. (I do not count the distant cousin living in Staffordshire.) But there are other responsibilities in life, and mine are towards my customers. Clockmaking is a very precise craft, and my father would have been proud of the way I had carried on the business I had inherited. 'Brooke, my boy,' he would have said, 'you can be proud of what you have achieved.' Although he would have added: 'Not too proud, mind.' He was strict on self-pride and the vanities.

What he did often say was that I needed a son to carry on the business. 'A good, steady boy who can continue Crutchley's Clockmakers,' he used to say. 'So take a wife, Brooke, and get a son, and remember it's better to marry than to burn.'

I would certainly have taken a wife, if there was any possibility that the wife I wanted – the only wife I could ever have taken – was likely to accord me a second look.

Elizabeth Marston. The simple act writing the name on this page sends a spike of such fierce longing through me that—

Perhaps I shouldn't go into that. Instead, I'll record that she's daughter of the Honourable Roland Marston of Marston House. The Marstons are landed gentry, padded against the world's chills by old money, and there's even said to be some kind of connection to royalty, although personally I've always doubted that.

But what with their money and their land and their fabled link to Saxe-Coburg, no matter how much I might yearn for Elizabeth – and yearn I have done – no artisan clockmaker could aspire to such a marriage.

I haven't exactly *aspired*, but I have hoped. I have hoped for many years, and I have woven dreams in which I rescued Elizabeth from assorted dangers, or in which I became heir to fabulous fortunes and titles making me an acceptable suitor. I know it's absurd and even pitiful to recount a portly clockmaker visualizing himself braving burning buildings or runaway carriages, but I did.

Today those dreams and hopes have died. They died between the eggs and bacon and the morning post, on a spring morning, with the birds gossiping in the trees and the meadows just becoming spangled with yellow and gold.

It was in my newspaper, in black, hateful print. And I am writing this at my little dining table, my breakfast congealing on my plate.

> 'The betrothal has been announced between William Lee, son of Sir James and Lady Lee of Shropshire, and Elizabeth Alexandra Marston, only daughter of the Honourable Roland Marston of Marston House. The marriage will take place on New Year's Day, 1881.'

Later

I've cut it out, that detestable oblong of print, and pasted it into this diary. I keep rereading it and, every time I do so, the words burn a little deeper into my soul.

William Lee. Thin and pale, with a scholar's stoop and an arid soul. How much say did old Roland Marston give Elizabeth over the match, I wonder?

They never tell you, those poets and those lovers, that hatred and agony can take on solid substance on a green and gold spring morning, or that it can smell of newly-fried bacon and eggs.

January 1881

The marriage has indeed taken place. I was not invited, of course – I dare say neither the aristocratic Marstons nor the patrician Lees are even aware of my existence, and if they were, they would hardly include a common clockmaker in the guests.

I was there, though, watching the ceremony from behind a pillar in the church. She wore white velvet, with a little fur-lined cape, and carried a sheaf of Christmas roses. While they signed the register, I slipped out through the chancel door and stood in the concealment of the yew tree until they came out.

I don't care for that Paul Pry image of myself, but it's what I did. I stood there, on the crisp, cold January morning, and I saw those two – my Elizabeth and that man – come out through the church doors, with bells ringing and choirs caterwauling and everyone laughing and throwing rice, and my stomach rebelled and I had to turn away to be sick behind a wall, because I could not bear it – I simply could not bear seeing them together. Mr and Mrs William Lee. I think it was then, straightening up from the spasms of sickness, wiping my mouth on my handkerchief, that the black madness entered my heart.

Tonight I shall lie wakeful in my bed upstairs, imagining the marriage night, every step of the way. A firelit bedchamber in Mallow House, snow crusting the window panes outside . . . She will lie warm and soft in scented sheets, waiting for him . . .

He'll go to her bed with a book of sonnets or some meta-physical poet's works, and I wouldn't put it past him to forget to remove his spectacles from his nose when he turns back the sheets . . .

April 1881

Today I sat three rows behind my Elizabeth in church and feasted my eyes on the little tendrils escaping from her bonnet and clustering over the nape of her neck. And the whiteness of her neck as it emerges from the collar of her gown . . . Is she happy with him? Is he good to her? When he bends his head in prayer, he looks exactly like a pale-brown vulture. I never before wished a man dead, but by God, I wish this one dead!

My father used to say that hatred is one of the devil's favourite guises.

November 1881

> 'Mr and Mrs William Lee of Mallow House, Marston Lacy, in the County of Shropshire, are happy and proud to announce the birth of a daughter, Elvira Victoria, on 10th November.'

Of course I should have expected that! Or did I believe theirs would be a marriage of convenience: separate rooms, separate beds, separate bodies? Didn't I know, deep down, that the grasshopper, the juiceless bookworm, would mate with the dragonfly? Oh Elizabeth . . .

The hatred walks through my workshop and my house every night now. The only place where I can find the smallest fragment of peace is in my workshop. But sometimes even there I feel the darkness enclosing me, and it's a darkness that whispers there are things that can be done to soothe an aching heart and burning loins, and ways to make an unwilling lady yield her body, if not her heart . . . If only I could have one night with her I believe this hunger would be quenched for ever. Just one night . . .

'The writing changes a bit on the next page,' said Nell as Michael paused to reach for his wine.

'Yes. It's the same person writing it, though. D'you want to keep reading?'

'No,' said Nell, 'but it's like opening up the cellar earlier – not knowing will be worse.'

'There's rather a lot still to read,' he said, looking at the papers.

'Are you saying we could be here all night?'

Michael turned his head slowly and looked at her. Nell had thought she was being very cool and very controlled about this, but when he looked at her in this way, a bolt of desire seemed to slice through her entire body.

'I wish I could be,' he said, then made a half-angry gesture, as if there was something he could no longer bear to resist, and pulled her against him.

His first kiss was gentle and almost questioning, but when she responded instantly and eagerly, the gentleness accelerated into passion. Through mounting delight and desire, Nell thought the emotion flaring up between them was so intense it was as if the air around them was becoming charged with electricity. She clung to him, lost to everything but the intense pleasure coursing through her. So, after all, those nerves and emotions she had thought gone were still there – alive and clamouring for attention.

When he finally released her, she leaned against him, strongly aware of the warmth of his body.

'Do I apologize?' he said, his arms still round her. 'Would you like to smack my face?'

'Oh Michael,' said Nell, turning her head upwards to look at him. 'That's the last thing I want to do to you.'

He smiled, his eyes narrowing in the way that was already familiar. 'I think I wanted to kiss you like that since that first day,' he said.

'I think I wanted it since about the second day.'

When he kissed her again, this time Nell leaned back against the settee's arm and he moved closer until they were lying against each other, their bodies locked together. And incredibly and blessedly, there was no shadowy ghost – these emotions were so different from the ones she had felt for Brad, it was as if they were coming from a wholly different source – a source she had not suspected existed.

Eventually, he sat up, his hair dishevelled, a faint colour touching his cheekbones. 'I should stop,' he said. 'Otherwise I don't think I'll be able to stop . . .'

'I got beyond that point ten minutes ago,' said Nell. 'I can't stop at all now. I don't want to stop. Kiss me again – oh God, yes, that's good . . .'

It was natural and unforced, and it was so wildly exciting that Nell thought she might either faint or burst into tears from sheer delight. His hands on her body were tentative and then not tentative at all, and it felt as if they were melting into one another.

He drew back briefly before entering her. 'Oh God,' he said. 'Is it all right – I mean can we— Because I haven't got—'

'It's all right,' said Nell, understanding. 'Long-term contra-
ceptive implant.'

She thought, afterwards, that the words ought to have
shattered the mood, but they did not. The firelight danced
over the walls, and the scent of woodsmoke and wine filled
the room, and the climax, when it came, was a sweet, deep
explosion. He cried out and pulled her against him, his hair
soft against her naked shoulder, and Nell wanted to stay like
this for ever. Against his shoulder, she said drowsily,
'Skyrockets and exploding rainbows. Oh Michael,' and felt
his arms tighten.

'Shooting stars and supernova,' he said. 'Thank you, my
love.'

'Did you call me your love?' said Nell, registering this after
several minutes.

'I did, didn't I? I think I was trying it out,' said Michael.
'But it sounds good, doesn't it? As if it fits?'

'Yes,' said Nell slowly. 'Yes, it does.' She sat up. 'D'you
know what I'd like now? Don't grin like that. I was going to
say a cup of tea.'

'You're a constant delight,' he said. 'But now you mention
it, a cup of tea would be exactly right.'

Nell stood up and pulled on the shirt she had been wearing
and that had been discarded so frantically a short while
ago.

'You look amazingly sexy wearing just a shirt,' said Michael,
watching her.

'You look amazingly sexy wearing nothing at all. Oh, are
you getting dressed? What a pity.'

'Well, just for a while,' he said, reaching for his sweater.
'I wouldn't guarantee that it's for the entire evening, though.'

Nell went out to the kitchen to put on the kettle, and Michael
followed her. It seemed entirely natural that he should reach
for the mugs and set them out while the kettle came to the
boil.

'After we've drunk the tea, do we return to Brooke?' he
said.

'Yes, let's. We might have to hand the journal over to the
police or the coroner or somebody in the morning, so let's
find out as much as we can before we do that.'

'At the moment I feel quite sorry for him, although I feel

sorry for anybody who isn't me tonight,' said Michael. 'Poor old Brooke and his unrequited passion.'

'But he had his work,' said Nell. 'And his books.'

30th November 1884

Like many another man suffering from an unrequited passion, I have turned to books for solace over the last few years. My father had a large library – although his tastes ran to the collected sermons of worthy churchmen and such moral tales as *The Pilgrim's Progress*. I grew up with Bible tracts and the New Testament – my father was inclined to eschew the Old Testament on account of the more robust activities of some of its peoples. He did not consider, for example, the Genesis account of the sin of Onan to be suitable for mixed congregations, although I always felt rather sorry for Onan, who was slain by the Lord for the mere accident of spilling his seed on the ground. These things happen. Nor did my father condone all of the Old Testament, considering St Paul on the subject of temple prostitutes, and Leviticus talking about fornication, unnecessarily descriptive. I believe he told the vicar at St Paul's that if these passages were ever part of a sermon, he (Father) would walk out. The vicar agreed with these views, although pointed out that a good deal of blame must be laid at the door of the later translators, King James included.

Given my father's outlook on matters of the flesh, I sometimes wonder how I ever came to be born at all, and I'm not surprised my mother died, quietly and unobtrusively, when I was two years old.

However, as well as the religious works, my father also had a shelf of local legends and folklore, in which he took considerable interest. As a boy I was not allowed to read them, and it was only after his death that I did so.

You'd think it a relatively harmless subject. Admittedly, there were a few slightly prurient explanations as to the tribal deflowering of virgins and how best to achieve this without loss of honour or prestige before the rest of the clans. Also directions for what apparel to wear when leaping through the bonfire – although authorities differed on that point, the purists holding the ritual would be tainted if undergarments were worn, the pragmatists recommending several thick layers of

flannel in case of errant sparks from the fire. But in the main
the books were innocent enough, although I'd question the
symbolism of some of the practices.

But – and here's the real nub of the matter – there's a
dangerously thin line between legend and lore and— Well,
the deeper, darker forces.

We've lost most of the old beliefs – we've forced them out
with our machines and our smoke-belching industries and our
mechanical dragons rumbling along iron tracks: I heard only
last week that the railway is to be brought quite near to Marston
Lacy, and while I suppose that's progress and necessary, I'm
sad at the despoiling of the countryside.

Despite all this, the ancient beliefs still linger. They've come
down to us from a time when the world was young, and when
strange things still lingered in its crevasses and chasms and
in the lairs of mountains and subterranean caverns. And for the
prepared or the curious mind, there are signposts pointing
them out.

For me, the first signpost appeared when I found a book on
my father's shelves called *The Ingoldsby Legends*, collected
by the Reverend Richard Barham, purportedly written by one
Thomas Ingoldsby of Tappington Manor. I suppose my father
acquired it because he thought anything written by a minister
of the church was suitable and praiseworthy. But although I'm
not a betting man (too cautious!) I'd lay any money that he
never read it. In fact, Thomas Ingoldsby was Barham's pen-
name. The legends he's plundered are parodies or pastiches,
but they are based on genuine old myths and beliefs.

Living quietly in this small corner of the English countryside,
making a modestly prosperous living, I have begun to trace
some of those beliefs. It's a curious experience – like picking
up a black and bloodied string and feeling your way along
until you reach its core. I'm not entirely sure I ought to be
doing this, but that dark string, once picked up, is impossible
to put down. I shall go just a little further along.

At times, emerging from reading of old tracts and ancient
chronicles, I am uneasily aware of something seeping into my
mind, like a thin trickle of brackish water. Is that how madness
starts? No, I won't believe that, I *won't* . . .

I shall go on with my research – I want to find the genesis
of those legends.

June 1885

My studies over these past months have been innocent enough, although – I shall be frank – they have not been studies I should want my neighbours to know about. That fine line between legend and something more dangerous, again. That trickle of brackish water . . . But it has stopped now, I know it has. I am entirely sane.

I have reread that last sentence and am shocked to see how deeply my pen scored into the page when I wrote that I was sane. I think I shall not write in this diary again. It sometimes frightens me.

TWENTY-FOUR

January 1886

I am coming to the conclusion that my books must be stored somewhere less visible. As the collection grows, they become more noticeable to visitors to the house, and some of the titles on the spine are – well, I'll use the word *dubious*.

Over the last few years I've made a number of trips outside Marston Lacy to scour second-hand bookshops – that despised railway has proved its value after all, for travel is now very easy indeed! Sometimes private libraries are broken up and sold when the owner dies. I've attended several of those; in fact, I believe I've become known as a collector of curios. 'Ah, Mr Crutchley,' a book dealer said to me last month at a library sale near Chirk. 'We wondered if you might be along. Now there's a little volume here you might fine interesting.' And twice I've been sent an invitation to such sales. That pleases me greatly.

It will be very inconvenient to move the books. But it might be worse to leave them where they are. People often come to my house – I am a church sidesman at St Paul's and also on its John Howard Committee for prison reform and visiting. This last is a very worthy organization – I was flattered when they invited me to serve on it, and I like to think I have been of value. Prison reform is a worthwhile cause – no matter a man's crime, depriving him of his freedom and liberty should be sufficient punishment without forcing on him the indignities and deprivations rife in so many gaols.

All this means there are frequent meetings to attend or arrange, and it has become the custom for many of these meetings to be held at my house. St Paul's is an estimable old church, but the vestry is shockingly draughty and a man could catch his death there in cold weather, even swathed in wintergreen. (I am convinced my chilblains can be directly attributed to several overlong meetings in the place.)

As well as church and prison reform meetings, salesmen call at my house, representing the manufacturing concerns that supply copper, brass and enamel for my clocks. I am a respected customer – I order liberally and settle my accounts promptly.

Then there are my own customers: often important people such as estate managers for the big houses hereabouts. Lord Somebody will decide he wants a long-case clock for his drawing room. Sir Someone-Else wishes to commission a carriage clock for his mantel. People want wedding presents, christening gifts. I like to invite them into my sitting room and offer refreshment. A glass of Madeira for the gentlemen, sherry for the ladies. It amuses me to see the surprise on their faces – they don't expect such refinement from a common clockmaker.

It would not do for any of these people to see some of the books I possess. The *Compendium Maleficarum*, or the *Petit Albert*, which is subtitled '*An eighteenth-century grimoire of natural and cabalistic magic*'. Or the *Sworn Book of Honorius*. That's an abridged version, of course, and printed about a hundred years ago, but much of the material is genuinely from its thirteenth-century source, and it's as forceful and awesome as when Honorius of Thebes gathered together a conference of magicians who agreed to combine their knowledge into one volume. I also have a late eighteenth-century copy of the words of the legendary sorcerer St Cyprian, (before his conversion to Christianity, naturally), but the provenance of the original work is so dubious that I do not give this one especial value in my collection. Still, it would not do for people to see it.

The ground floor of my house is a showroom, displaying finished clocks available for sale. A public area. The workshop across the courtyard is also open to people who care to look round at clocks on which I am currently working.

But beneath the workshop is a surprisingly large stone cellar. It's considerably older than the house itself – my father believed there had been a lodge on the land before our own house was built. He said it would have been the gatehouse to a long-vanished estate owned by some forgotten feudal baron, and that we trod in exalted paths.

Later

I have inspected the underground room, and I believe it can be made into a very good secret library. The trapdoor leading down to it is inconveniently tucked away by the side of the stove, but I do not mind that. It means the entrance is hidden from view.

July 1886

I have done the deed. I have built shelves to line the walls, and my books are arranged on them. After a struggle, I managed to bring a desk down the steps and a small wing chair to stand in one corner. There are oil lamps, of course. Rugs on the stone floor to soften and warm it. And this diary. I shall keep it in a drawer, wrapped in oilskin to preserve it.

And, as I thought, I find it easy enough to lift the trapdoor and go down the stone steps. I even fashioned a handle for the underside of the trapdoor so it can be easily lowered while I am down here. I am toying with the notion of fixing a bolt as well, in case I should ever have reason to hide. I cannot imagine why I would want to hide from anyone, but life is strange and unexpected.

I like it down here. The stone room is as snug and dry as any man could wish, and as I read or write, the oil lamps cast pools of light over the rows of books. I'm writing this entry here now. And every time I descend the stone steps, pulling the trapdoor closed over my head, I have the feeling I am entering a different time – a time when the world is still shrouded in myth and magic, and when it is still raw from the agonies of its own birth.

Fanciful words for a common clockmaker! But I've reread them and I will not scratch them out! They make a good note on which to end these chronicles!

August 1888

I had not intended to take up these diaries again, but today something has happened that I must record.

I see it's two years since I wrote anything, so, for tidiness's sake (and my own self-esteem), I shall set down that the two years have been filled, not unpleasantly, with work, with study, and with being part of the small community which makes up Marston Lacy and the surrounding villages. Recently, I was even asked to join a new Chamber of Commerce body, which is to come under the aegis of Shrewsbury and one or two of the other big nearby towns. I agreed, of course.

But this morning I received a letter that scrapes at the old inner agony afresh and sets it bleeding again. It is from that stoop-shouldered, droop-necked bookworm at Mallow House! Here it is, copied down in its entirety. As I write it, I feel as if venom drips from the nib of my pen on to the page.

> Mallow House,
> Marston Lacy.
>
> Dear Mr Crutchley,
>   You are recommended to me as a clockmaker of some repute . . .

'Some repute', he calls it! I am quite simply the finest clockmaker he will ever find!

> . . . and I should therefore like to commission a long-case clock from your workshop. It is to be a gift for my wife at Christmas.
>   Please call upon me on Friday of this week at midday to discuss your terms.
>   Yours very sincerely,
>   W.S. Lee Esq.

It's gall and wormwood to me to be summoned to Mallow House with no regard for my own convenience. People come to *me* – they seek me out in my workshop.

Shall I go? Dare I? Will *she* be there? The thought of perhaps meeting her – speaking to her, taking her hand – is causing me to tremble violently. I cannot do it.

Later

But I will do it, of course. But oh God, if she is there, let me not stare at her like a moonstruck idiot.

Friday

She was not there. I veer between sick disappointment and relief. Only William Lee was there, and I am glad to report I did not like him. He is dry and dull, and I hope he withers and desiccates like the old parchment of his own books. (Yes, but he is in bed every night with her . . . He fathered a child on to her . . .)

Our discussion took place in the library. It overlooks gardens – gardens where she must often walk, and where she must gather flowers for their rooms or their table. He said he likes to spend most of his time in that room – he sits in it every evening after dinner. Does she sit with him? Perhaps embroidering or reading?

We discussed the commission, and it was agreed that I should prepare sketches and designs for his consideration. The clock is to be a surprise gift, so I am asked not to talk of it to anyone.

I am very glad that I insisted on a price of 150gns for the clock!

August 1888, cont'd

Today Lee came to my workshop and approved my design, which is for a moon-phase clock, with the face of the moon in its own secondary arch-dial above the main dial. It's an intricate task to fashion that part of the workings and ensure the moon's silhouette really does move round to echo the moon's phases, but I have done it before and I shall do it now. I will use blue enamel for the moon and brass for the figuring.

For the rest, there's a bell strike on the hour and an eight-day mechanism. The case for the pendulum will be mahogany, inlaid with rosewood, with a gimp of ebony.

September 1888

This evening, while I was planing and smoothing the mahogany for William Lee's clock, (it's like silk, and it's the colour of *her* hair, glossy and dark), I thought something leaned over my shoulder as if to look more closely at what I was doing: there was a whiff of foetid breath and the impression of a bony finger digging into my neck. I spun round at once, but there was nothing there.

I dare say the cheese I had for supper is to blame. It's well known that roasted cheese can upset the digestion. I shall leave a note for Mrs Figgis, telling her not to serve cheese with my supper in future.

But I can't get rid of the notion that the burning jealousy and the hatred I harbour for William Lee is somehow taking on substance – that it's striding through my workshop, watching its chance to take possession of my mind . . .

I've reread that last sentence, and I know it sounds like the ravings of a disordered mind. But there *is* something in my workshop that wasn't there before, and whatever it is I don't like it.

October 1888

The more I read, the more I find references to music in the ancient beliefs. Music that possesses power over men's minds and souls . . . Orpheus with his lyre, charming the denizens of hell into giving him back his lady . . . The medieval dances of death, with the victims forced by demons to dance until they dropped . . . The beckoning cadences of the Plague Piper wearing his glaring red mask of agony, leading his victims to the twin Towers of Fever and Madness . . . The *el diablo* chord, which the medievals believed could summon the devil.

And a strange and eerie chant from the world's earliest time that is believed to have power over the dead and the ability to cast men into deep, dreamless sleep.

October 1888, cont'd

William Lee's clock is almost finished and will remain in my workshop until just before Christmas, when it will be taken to Mallow House. It's a beautiful piece of work. I never made a better clock.

And yet, and yet.

When I look at it I see that something has got into the making that I never intended. Is it the outline of the moon in the arch-dial? Has it a sly, leering look as if something has given the serene features a vicious tweak? And the pendulum case itself – if I look at it in a certain light, the grain seems to form itself into a writhing human creature. Does it resemble Hogarth's images of Bedlam, with the poor lunatics trying to escape their bleak prison? Looking out at the world with despair and hatred?

Hatred. That word again.

Only last month I witnessed a case of hatred that had tragic results. A fight between two men in the Black Boar – one accusing the other of violating his sister. I was there, drinking a glass of ale with one or two acquaintances – it's a convivial place of an evening, the Black Boar, and I like to share the company of my fellow men sometimes. It reminds me that there's an ordinary and sane world beyond the shadowy, secret library.

But on that night an ugly fight broke out between the brother and the seducer. It began as a verbal battle, but it ended with the seducer being felled to the ground and smashing his head against the stone chimney breast. They summoned the local medic at once, and I helped in staunching the blood, but the man was already dead, and the jealous brother was taken to Shrewsbury Gaol. He stood trial and was found guilty. He will hang this coming Monday. A dreadful waste of two lives – three, if you count the girl, for this will taint her life for years to come. It determines me to fight and vanquish this scalding hatred that courses through me and fills me with bile.

October 1888 cont'd

But all the resolve and determination in the world does not quench this overwhelming desire for Elizabeth. Perhaps if I had not been inside her house – if I had not sat on chairs where she must have sat, touched doors and walls she must brush past every day . . .

Just once. If I could have her just once. But how? *How?* I would not use force on her, but if only there was some way . . .

Some months ago Barham's *Ingoldsby Legends* led me to the dark root of his parody of the Hand of Glory legend. He clearly knew the original source of the belief, of course, and after some searching I knew it as well. It has its core in music – music again! – in an eerie sequence of music that is credited with the power to open locks and cast every person in a house into a deep and dreamless slumber.

Every person in the house . . . William Lee, the child, their servants . . .

How far can I believe this? How much of it is old wives'
tales, the beliefs of the credulous, the wish-fulfilment of the
bereft or the lonely?

Even if it were true, I cannot do it. I dare not. In any case,
my reading has informed me of what's needed to set the
enchantment working and the ingredients are impossible to
obtain.

Or are they? For on Monday morning, by nine o'clock, the
one ingredient that would normally be beyond my power to
acquire will be there for the taking.

Next Monday afternoon I am to attend a meeting of the
John Howard Group at Shrewsbury Gaol.

And at 8 a.m. on that day they will have hanged the murderer
who killed his sister's seducer in the Black Boar.

October cont'd

I am moved to copy down parts of the recipe for creating the
Hand of Glory – partly so I have the information in a safe
place other than on my shelves. There are several versions,
but this one, from *Petit Albert*, dating back to 1722, is the
most detailed.

> 'Take the right or left hand of a felon who is hanging from
> a gibbet beside a highway. Wrap it in part of a funeral pall
> and, so wrapped, squeeze it well to drain all blood. Then
> put it into an earthenware vessel with zimat, nitre, salt and
> long peppers, the whole well powdered. Leave it in this
> vessel for a fortnight, then take out and expose it to full
> sunlight during the dog days until it becomes quite dry.
> Next, make of it a candle with the fat of a gibbeted felon,
> virgin wax, sesame and ponie, and use the Hand of Glory
> as a candlestick to hold this candle when lighted.'

The practice of hanging a felon from a gibbet hasn't existed
in this country for a century or more so I cannot follow this
part to the absolute letter. But I believe – and trust – that the
hand of any hanged murderer will suffice. The dog days are
a difficulty – October in England can scarcely be called sufficiently hot to warrant that term; however, there is another
version of the enchantment which says this:

'If the sun be not powerful enough, dry the Hand in an oven heated with vervain and fern.'

That I can do with no difficulty.

The poet Robert Southey places the Hand in the possession of the enchanter Mohareb, when he would 'lull to sleep Yohak, the giant guardian of the caves of Babylon'. Southey writes:

> 'A murderer on the stake had died;
> I drove the vulture from his limbs, and lopt
> The hand that did the murder, and drew up
> The tendon strings to close its grasp;
> And in the sun and wind
> Parch'd it, nine weeks exposed.'

Nine weeks is a long time, but everyone knows poets are given to exaggerating, so I shall accept the *Petit Albert* direction of two weeks and use the oven instead of the hot sun.

29th October 1888

In two days' time I will be in the grounds of Shrewsbury Gaol, and it will rest on my ingenuity as to whether I can do what has to be done to the body of the hanged murderer. It seems fitting, although macabre, that I shall carry out my grisly task on the Eve of All Hallows. Will the powers said to walk abroad on that night stand at my side as I go about my work?

If ever I believed myself to have crossed the line from sanity, I think I have done so tonight. Tonight I believe I am mad.

TWENTY-FIVE

1st November 1888: 10.00 a.m.

I have resolved to set down a clear and concise account of what has happened.

I rose early on Monday 31st and sat quietly in the room above the showrooms, looking out on to the High Street, waiting for the town clock to chime eight. I was not seeing the familiar shops and people though; in my mind's eye was a vivid picture of the condemned man being led from his cell in Shrewsbury Gaol across the courtyard to the execution shed. It's quite a short walk – I know, for I've visited the place twice with the Howard Committee. So I was able to walk with the doomed man in my imagination, my steps matching his – although when the clock finally struck the hour it coincided with Mrs Figgis, who, according to custom, had arrived to cook my breakfast. My mental images of the condemned man being lead to the execution shed became inextricably mingled with Mrs Figgis's voluble catalogue of local gossip and the scent of bacon and eggs frying in the pan.

I made a good breakfast, though. It would not have done the man any good if I had gone hungry for the morning,

The Howard Committee set off sharp at half-past one. Measured in miles, Shrewsbury is not a very long way from Marston Lacy, but it's not an easy journey, and so we had hired a conveyance. There were six of us in all, so it was somewhat crowded. I am not overfond of travelling – the jolting of the carriages always makes me feel sick. My father used to say it jumbled a man's insides to travel at such unnatural speeds, and on that journey I had the feeling he might have been right, because by the time we reached Shrewsbury town I was sweating and dabbing a handkerchief to my lips. This, however, was usual for me on any journey, although I will say the knowledge of what I intended to do after the meeting would not have helped.

We toured the prison as arranged and afterwards made our

representations to the governor – a very gentlemanly person he is, humane and far better than some governors we hear about. He was agreeable to our suggestions as to how prisoners might have their lives made a little easier and promised to bring our points up with his superiors.

Tea was served to us – a good blend of tea it was, none of your floor-sweepings for the Howard Committee! It was all very civilized, and I should have found it interesting and worthy if I had not been churning like a seething cauldron inside at the prospect of what lay ahead. I had a plan, of course, but of necessity it was a very sketchy one – there were so many imponderable factors. But I had already marked out one warder as having a shifty and venal eye, whom I thought might make an ally.

The morning's execution was mentioned during our interview with the governor, of course. He said it was a sad affair – a young man's moment of hot-temper and jealousy causing him to take a life and lose his own as a result.

I said, 'At least there is now the long drop, which I think is believed more merciful.'

'Indeed it is. A matter of seconds only. Yes, there have been some dreadful cases of bungling in the past – I have witnessed more than one myself.'

'Tell me,' I said quickly, before the conversation could drift, 'do you still have the tradition of leaving the body to hang for an hour after the execution?'

'Yes, certainly. A small mark of respect. The poor wretch has precious little more.' He paused, and I willed him to go on. After a moment he did. 'We bury them quickly enough afterwards,' he said. 'That man this morning, for instance. He is even now lying in the grave in the yard.'

'And already covered with quicklime, no doubt,' I said. My tone was so light that it could have floated away, and I do not think I betrayed how much depended on his answer.

He said, 'The quicklime will be sprinkled over him tomorrow morning. We allow them twenty-four hours in the grave before we do that. Another mark of respect, and a purely personal one on my part. Quicklime is a vicious agent, you know.'

A rush of relief coursed through me so fiercely I could not speak, only nod, as if the information was of vague interest. I had been prepared to dig through soil and lime – I was wearing thick leather gloves and strong boots – but it would be so much easier and safer without that layer of corrosive, burning lime.

Even so, my courage almost failed me at that point – I wished for nothing but to return home and sit down to the supper Mrs Figgis would have left out for me. But as the group made its way through the prison, I said, 'I shan't be travelling back with you. I have an old aunt in Shrewsbury town I should like to visit.'

This was seen as a perfectly reasonable arrangement. I was considered sensible to take advantage of the opportunity of being in Shrewsbury. There was some slight concern as to how I would get back, however.

'I can spend the night at my aunt's house,' I said, 'and walk along to the railway station in the morning.'

It satisfied them. Shrewsbury General Station is the Shrewsbury to Chester line – part of the Abbey Foregate loop – and a great many trains go through it. I would be able to travel to the halt at Marston Montgomery. It's a three-mile walk from there to Marston Lacy, but there are any number of drays and carters coming and going who would happily take me up.

As we were ushered through the prison precincts, with doors and gates unlocked by the warders every fifteen yards, I deliberately lagged behind and caught the eye of the warder I had noticed earlier. A weasel-faced fellow he was, with a darting, acquisitive eye. Speaking quietly, I asked him in which direction the burial yard lay.

'It's over there,' he said, pointing furtively. His lips formed a sly curve. 'You'd like to take a look, sir? See where we put the murderers?' The words were respectful, the tone was not.

I said, 'It could be interesting. Worth my while.' A pause, the count of five. 'Worth yours too, perhaps,' I said, softly so the others could not hear.

'How much worth?'

'Half a sovereign.' It was a lot, but there was no point in penny-pinching.

'Souvenir of a murderer?' he said. 'Lock of hair, bit of shroud to brag about and make money on? Is that what you're after?'

I said, as frostily as I could, 'Indeed not. But as one of

the Howard Prison Reform Organization, I should like to see the exact conditions in which an executed murderer is buried.'

'Call it what you want,' he said, shrugging. 'Listen, then. Pretend to turn your ankle on the cobbles. I'll take you into the warders' room to strap it up.'

The facility with which he came up with this small plan – a much simpler and better one than my original idea of hiding and waiting until nightfall – indicated he was not unused to such an arrangement. It's a sad reflection on the curiosity of men, but I am in no position to level criticism.

I flatter myself I staged the ankle-turning business neatly. A stumble, a startled cry of pain, and within minutes I was helped into a small room opening off the courtyard, furnished with battered chairs and a table.

'Now then,' said the warder briskly, 'how long d'you want?'

'An hour at least. Two would be better. At a time when no one is around.'

'Ah,' he said. 'I *thought* it was souvenirs you was after. In that case, half a jimmy o'goblin won't be enough. Make it whole one.' It was extortion, pure and simple. I hesitated, and he said, 'You pay me that and I'll come back later and unlock a door to get you out.'

I had worried about this part of the proceedings quite a lot. My plan had been to remain inside the prison all night and find my way out when the morning contingent of warders came on duty. But this new twist would solve it very well for me. I briefly considered how far I could trust this man – it would be easy for him to leave me in the prison all night and deny all knowledge next morning.

But these things work both ways, and I said, very coldly, 'If you cheat me in any way, I shall see to it that you lose your position here and are prosecuted. I am a man of some standing, and I think my word will be believed over yours. I hope that's clear?'

'I won't cheat you,' he said, and I thought there was a ring of sincerity in his tone, so I nodded and handed over the sovereign.

'Good,' he said, tucking it in an inner pocket. 'You got until seven o'clock tonight when the night guard goes round. That do you?'

It was ten minutes to five and already dark. I said, 'That will do very well.'

'I'm off duty at seven. I'll come back just before the hour and we'll go out together. You'll appear to be a visitor I'm seeing out. Simple as can be. From there on it's your business how you get back to wherever you live.'

Any burial ground is a grim place, but that piece of land on the side of Shrewsbury Prison is the eeriest place I have ever encountered.

It was not very large, and although sparse grass grew here and there it had a sick look, as if there was some disease in the soil beneath. It was very dark, but a thin, cold moonlight oozed through the clouds so that I could see the outline of the newly-dug grave near one wall. It's extraordinary how that shape strikes such terror into the heart; seeing it brought every superstition and every grisly legend ever read or dreamed or remembered into my mind. Because one should not disturb the resting place of any man, even that of a murderer, perhaps especially that of a murderer.

The words of the Ingoldsby rhyme ran maddeningly in and out of my head as I approached the grave.

On the lone bleak moor, at the midnight hour,
Beneath the Gallows Tree . . .
The Moon that night, with a grey cold light,
Each baleful object tips . . .

It took considerable resolve to approach the open grave and look down into it and, when I did so, I think I came closer than at any other time to abandoning the whole plan. He lay, imperfectly covered in a winding sheet, his head lolling to one side at an ugly, ungainly angle, his thick, farm-worker's neck swollen and bruised from the hangman's rope. His skin was the colour and consistency of tallow.

I looked round. How likely was it that I could be seen? The burial ground was enclosed on three sides by a high wall, and there were no windows and only one door, which led to the main part of the prison. No one would see me.

And yet I had the feeling that someone did see me – that eyes watched from the shadows and marked what I did. Nerves, nothing more.

The grave was narrower than I had expected and also deeper

– I had assumed the gravediggers would be cursory in their work, and I thought it would be possible to reach down and do what I had to do from ground level. But it was not. Even kneeling at the rim and stretching my hands down as far as possible, I could not reach what lay there. So be it: I would go down into the grave itself. The prospect made my flesh creep, but I was too close to what I wanted to give up now. Down the centuries there have been mad, wild things done in the name of love, but I wonder if there has been anything wilder or madder than what I did that night for love for Elizabeth Lee.

I felt in my pocket to make sure I still had the knives and chisel wrapped in cotton waste, then I sat on the edge of the open grave and slid down into its depths. Showers of dry soil broke away like scabs from a wound, and I landed squarely on the body itself.

It was dreadful. His flesh was soft and pliable in places – I could feel its softness – but in others it was hard and marble-like. I remembered the old country saying about dead men: *they shall grow hard and they shall grow soft.* Rigor mortis, that grotesque solidifying of sinews and flesh, wears off after several hours, and the dead become lumps of flabby meat. This body was in the halfway stage.

I managed to move in the restricted space until I was straddling his stomach. The winding sheet fell back in the process, and the words of *Petit Albert* came into my mind – *take the hand of a felon . . . wrap it in part of a funeral pall . . .*

It was simple to slice off a section of the thin cloth, using one of the knives I had brought, and to fold the fragment in a pocket. But the worst was still ahead of me.

He was, of course, lying with his hands crossed on his breast, and I reached for the right hand. It was in the same semi-hard state as the rest of him – I had no idea if that would make my task easier, but using the larger knife I began my grisly work.

Joint, muscle, nerve . . . For the spell of the dead man's hand . . .

The flesh parted under the knife's blade. No blood, of course. I sawed determinedly, and presently the knife scraped against bone. This would be the difficult part. I reached in my other pocket for the small tooth-edged saw and the chisel.

The worst part was the noise – the rasp of steel against bone. Wrist-bones are quite small and thin, but there are joints, nubbly lumps of gristle and sinew . . . I was using the chisel by that stage, but my hands were so slippery with sweat that several times the blade slid off the bones and gouged into the chest below. But finally the hand lay free, and I lifted it and wrapped it in the fragment of shroud. It was easy enough to hide the stump of the handless arm by folding the rest of the shroud across.

I was shaking badly by the time I clambered out of the grave to wait for the warder's return. As I sat on the diseased grass, I was painfully aware of what lay underneath it. All those bodies of men hanged for murder – probably most of whom had gone to their deaths terrified and struggling, blinded by the hangman's hood, fighting every inch of the way . . . Small wonder the atmosphere of this place was so thick with emotion. Fear, despair, loneliness – they were all here.

It's a vicious thing, quicklime, as the governor had said earlier. It burns and eats its way through flesh and bone, through heart and liver and kidneys . . . When it came to Resurrection Day, there would be precious little left of the killers who lay in this poisoned earth. A few crumbling bones to struggle towards the Lord when he called to them, shreds of hair and flesh holding the bones together.

I make no apology for that dark rhetoric, for in a murderers' burial yard a man may surely become fanciful and see a few ghosts.

1st November cont'd. Evening.

I have followed the instructions of all the recipes as exactly as I can. I have scraped fat from under the skin of the hand and preserved it in a sealed jar. (I took the jar from Mrs Figgis's larder; it had contained potted meat. I washed it very thoroughly, of course.)

The hand is packed in an earthenware pot with the other ingredients and the whole is in the stove in my workshop. And at this time of year I keep the stove lit.

I shall count the next fourteen days very anxiously.

15th November

Today I withdrew from my oven the earthenware pot. The hand is dried and shrunken – the surface resembles old leather and the nails have cracked in the heat. It's repulsive to the touch, but if it gains me my heart's desire . . .

And now, in this secret room, I shall create the candle out of the fat squeezed from the hand. Tomorrow night I shall go to Mallow House. But tonight my thoughts and my dreams are filled with *her* – with Elizabeth.

In two days' time shall I have finally slaked this burning desire that has constantly gnawed at my heart and my loins all these years?

17th November

It's unlikely that anyone will ever read these pages, just as it's unlikely anyone will ever know the part I played in what has happened. But just in case—

I set out for Mallow House shortly before midnight. With me I had the objects fashioned in the secret library – the dried hand, the candle. A tinder box so I could light the candle. And the chant that seemed to me, from my readings, to strengthen the spell.

(Have I just written those words? Have I really admitted to believing I created a spell . . . ? The words are imbued with madness. If I was mad on the night I made the decision to do all this, I was certainly mad last night.)

No one saw me slink through Marston Lacy, of that I am sure. It's a quiet place in the main – that violent death in the Black Boar was a very exceptional case indeed. Once clear of the houses I turned into Blackberry Lane and, as I did so, I heard a church clock chiming. Midnight. The keystone of night's black arch. The sound came clearly across the fields and, as the last chime faded, in a nearby tree an owl gave a soft hoot and I heard its wings beating on the air as it went in search of prey. Was the midnight chime the spring that had released it from a daylight spell?

As I drew level with what had been the carriageway to the old manor house, I was startled to hear soft sounds very close by. They unnerved me for a moment, then I thought it must be the wind sighing in the trees, or the owl again, or a fox

– they sometimes give strange cries, foxes. But once past the ruined road to the old manor, I realized with a sick jolt that the sounds were of my own making. I was singing, very softly, the old Ingoldsby rhyme.

'Open lock to the dead man's knock . . .
Fly bolt, and bar, and band . . .
Nor move, nor swerve, joint, muscle or nerve,
At the spell of the dead man's hand!'

The rhyme meant nothing, and it possessed no power. It was simply old Richard Barham's mischievous version of the real spell. But I found it comforting to murmur the words and hum the cadences it seemed to form. It felt like having a companion, and midnight's a desperate and lonely place when your mind is cloaked in madness.

No lights showed in Mallow House – I was glad of that. The gate made a faint rasp as I pushed it open – a scratchiness that sounded like a hoarse voice whispering. *Beware.* The gardens were silver and black from the moonlight, and the house itself was drained of all colour. I looked up at it, wondering which window was Elizabeth's, then went round to the back. I did not know, not for sure, that there would be a garden door or a kitchen door, but a house of this size would not have just one entrance.

The paths were dry and soft, and my feet made no sound. Once something scuttled across my path, and I started back, and once I thought there was a movement at one of the downstairs windows, but it was only my own reflection in the glass.

The door I sought opened on to what looked like the sculleries. I felt for the handle and tried it. Locked, of course, and very firmly. My heart was beating so fast by this time that it would have been almost audible to anyone in earshot, but no one was there to hear. No one was there to see, either, when I drew the hand of glory from my pocket and set the candle in its wizened grasp. When I lit the taper it crackled sullenly, then finally flared into a thick, unpleasant-smelling light.

I took a deep breath, lifted the hand aloft, and very softly began to chant the spell. And now it was not Barham's light, mocking parody I had sung in the lane, it was the real thing. The ancient, powerful sorcery from the time when the world was still cooling from the fires in which it had been forged. The language and the music of gods and daemons.

Sweat prickled my whole body, and for a moment it seemed that nothing was going to happen. Sick disappointment flooded me. The spell was an empty charm, a blown egg, the enchantment was husked dry, and the sorcery that was to have given me that precious hour with my lady had frayed to cobwebs and vanished.

And then there was a soft click, and then another, and the sound of a steel bar being drawn back. The door of Mallow House swung ajar.

TWENTY-SIX

As I stepped across the threshold, the smeary light from the candle fell across the stone flags of the scullery floor. I lifted it aloft, and the light washed over a large dresser set against the wall. There was a big range, faintly glowing with heat, and a rocking chair in one corner with a rag rug in front of it. It was a kitchen that might be found in any fair-sized house in any part of the country – but it was *her* kitchen. She would often be here, ordering meals, supervising household tasks. Somewhere over my head she would be lying in her bed. Sleeping? I wanted her to be asleep. I wanted them all to be asleep. I believed myself beyond sanity, but not so far that I wanted to inflict hurt on anyone.

I went out of the kitchen to the big oak-floored hall where William Lee had met me that morning. A copper jug filled with chrysanthemums and dahlias stood on a low chest, and I imagined Elizabeth picking the flowers and arranging them. My heartbeat increased to a painful intensity.

It was very quiet. Through the half-open door of the library I could see the dull glow of a fire with a guard in front of it. There was a faint scent of woodsmoke, and I remembered how Lee had told me he liked to sit in his library in the evenings. Was he there now? If he was not, my plan would crumble into nothing, for I would not dare enter Elizabeth's bedroom with him there. I tiptoed forward. Let him be there, please let him be in his library, asleep over his books. It was only a little after midnight, not a late hour for scholars . . .

At first I thought the library was empty, then I saw the slumped outline in the big wing-chair near the fire. I watched him for a moment. If he slept the normal sleep of a man nodding over a book in a warm room he must surely sense the presence of an intruder. The shrivelled hand felt warm now to my grasp, and once the foetid tallow dripped on to my skin, making me gasp. But William Lee did not move. Dear God, it was working, the ancient shred of sorcery was actually working.

I went from the room and began to ascend the stairs. The light came with me, the grisly lump of flesh taken from the burial ground shivering and sending shadows chasing across the walls. Did I sing at that point? Truly, I have no idea, but I could hear the chant clearly inside my head.

At the head of the stairs was a large landing, L-shaped, with doors opening off and two windows with low sills, partly curtained. Which one was *hers*? I chose at random, moving softly, still not knowing who else might be in the house – a servant, a cook, someone to look after the child.

The first room was empty, but comfortably furnished as a guest room. Did they have guests to stay – his family, hers? Friends? Bitter jealousy rose up at the thought of them smiling and welcoming people into the house – of Elizabeth preparing this room, planning meals . . .

She was in a big, square room at the back of the house – it would overlook the lawns and the herb garden. She lay in a wide bed – the jealousy jabbed again, but I had been prepared for this – the covers drawn over her. Her hair was braided for the night. In the flickering light it was like two ropes of polished chestnut. Her eyes were closed, and there was a faint sheen of moisture on her eyelids, and a shaft of such love for her sliced through me; it felt as if something was wrenching my heart in two pieces.

I put out a hand to touch her face – her skin felt like cool satin and her hair was so soft and sensuous . . . But then, between one heartbeat and the next, I knew this was as far as I could go. She was too defenceless, too serene. I felt the madness drain from my heart.

I am not sure how long I stood there, the house silent and still all around me, the light still flickering over the bed, but I think it was quite a long time. Then there was the soft beating of wings beyond the window and the shriek of some small creature in the dark gardens as the owl pounced on its prey. It penetrated my frozen stillness, and I turned to the burning tallow and blew it out. It guttered almost at once, but it left a thin ghost-trail of itself on the air and a thread of evil-smelling smoke.

In the bed, Elizabeth turned her head and opened her eyes.

She saw me at once – I was standing against the partly-curtained window, the light behind me, and she must have seen an anonymous outline that she recognized was not her husband. She started back in the bed, one hand clutching the sheets about her in a gesture of defence – needless, of course, for I would not have hurt her. A door opened and closed below us, and there was the sound of someone coming up the stairs. Elizabeth screamed, and the footsteps quickened at once. I heard William Lee's voice calling out.

'Elizabeth? What's wrong?'

He ran along the landing and burst into the room, and his eyes widened in horror. What he saw must have been as clear as a curse – the dark figure of a man standing in the room, his wife half sitting up in the bed, her hair tousled. I thrust the now-cooling candle and its macabre holder into my coat pocket and prepared to make a bolt for it, although where I would have bolted to, I have no idea. William stood between me and the door, and there was a forty-feet drop from the window, even if I could have got it open.

That was when he shocked me. He said, in a dreadful, sneering voice, 'So this time you've brought your filthy whoring into the house, you cheating bitch.'

He was across the room in two strikes, his hand raised, and I waited for her to flinch, to defend herself verbally and physically. Indeed, I was ready to leap to her defence and be damned to them recognizing me.

But she said – and her sneer matched his and overrode it, 'If I'm a whore, who made me one! If you could ever raise your manhood above half-mast I mightn't have looked elsewhere!'

'A decent woman would know nothing of such things,' said Lee. 'You were a slut before I married you – and your father glad to pay me to be rid of you and your whoring! If I had known that at the time—' He turned to me. 'As for you, whoever you are, get out of my house, for there is no gratification for your fornication here tonight!'

Through my panic and horror I realized I was standing with my back to the bedroom – in the dark bedroom he could not see my features. I started across the room, keeping my shoulders hunched and my face turned away, hoping I could get to the stair before he saw who I was, praying he would not attack me. But once outside I paused on the landing. My mind was still reeling from what I had heard, but if Lee intended violence towards Elizabeth . . .

I heard him say, 'Tomorrow, Elizabeth, you will leave this house and go to wherever you choose. You will leave our daughter with me. I will not have her brought up by a trollop.'

'Did you really think Elvira was your daughter?' said Elizabeth, and she laughed.

I felt, rather than heard, Lee's recoil. He said, 'Oh God, you bitch. But on our wedding night—' There was a pleading tone in his voice. 'Elizabeth, surely that night—'

'Did you count *that* as a demonstration of manhood?' she said. 'Or of fertility? I promise you, William, those few drops you managed to wring out that night would not have spawned anything!' There was such derision in her voice that I winced.

'But Elvira— Elvira isn't my daughter?' It was half a question, half a sob, and I felt a deep pang of pity for him.

'Of course she isn't. An inch of flabby skin that hangs like a turkey's wattle, and you think it would father a child!'

'Who—?'

'Oh, the butcher, the baker, the candlestick maker. The stable boy, the pot boy. Who knows?'

William Lee gave a low cry of pain and fury, and I heard him lunge across the room. Elizabeth screamed with real fear, and I took a step back to the open door. I no longer wanted to shield her from all the world's evils – in these few moments I had seen the sweet, serene carapace ripped away and glimpsed what was beneath. It was like biting into a ripe juicy apple and feeling your teeth sink into pulpy rottenness. But even so, I could not let William Lee harm her.

I was too late. He had dragged her from the bed, and seized a heavy pewter figure from the washstand. He brought it smashing down on her skull – I saw it crunch against the white skin, and I saw the skin and the bone crumple and blood spatter the bedclothes. She gave a grunting cry and slumped back, her eyes falling open.

Lee's face contorted with horror and disbelief. He stood there for several minutes, his hands trembling, then he seemed to give himself a shake like a dog emerging from water. Setting down the pewter figure, he took hold of her body by the arms and began to drag it across the floor. I believe in those moments he had forgotten I might still be in the house – I think he had virtually forgotten my existence.

I pressed back into the window alcove, partly hidden by the long curtains, and watched. He dragged her to the head of the stairs, then straightened up briefly, clearly out of breath from the unfamiliar exertion, and wiped the back of his hand across his forehead, which was slicked with sweat.

Then taking a deep breath, he tipped his wife's prone body down the stairs.

She fell in a series of thudding bumps, almost stopping on the half-landing, then sliding down the rest of the way, until she hit the bare oak floorboards in the hall. Blood oozed from her head.

William clapped his hand to his mouth and stumbled back into the bedroom. I heard him retch, then there was the unmistakable sound of him being sick. I was just gathering my resolve to make good my escape – in fact, I had stepped out of the concealment of the alcove – when a door opened at the far end of the landing, in the shorter half of the L-shape. A small figure clad in a long nightgown walked rather timidly towards the stairs.

'Mama?' She had a sweet voice, high and clear. Elvira. Her hair was the same colour as her mother's, but the features might have belonged to anyone. The butcher, the baker, the pot boy . . . 'Mama, I heard cries . . .'

She saw the tangled figure of her mother lying below, and then she saw me. She stopped dead, as if something had jerked a string. Our eyes met, and for several appalling seconds we stood motionless, staring at one another. Her eyes widened in utter horror, and I saw her mouth open to scream. But before she could do so, I had moved to the stair and I was running down them, slithering and half-falling, saving myself from falling by grabbing the banisters. I reached the foot where Elizabeth lay, and – oh God, the worst yet – my foot skidded in the mess of blood and brains. I gasped, righted myself, and ran to the back of the house, dragging open the scullery door through which I had entered. (Was it unbolted? I can't remember – I was in no state to see such details.)

I have no recollection of going along Blackberry Lane and along to the village, but clearly I did so because I am back here in my secret room, writing these pages.

A short while ago I went back up to the workshop and stood

listening. Did I expect to hear the sounds of a hue and cry coming through the streets towards me? If I had to hide from the police, could I do so in the secret library? How long could I remain down there?

But nothing moved, and I went across the cobbled yard to the front of the building. The street was deserted, but, as I stood there, I heard, very faintly, the chimes of St Paul's. Two o'clock. I came back down the steps to finish this journal entry.

A sensible man would go to bed and try to sleep. But I am not sensible – although I don't think I am mad any longer. My sanity returned in that bedroom when I heard Elizabeth exulting in her own promiscuity, scorning her husband for his impotency, flinging her daughter's paternity in the poor wretch's face. I think that might be when my own madness entered William Lee, for if ever raging insanity glared from a man's eyes it did so in that moment.

It is now almost three o'clock, and I must at least make the attempt to sleep – and to appear shocked and horrified tomorrow when the news reaches me that Elizabeth Lee of Mallow House has died in a brutal attack.

I find I cannot mourn for her. I can mourn for the creature I thought she was, but I cannot mourn for the sluttish shrew she really was. I can mourn a little for William Lee, though, and for the madness that had him in its grip when he killed her.

But if I am going to mourn for anyone, it will be for the child – Elvira.

18th November

The news of Elizabeth's death is all over Marston Lacy. I heard it from the dairyman when he left the churn of milk, and again from the postman. Mrs Figgis was voluble on the subject and eager to impart all the information she had gleaned on her way to my house. Most of it was wrong – how I ached to correct her. I did not, of course.

20th November

It's becoming known, by gradual stages, that the police have questioned William Lee, and that he has said a burglar entered the house and resisted Lee's attempts to throw him out. His wife came to his assistance, and in the scuffle the intruder lashed out at her, landing a blow which sent her tumbling down the stairs to her death. Lee is known to be distraught at his loss and is seeing no callers.

Everyone in Marston Lacy is quivering with sympathy and a ghoulish curiosity. There is genuine concern for the child. I have concern as well, but I am ashamed to write that alongside the concern is a selfish anxiety. Did she recognize me when we stared at one another on the landing? She cannot have done – as far as I know she has never seen me before.

But if she sees me in the village at any time, will she remember who I am?

21st November

The police have asked everyone in the village if a stranger has been seen in the area. Clearly, they are taking William Lee's statement of a burglar seriously. I was in the Black Boar last evening, and the four-ale bar was alight with speculation. The village constable, seated morosely in a corner with his notebook and modest glass of cider, made notes of everything that was said, and as the evening wore on it began to seem that three-quarters of Marston Lacy had seen a sinister stranger on the very day of Elizabeth's murder. A shifty fellow he was, they said, egging each other on. Wall-eyed and low-browed He shambled through the main street, muttering and cursing to himself, opening and closing his hands as if looking for a victim to throttle. This last was hastily corrected to 'looking for a victim to push down the stairs'. By closing time, the stranger's appearance had attained the grotesque proportions of the deformed bell-ringer of Notre Dame and was possessed of much the same attributes and lusts as R.L. Stevenson's Mr Edward Hyde.

I contributed my own mite by a vague half-memory of having noticed a tall, thin man wearing a trailing coat and worn boots walking through the village at dusk. I did not embellish this thumbnail sketch – I have always found far more notice is taken of a brief, unemphatic statement than of the hyperbole of the ale-flown.

It may be the beer I drank tonight, but I am starting to feel safer. There have been no police enquiries at my door, and I am daring to believe that either Elvira Lee was unable to give the police any useful information – or that her father has not allowed her to be questioned by them.

They have been glimpsed briefly in the area, sad figures in their black clothes, the child holding tightly to Lee's hand.

23rd November

A difficulty now presents itself. The clock commissioned by William Lee is finished, and I cannot decide what I should do about it. But I am loath to lose 150 gns, and the clock was made to a specific and approved design, so it may be months before I find another buyer for it. The cost of the materials was quite high – rosewood is expensive, and the blue enamel for the face was specially cut.

I have drafted a letter to Lee that is partly-condolence, partly-business . . .

> My dear Mr Lee,
>   Permit me to offer my deepest sympathy on the tragic death of your wife, and to condole with you on the terrible circumstances surrounding it. I had never met Mrs Lee, but had seen her occasionally from a distance and believe her to have been a gracious and lovely lady, well-respected in these parts.
>   I am in something of a quandary, since the long-case clock you were so kind as to commission from my workshop is now complete – indeed, has been so for some three weeks now. If acceptable, I could arrange for its delivery to Mallow House in the next few days. I would be most grateful if you would let me know if that is a suitable arrangement.
>   Believe me, sir, your very humble servant,
>   Very sincerely,
>   Brooke Crutchley
>   Master Clockmaker

I have posted the letter and await a reply.

24th November

The reply has come already.

> My dear Crutchley
>   I am in receipt of your letter and thank you for your
> kind sentiments and condolences.
>   You will appreciate, I am sure, that in the present
> circumstances I had forgotten the commission for the
> clock. However, I am aware you will have expended
> considerable time and cost in its making, so would be
> happy if it could be delivered here any time on Thursday.
> A note of your account will oblige.
>   Yours etc.,
>   Wm. Lee

I have decided to accompany the clock when it is taken to
Mallow. It's risky, but it is my custom to do so with all new
clocks. On this occasion it will resolve in my mind whether
or not Elvira recognizes me. I cannot continue in this dreadful
state of unknowing.

I believe I shall destroy those books that set out spells and
enchantments. They seem to me to represent a period of my
life when I was not sane. Do I believe in them any longer, I
wonder? I don't want to. And yet I cannot forget how the
locks clicked open before the Hand of Glory that night, and
how both Elizabeth and William seemed to sleep so deeply
and only woke when I snuffed the light . . .

TWENTY-SEVEN

26th November

I have spent the night in tumult. I have no idea what to do, but I have finally been able to come down here, and I hope that setting down the events of the last twenty-four hours may serve to calm my mind.

Yesterday the carter arrived at the workshop as arranged, to load the clock on to the dray. We swathed it in dust sheets, and I protected the mechanism with plenty of cotton waste.

Blackberrry Lane was shrouded in autumn mist – wisps clung to the bare branches of the trees, and everywhere was touched with hoar frost. Mallow House, when we reached it, seemed lonely.

William Lee himself admitted us to the house. He looked pale and haggard, but he was courteous and asked that the clock be taken to his library. It was to stand against a wall near the windows.

The carter helped me to carry the clock inside, then took himself off – he had another delivery to make, but offered to call in an hour's time to take me up and so back to Marston Lacy.

'I will leave you to your work,' said Lee. 'I have a task in the orchard – a tree whose roots have spread to unfruitful soil. My gardener uprooted it yesterday, and it is to be replanted in more wholesome earth.'

One somehow doesn't associate murderers with homely tasks like replanting trees. From the windows I watched him walk through the gardens. After a few moments the child joined him. She was wearing a scarlet scarf and a little scarlet hat. The colours were too bright for her – she's a rather sallow child – but they were vivid and warm against the grey morning.

I gave the shining mahogany of the clock's casing a final polishing – it had picked up a few fragments of straw in the cart. Then I opened the door to set the mechanism going. It started at once, sweetly and smoothly, the measured tick making a pleasant, slightly soporific sound in the quiet room. I waited to make sure the hands moved round correctly. Once I would have imagined how *she* would have looked at the clock many times during the day, seeing the minutes and hours pass, seeing how the secondary face showed the months.

I put the cloths and beeswax away and left out a small phial of thin oil for occasional use within the mechanism. I always do that with a new clock. Then I went to the window.

There they were, at the bottom of the gardens – I could just make out the scarlet of Elvira's scarf and cap through the trees. My heart began to bump, for this was to be the test. I was resolved to walk down to the orchard and tell William Lee his clock was in place and working satisfactorily. I would smile at the child and see what happened.

It was not easy to go along the gravel paths, between the smooth lawns and the herb garden in its enclosure of box. Even on a day like this there was a faint drift of rosemary and thyme and mint, and the acrid tang of the box.

The orchard was only just about worthy of the name. There were four or five trees – mainly pear and plum, but I could see the apple tree to which Lee had referred. It lay on the ground, its branches like burned bones.

They had not heard my approach, and I paused in the shadow of some shrubbery, trying to summon up the resolve to go forward.

Lee was telling the child how the tree would be replanted. 'Today we will trim it, and tomorrow the gardener will put fresh soil and compost in so the roots can be nourished. Then we shall have juicy apples.'

Elvira appeared to consider this. She stared down at the tree and at the newly-dug patch of earth.

Lee said, in a very casual voice, 'How much do you remember about the night your mamma died?'

'I remember bits, but I don't understand them,' said Elvira, frowning.

'What bits?'

'You were there,' she said. 'If I keep looking at you, I remember you shouting and standing by the stairs.'

'Do you?' he said, very softly. 'That's a pity, Elvira.'

'I want to remember properly,' she said. 'Because you did something that night – what did you do?' She broke off, and even from where I stood I saw a horrified realization come into her face. She was staring at Lee, and I saw she was starting to remember.

Lee saw it as well, and that was when the change came over him, as it had done in the bedroom that night. He had been idly holding a big spade, presumably left by the gardener, and I saw his knuckles whiten as he tightened his grip on it. A tremor of fear went through me, and I came out from the shelter of the trees.

He saw me at once and half-turned. I saw with horror that the madness still glared from his eyes. In a dreadful, slurry voice – a voice that was somehow no longer that of William Lee – he said, 'Who are you? What do you want? Have you come to stare at me like she does? Those great accusing eyes . . .'

'Mr Lee – it's Brooke Crutchley. You know me. You let me into your house an hour ago.'

He was staring at me with more attention. 'You were there,' he said, suddenly. 'You were the man in Elizabeth's room.'

'No . . .'

'You were,' he said, and the child gave a cry of sudden fear, staring at me. Lee ignored her. 'So that open-legged whore added the clockmaker to her conquests, did she?' he said.

'No,' I said again, more firmly this time. 'Never.'

'No matter,' he said. 'One more is neither here nor there. But you saw, didn't you? You *know* what happened.' The dreadful maniacal glare was fading, but he said, 'You do realize I can't allow you to speak out?' He took a step towards me, and for a moment I thought he was going to attack me. But he did not, and after a moment I felt safe to look away from him and at Elvira. She was huddled on the ground, staring at me with panic, and pity sliced through me.

Lee glanced down at her. 'She's remembering it all,' he said. 'A little at a time, but soon she will remember it all. I can't allow that.'

'If you make any attempt to hurt the child, be very sure I shall see you brought to justice.'

'What could you do?' he said, dismissively. 'Who would listen to you?'

'I mean it,' I said. 'Elvira is not to be harmed.'

*   *   *

I have spent the rest of the day and most of the night in a ferment of anxiety. I cannot believe William Lee will really harm his daughter—

But writing that, I'm reminded that she isn't his daughter – or so Elizabeth said. Has that engendered in him a hatred towards her? And added to that is the fact that she knows he killed her mother. And that I saw it happen.

I have no idea what to do. I think he might try to silence me, although I don't know how. But I believe I can protect myself against him.

What worries me is how I can protect Elvira.

27th November

Marston Lacy is buzzing with shock. No one knows the exact truth, but the word is that Elvira Lee has been admitted as a patient in Brank Asylum. Gossip and speculation is running everywhere like wildfire. Everyone insists it's too incredible for belief, but then agrees that the poor scrap's reason might have been overturned by the death of her mother. From there it's been a short hop to people remembering that the Marston family – Elizabeth's people – were not noted for their restraint or self-control. Old Roland Marston, say the older members of the community, was much given to boisterous behaviour and even fits of ungovernable rage.

It's generally agreed that if Elvira's mind has given way under the shock, it's tragic that there's no family to whom she could be sent. But William Lee's parents are both dead, and so are Elizabeth's – in fact, Roly Marston fell down of an apoplexy while rogering the barmaid from the Black Boar, and her mother expired from the shame.

For myself, I believe Elvira has started to remember more and more of what she saw the night her mother was killed, and that this is William's way of ensuring she never talks of it. Then I remember that flare of vicious anger in his eyes and the way his grip tightened on the spade, and I'm dreadfully afraid for her.

Is it possible his action might be more altruistic, though? Is he afraid he might harm her, and is he therefore putting her beyond his reach? I don't know. What I do know is that I would do anything to keep her safe from that terrible fury I glimpsed.

He hates her – not only because he thinks she could speak the words that would hang him, but also because she's a bastard from some unthinking liaison of Elizabeth's.

I believe I shall now close these diaries, and this time it really will be for good. The lamps down here have burned very low, and shadows are creeping forward from the corners.

A few minutes ago I fancied I heard sounds above me. Could someone have broken into the workshop? But it's unlikely. And I see that it's past midnight, and that's an hour inclined to make a man feel a little nervous.

The sounds have come again. Someone *is* up there. There are footsteps . . .

The trapdoor is being lifted – someone is coming down the stone steps towards me . . .

A sense of tidiness prompts me to take up Brooke Crutchley's pen and make a closing entry in what is clearly a journal of many years' standing. As I write that, I hear my wife jeering at me. 'Tidiness, William?' she would have said. 'You never had an iota of tidiness in your entire body – you strew your belongings everywhere in the house with no consideration for anyone else.'

Perhaps she was right – occasionally she could be, the whoring bitch. But I believe I have a tidiness of mind – a scholar's mind – and that's what has compelled me to take the virgin pages from Crutchley's desk and record what I have just done.

I have killed him. I stole out to his house in the village earlier on and hid in his workshop. I saw him open the trapdoor at the side of the old stove and descend the steps. And I thought – haha! my fine sly gentleman, so you have a bolt-hole, do you? But now I have you cornered.

He could not be allowed to live, you see. I'd like anyone who might ever read this to understand that. And once a man has committed one murder, the second does not seem so very bad. You can only be hanged once. You can only suffer hell for one eternity.

Brooke Crutchley knew I killed Elizabeth. And I believe him to be an honourable man – a man who would think the law should extort its due punishment. Two days ago, in the gardens of Mallow House, I knew I should have to silence him to prevent him talking. And tonight I have done precisely that.

It was remarkably easy. Murder is easy – the books never tell you that. Killing Elizabeth was easy – that blow to the head in the bedroom, then the push down the stairs. Several years of fury and jealousy were behind those two acts, of course. The taunting, the humiliations, the sheer bitter hatred . . . It is not given to all men to have rampant appetites or capabilities, and I was brought up to believe it was not within a lady's nature to possess those appetites. (Street women are different – they are coarser-fibred, their sensitivities are less delicate. Or so I am led to believe.)

Killing Brooke Crutchley was easy as well. He had been diligently writing away in this room – and who would have thought an ordinary, rather stout clockmaker would have created this remarkable underground room? I have not inspected the books on the shelves in any detail, although I shall do so before I leave. But even a cursory glance by the flickering lamplight suggests he has some rare and curious treasures in his collection.

He was seated behind the desk when I came down the steps, and he stared at me, his mouth in a round *O* of surprise. I didn't hesitate. I had brought with me what I believe is called, among street ruffians, a sandbag a receptacle filled with ordinary garden soil. I had taken a silk bag from my wife's sewing table (she did have one or two ladylike pursuits) and filled it with the soil from around the old apple tree. There is a drawstring at the top – I pulled this tight and fashioned a loop.

Crutchley started out of his chair when I entered, demanding to know what I was doing there, but I gave him no opportunity to say any more. I swung the bag high above my shoulder and let its own weight carry it straight towards his head. It struck him squarely on the temple, and he went down like a poleaxed bull.

I believe I stood staring down at him for quite a long time and – this is a curious thing – it was as if something stood with me. Something that approved of what I had done, something that nodded a scaly head and patted me with a fleshless hand, and huffed foetid breath into my face as it leaned forward to whisper, 'Well done . . . Oh, well done . . .'

The devil, they say, likes murder very much – not that I'm imagining the devil has condescended to stroll into this very ordinary workshop and insinuate himself down the stairs to this room. But there's *something* here, for all that . . .

I've managed to drag Crutchley's body back to the chair behind the desk and prop it upright. He has no heartbeat – I'm quite sure he's dead. I shall have to read the journal, of course – it's almost certain he will have recorded seeing me kill Elizabeth.

Dare I take the journal back to Mallow to read? No, it's too much of a risk. It could be seen – there are callers to the house. The vicar from St Paul's has been twice already, and there will be people from Brank Asylum, to talk about Elvira.

Elvira . . . She went so obediently into that place. I could wish she had resisted and cried, but she did not. She sat in a corner of the room as I talked to the doctors, her big dark eyes fixed on me. Delusional, I said. Given to fits of hysterical rage. At such times I can't control her – she bites and screams and sees nightmare figures while awake.

'Nightmare figures?' said the doctor.

'Men wrapped in black cloaks she believes mean her harm – although she can't describe what that harm could be.' I had thought very carefully about this beforehand – it seemed to me that this was more believable, more sinister, than the traditional child's terrors of giants and witches.

They agreed to keep her with them for a few days to see if some form of calming treatment could be given. For the moment that will have to suffice, although I will have to think of some better solution. The memories were starting to come back to Elvira, and I can't risk her telling people she saw me kill her mother, I cannot . . .

It's two o'clock, and for now I shall return home. But tomorrow night I shall come back here, very late, and sit in this room and read Crutchley's outpourings. If there is anything damning in them, I shall burn them in the stove above this room.

29th November

So. So Crutchley knew it all. More, he *caused* it. For if he had not crept out to Mallow that night with his stupid superstitions and the repulsive lump of graveyard flesh . . . Well, perhaps Elizabeth would still be alive and I should not be a haunted man, going in fear of discovery. The irony is that he could have had her, just as any man could have had her. She was not discriminating, the harlot.

He still sits where I left him last night, stiffening in death's grotesque pose, his eyes wide open and staring at nothing. Or are they? Aren't they staring at *me*? Just as Elvira's eyes do . . .

Elvira. Spawn of God-knows what pot boy or stable lad.

I can't bear Crutchley's dead eyes watching me. I have walked round this room and swung quickly round to take them by surprise, and each time they are fixed on me. *Something still lives behind those dead eyes . . .*

In Crutchley's workshop upstairs are a number of tools for the fashioning of intricate clock mechanisms – I saw them while I hid there, waiting for him. Tiny, sharp-ended implements they are – miniature chisels and screwdrivers. Among them are several long needles . . .

It was easier than I expected.

When I return tomorrow to finish reading the journals and destroy them, the man will no longer stare at me with that condemnation and knowledge. He will no longer be able to stare at anyone or anything, for he no longer has any eyes. He will have to feel his way through eternity.

Tomorrow afternoon I must go out to Brank Asylum. They will allow me to see Elvira – they will leave me alone with her. She will stare at me with those accusing eyes – silent and condemning, just as Crutchley's did. I don't think I can bear that.

But I still have the long needle in my pocket . . .

TWENTY-EIGHT

Nell and Michael came up out of the last years of the nineteenth century with difficulty. The journal ended with William Lee's avowal to visit Elvira.

'But afterwards he never went back to the underground room,' said Michael, eventually. The room had been silent for so long that the sound of his voice was slightly startling.

'He couldn't,' said Nell. 'Look at the date on the last entry. The twenty-ninth of November. And according to that newspaper article he was arrested on the thirtieth. He had no chance to go back.'

'And Brooke's body was never found,' said Michael thoughtfully. 'William blinded him, didn't he? Put out his eyes. Even though Brooke was dead, William believed he was watching him – knowing him to be Elizabeth's killer.'

'I hope Brooke *was* dead when he did it,' said Nell, uneasily. 'I hope that blow to the head didn't send him into some sort of coma. But Michael, you realize it's been Brooke we've been seeing or hearing – or the residue of him, or something. I don't pretend to understand that side of it. But whatever he is, or whatever's been wandering around, it hasn't been threatening us. It's been frightening because it's – well, spectral. But he never intended any harm to anyone.'

'The reverse, in fact,' said Michael. 'He was looking for Elvira. Trying to keep her away from William because he believed William wanted to silence her – maybe to kill her.'

'Yes, of course. And Beth said that day that whoever took her didn't mean any harm – that she wasn't the one he was looking for. Ellie said something like that as well, didn't she? And Brooke took Beth to the church, remember – his own church where he was a sidesman and on that prison reform committee.'

'He took those other girls there, as well,' said Michael, remembering. 'That one in the nineteen sixties. And there was a mention of one in the thirties, too.'

'He thought he was putting them in a safe place – somewhere William couldn't hurt them.'

'Yes. And d'you remember Harriet's account of someone tracing her features that day at Charect? It's what a blind person would do – trying to identify someone by touch. But,' said Michael, 'he was already too late to save Elvira. William got to her in Brank Asylum. Don't cry, Nell, darling.'

'That poor child, Elvira,' said Nell, shakily. 'I keep seeing her with Beth's face. She must have thought William was the one person in the world she could trust – the one person she had left to cling to after her mother died.'

'I know.' He held her to him for a moment.

'Sorry,' said Nell, presently. She sat up and reached for the remains of the wine. 'Elvira thought it was Brooke she had to be frightened of,' she said. 'She saw him that day in the garden – when the apple tree was being replanted. She had seen him in the house the night her mother died, as well.'

'And so she allotted it all to Brooke,' said Michael, thoughtfully.

'Yes. D'you know,' said Nell thoughtfully, 'at the start I didn't much like the sound of Brooke Crutchley – I still don't like that clock he made, and I definitely don't like all that brooding over books on magic, or that grisly night in the burial yard at Shrewsbury Gaol. But I've got to say, I feel rather sorry for him. I do think he was a bit unbalanced by Elizabeth.'

'I wish I could have seen Elizabeth for myself,' said Michael speculatively, and he grinned at her. 'I'll bet she was quite a girl.'

'You wouldn't have liked her one bit,' said Nell firmly, and he laughed.

'I like what I've found here,' he said and pulled her to him.

'Michael,' said Nell, an appreciable time later, 'do you realize it's well after midnight? Will you be locked out of the Black Boar?'

'Probably not, but I think I should go,' he said. 'I won't assume that I can stay the night here, Nell, in case you were wondering about that.'

'Well—'

He took her hands. 'There are going to be some nights though, aren't there?' he said. 'When I don't have to leave?'

'Oh, I hope so,' said Nell eagerly. As he got up to go, she said, 'Michael – Brooke's body. What will happen?'

'I should think the police will carry out some forensic tests,' said Michael, 'but they'll probably start with the assumption that it's Brooke. There was that presumption of death notice, wasn't there?'

'There'd be a proper funeral?' said Nell.

'I imagine so. Were you thinking that might lay the old boy's spirit to rest or something?'

'I suppose I was. Don't laugh at me, I know I'm being romantic and clinging to the old traditions of all good ghost stories.'

'I wasn't laughing,' said Michael, coming back to kiss her. 'I'll see you in the morning, my love. I've said it again, haven't I? "My love". It does sound good, doesn't it?'

'Better each time you say it.'

'I think so as well.' As they went down the stairs and through the shop to the street door, he said suddenly, 'There's another thing I think should be explored before we can regard all this as over. And I think it should be done before Jack and Liz get here.'

'What?'

'The attic at Charect House.'

Michael was pleased to find, when he reached his room at the Black Boar, that a phone message had been put under his door. It had been carefully written out by the receptionist.

'Dr Flint – phone message from Dr Jack Harper in Paris. Apologies for not being in touch – his cellphone was stolen at Charles de Gaulle airport. He will get another one when he reaches London tomorrow so he can use a UK network while he's here. Will contact you then.'

So Jack's long silence was explained as easily and as ordinarily as that. Michael was immensely relieved – he had been visualizing all manner of things happening to Ellie. But it looked as if they could come to Marston Lacy for Christmas as planned, and Ellie would be perfectly all right. As he got ready for bed, he was smiling at the prospect of introducing Nell to Jack and Liz, and of seeing Beth and Ellie together.

It had been difficult to get the builder to come out to Charect House again so near to Christmas, but Inspector Brent had added his persuasions to those of Michael and Nell, and a lorry and a couple of men had finally trundled along Blackberry Lane.

Charect House was silent and still. There's nothing here now, thought Michael, standing in the hall with the scents of new timbers and paint around him. Whatever was here – some lingering fragment of that strange, unhappy man who loved Elizabeth Lee beyond sanity, and who saw her die that night – it's gone.

The builder went up to the attics, admiring the renovations along the way.

'Nice piece of oak for that banister,' he said. 'And that coving on the landing – you wouldn't believe the problems we had putting that up. High ceilings in these old houses, see.'

He stood in the attic, which had been opened up for Ellie's playroom and which was due to be papered with bright wallpaper chosen by Liz, and looked disapproving.

'Crying shame to disturb all this,' he said. 'Still, if it's police orders.' He tapped the wall and nodded. 'Be a breeze to break that down. I'll get the sledgehammer.'

As he clattered down the uncarpeted stairs, Michael stood for a moment in the attic room with the views towards the smudgy Welsh mountains. Ellie would love this room – it would be her hideaway, and she would make up so many stories about the people who had lived here. But let them be happy stories, thought Michael. Because this house must have had happy times. He looked back at the wall that the builders were going to demolish and hoped he was doing the right thing. But I think you're still here, Harriet, he said in his mind. I think you've been part of whatever's lingered here.

The builder and his assistant came noisily back up the stairs, and Michael stood back as the sledgehammer swung through the air. It landed squarely on the centre of the wall, and this time it gave way almost immediately. Huge sections of old, dry plaster fell away, and there were several confused moments when the entire attic was a mass of whirling dust. Fragments of plaster and shards of brick seemed to go on and on cascading down, catching at Michael's throat, making him cough and stinging his eyes.

Then, little by little, the dust cleared and began to settle, and it was possible to make out what was beyond the huge, jagged hole. Huddled against the inside of the wall was something that might, at first glance, be household debris. But as the dust cleared—

'Jesus Christ,' said the builder. 'Oh, Christ Al-bloody-mighty, it's a sodding body.' He turned to Michael, his face, beneath

the plaster dust, patchily red and white with shock. 'A corpse,'
he said, his lips flabbering over the word.

'Yes.'

Michael had hoped very strenuously that she would not be
here – that he would be able to think of her escaping, returning
to Cheshire, perhaps becoming involved in some interesting,
useful war work. Even that she might have met someone to
replace her beloved Harry.

He brought his mind back to the builder who, white-faced,
was asking if the police should be called. 'Will I go down to
phone them?'

'I think you'd better. Ask for Inspector Brent, if possible.
But tell him there's no frantic rush.'

'You don't mind staying up here with – with that?'

'Not in the least,' said Michael, and he turned back to the
jagged hole and to what lay just inside it.

Harriet Anstey's bones were small and fragile, and Michael
found them unbearably sad. The hands were stretched upwards
as if the last act might have been to bang vainly on the wall
for help. Clinging to those hands were shreds of what might
once have been striped cotton.

'Oh, Harriet,' said Michael softly. 'I'm so sorry no one
found you.'

It seemed incredible there had not been a search for her.
But perhaps there had. Perhaps people had tried to find her,
but been unable to do so. And it had been 1939 – the lights
were about to go out all over Europe for the second time that
century and England stood on the brink of chaos.

How long had it taken her to die? Had she died in darkness
or had it at least been when a few threads of light were coming
in through the small, round window – the window at which
she had stood, trying to attract attention? The window where
Michael had seen her that day . . . ?

In the same soft voice, he said, 'I don't know if I can arrange
for you to be buried next to Harry, because his body's probably
in France. But if I can, I'll find out where he is, and if there's
any way of ensuring you lie alongside him, I promise you shall.'

With the words, he had the vivid impression that a small,
soft hand slipped into his and held it firmly for a moment.
He stood very still, wanting the sensation to go on, willing
there to be more.

But there was not. The feeling melted, and there was only the dusty attic.

Brooke Crutchley's body was cremated in a brief, private ceremony one week after Christmas. Michael and Nell attended, together with Inspector Brent.

'Unusual case,' said the inspector as they walked away from the crematorium. 'Very distressing for you to find a thing like that in your house, Mrs West.'

'Yes, it was. At least we can give him an identity, though,' said Nell.

'Forensics confirm he died from a blow to the skull,' said Brent. 'We'll never know the truth, but I expect some kind of long-ago local feud was at the heart of it.'

'I expect so,' said Michael, in an expressionless voice, and Brent glanced at him.

But he only said, 'I looked in the files for the account of the William Lee case, as you asked.'

'I got interested in some of the area's history,' said Michael, sounding slightly defensive. 'And there were all those stories about William Lee still walking—'

'People like a nice ghost story,' said Brent indulgently. 'As long as they don't actually have to meet the ghost themselves, of course. But in the main, Lee's case seems straightforward enough. He was arrested on the thirtieth of November, 1888. There was one odd thing, though—'

'Yes?' said Michael again.

'The arrest took place in the old asylum – Brank Asylum. One of those grim old Victorian institutions from all accounts. Long since gone, of course. But seemingly Lee had gone there to visit his daughter, and the attendants heard her screaming. When they got to him, Lee was cowering in a corner of the room, flailing at the air with his hands as if he was trying to hit someone who was attacking him.'

Michael and Nell exchanged a quick look, then Nell said, '*Was* someone trying to attack him?'

'What? No, there was no one there except the child, and she was lying on the ground, her face covered in blood. Lee had assaulted her. They arrested him, and once he was in custody he confessed to the murder of his wife. Open and shut case. They hanged him soon afterwards.'

Charect House, January 20—

Michael—

I *knew* you'd get Wilberforce into print! It's terrific news
about the publishing deal, and I hope you screwed a huge
advance out of them. We'll want signed copies next November,
of course. Good date to bring out a kids' book as well – exactly
right for Christmas. And I don't know why you're worried
about balancing *Wilberforce* with Oxford. If C.S. Lewis and
Tolkien could do it, so can you.

Liz and I are knocked out by Charect House. It's the most
beautiful place ever, and we don't know what persuasions you
used on the builders to get the work done, but they've made
a great job of everything.

We loved being with you at Christmas and staying in the
Black Boar, and we think Nell is one very cool lady. How is the
hunt for antique premises in Oxford getting on? Liz says when
Nell finds a shop, she should expect us to be the first customers.
Ellie is wringing promises out of us that we will bring her to
Oxford to meet Wilberforce, so you're both likely to be invaded.

Ellie is entirely fine now. The nightmares have vanished,
and she loves England. There's been no more mention of
'Elvira', I'm relieved to report. Although Ellie does seem to
have found another imaginary friend – can you believe that?
This time it's an English gentleman who likes to walk round
the gardens here and sit in the orchard. I swear that kid's mind
is so full of stuff . . . There's no man, of course – we've made
sure of that. The gardens are perfectly secure, and Liz keeps
a watchful eye.

But an orchard, for pity's sake. There might once have been
an orchard at the far end of Charect's garden, but there certainly
isn't one now. But Ellie insists that tomorrow she's promised
to help this man dig up some old apple tree.

   We'll let you know what happens!
   Jack